little minnow

A SARA RANDOLPH NOVEL

little minnow

A SARA RANDOLPH NOVEL

RICHARD SNELSON

STIRLING PRESS

an imprint of
THE OGHMA PRESS

OGHMA
C R E A T I V E   M E D I A
Bentonville, Arkansas • Los Angeles, California
www.oghmacreative.com

Library of Congress Cataloging-in-Publication Data

Names: Snelson, Richard S, author.
Title: Little Minnow/Richard S. Snelson |
Description: First Edition. | Bentonville: Stirling, 2021.
Identifiers: LCCN: 2022933868 | ISBN: 978-1-63373-716-7 (hardcover) |
ISBN: 978-1-63373-717-4 (trade paperback) | ISBN: 978-1-63373-718-1 (eBook)
Subjects: | BISAC: FICTION/Thrillers/Suspense | FICTION/Women |
FICTION/Small Town & Rural
LC record available at: https://lccn.loc.2022933868

Stirling Press hardcover edition May, 2022

Cover & Interior Design by Casey W. Cowan
Editing by Chelsea Cambeis & Amy Cowan

Published by Stirling Press, an imprint of The Oghma Press, a subsidiary of The Oghma Book Group.

This story is dedicated to an Army veteran of the Iraq War.

From the first day I met Fatima, her story of war and her recovery from it inspired me to write The Sara Randolph Series of novels.

one

HER FATHER SAT AT THE helm of the jon boat steering around the sunken logs and the day's hazards on the river. A spring breeze kissed the surface of the river's cold water and then rose over the bow of the boat to caress Sara Randolph's face. Her hazel eyes were hidden behind the large Ray Bans that had become her addiction in the deserts of Iraq. Now the dark glasses not only muted the sun's rays flashing off the water, but they also hid her shame. Shame and painful memories the burn scar on the side of her face brought back to her. She'd returned two days earlier hoping it would feel wonderful to be home and back on the river where she'd grown up.

It wasn't turning out the way she'd hoped.

Sara ran her finger over the weathered *L* and *M* letters her dad had carved on the front boards of his jon boat the day she left for Iraq. He told her, "You'll be there in front of the boat, riding with me each day, Little Minnow." She'd thought of those initials and her dad fishing the river many times when she'd gotten up to face the days filled with wind, sand, Iraqi prisoners, and always feeling afraid. Afraid of never being home again.

She leaned against the bow, feeling the drumbeat of the boat's flat bottom kissing the waves and echoing against her bosom in song—a welcome home song for the soldier. It seemed to say, "You've been away far too long."

But she didn't deserve such a welcome.

Turning to her dad back at the tiller, she shouted over the engine noise. "I've missed you."

He smiled and pointed at her. "You, too, Little Minnow."

She turned away, knowing he wouldn't hear what she said next. "Sorry, Dad. Little Minnow got left back in the Sandbox."

Sara skimmed the water with her hand, reaching out to touch the ripples even before they caressed the bow of the moving boat. Lifting her camo cap, she rubbed a wet hand across her hair and pushed it back into place. The current splashed over gunwale and tossed spray across her lips and face.She pulled back into herself, though, when the dark turmoil of the water brought memories she fought to keep away.

Sara could tell her dad was looking for just the right spot to stop the engine and insist she toss a baited line. It was too soon, though. She wanted no part of the fishing. Fighting to push back the memories of her last day in Iraq was all that she could handle right now.

Dad shifted the boat to idle, and the boat slowed. He held out a rod and reel toward her. "Let's catch some supper."

"Later." She desperately wanted out of the boat to walk the bank alone.

"All right, then."

An hour later, after he'd caught and tossed back more than a dozen trout, she felt sure his patience with her had just about run out.

"Fish on, girl! It's a big one this time." He walked to the bow of the boat and shoved the rod into her reluctant hands.

She grabbed the rod's handle and held on. The pulsating fishing rod brought back memories of good times on the river with her mom and dad. She lifted the tip of the rod. The fighting pulls of the trout trying to escape had her in its grasp.

"Take up some line," he yelled, before starting the boat's motor to follow the fish.

"I'm cranking hard, Old Man." A tiny bit of the home she remembered was coming through to her.

The screaming missile came at her from the left side of the boat.

"Incoming! Get down," she commanded and pancaked to the bottom of the boat, throwing the fishing rod in the air and cramming both hands over her ears. In a panicked quest for a breath, she sucked both legs tight against her chest.

"They're on the roof. Fifty cals, get on them! *Now!*"

Sara sprang up, rocked the narrow boat, and reached for her sidearm and grenades, glazed eyes staring after a distant enemy. Her hands came up empty and shaking.

"I'm going to kill you sons of bitches!" She dropped to her knees.

"Sara! My God." Her father grabbed her shoulders and shook. "You're home and safe here." The stark surprise on his face showed he didn't see this coming. He knelt beside her, reaching for her arm. "It was just a pissed off blue heron took off over us! This ain't Iraq, Sara."

"Oh, yes. I—"

"Easy, girl."

"I should have died with my crew!"

"Calm down, soldier."

"Go to hell, Old Man."

"I understand."

"Really?"

She regretted what she said immediately. She knew he had been through days of combat in the jungles of 'Nam. Sara hunched over, grabbed her stomach, and leaned over the edge of the boat to vomit.

When the wrenching stopped, she turned and reached for her father.

"I'm so sorry." She pulled him close.

"I have bad memories too. I see flashes of the jungles in 'Nam, Sara."

"I want it all to end," she said, wiping the tears from her eyes.

"I thought that for a long time."

"Mom told me that about you."

He didn't offer more, only, "Okay if we just drift a while?"

He killed the idling engine and picked up the paddle to keep the boat in the middle currents of the river. The quiet of the wooden boat lapping the waves and ripples of the shallow river started to relax her. When she turned toward her dad, he smiled. She wished the quiet part of their float would last the rest of the day. She didn't want to talk to him about what happened while she away. She kept hoping that if she didn't talk about them the bad memories would go away. The doctors at the hospital all said they wouldn't.

They wanted her to talk and write about them, instead. She didn't want to believe them.

———————————

HER DAD'S FISHING DOCK WASN'T far ahead. The covered dock had known more than one bank-clearing flood on the river in it's time. And after each flood, like clockwork, he would head downstream in his jon boat with a heavy tow rope, praying he would find the dock washed up on a sandbar just sitting there waiting for him. Once he'd told her he found it broken and bent, leaning against a stand of willows. Another time he found only the humpty-dumpty pieces—splintered boards, foam floats, and a bent tin roof turned upside down—all waiting to go home for him to work his magic and put them back together again.

She hoped Dad could work the same magic on her now.

Just before the boat bumped the back of the slip, Sara picked up the tie rope and jumped to the dock. The foam floats under the dock rebounded as she landed and then quickly settled. She tied the boat securely to the dock with a cleat hitch knot and then added another turn for good measure. When she pulled on the knot, it sent a sharp pain through the healing wound in her side.

"What's wrong, Sara?"

She stood rubbing her side. "I stretched a little too much."

"That wound still bothering you?"

"You still keep that bottle tucked away in the back of the bread box?" She turned and headed up the steps to her dad's cabin, taking the steps two at a time.

"Maybe I should fix us something to eat first?" John yelled after her.

"I'm not hungry, Dad."

Sara let the screen door of their cabin slam behind her and went for her dad's booze. After tossing her sunglasses across the counter she poured an inch of the bourbon in a water glass and downed the aged liquor. She shuddered, lifted the bottle, and poured another.

He paused after opening the screen door. "Bottle's been back there... well, a long time. After your mom died, the booze 'bout got me, Sara."

"Don't fucking lecture me."

Her dad pulled back a chair from the table and turned its back toward Sara before straddling it to sit facing her. She swallowed the second drink in a gulp and then wiped the drops of bourbon off her lips with the back of her hand.

"Was this the first time something like that happened?"

"I wish I could get away from it all."

"Do you want to talk?"

"No!" Sara rushed out the cabin's screen door and slammed it behind her. She went to stand alone with her face pressed against an aged cottonwood tree. She had the sudden realization that coming home to live with a war-scarred father might not have been a good idea. Her options had been few. So many things in the city had triggered her memories—delivery truck doors slamming, buses belching out clouds of black smoke—small things that shook her to the core. Finally, she'd hoped the quiet of the river she called home would help. Now that she was here, though, it didn't seem to be working.

two

PROTECTED BY THE TOWERING COTTONWOOD and oak trees, the red and pink colors of the redbuds were the first to announce the coming of spring on the river. Not to be outdone, the whites and pinks of the flowering dogwoods followed when the redbuds faded. The soon to come unfurling of the tree leaves would signal the celebration of warmer breezes and longer daylight hours. Tucked away in this year's colors, the cabin sat high on the river's bank hidden from passing fishing parties that wouldn't have known the cabin existed if it weren't for the dock.

She remembered her mother telling her when John built a second bedroom on the cabin and installed indoor plumbing with a shower and bathtub because they both wanted a family. The large cistern he hand-dug was the only source of water until he installed a pump to bring the clear water of the river into the house to use for everything but drinking.

He built the cabin's wooden deck after he came back from Vietnam. It extended to the edges of the surrounding flowering trees her mother loved. She asked him to get the lumber and build the deck, so she could have a place to sit next to him and talk. The deck became a place for them to share the day's bright spots without the glaring noise of the television relaying the day's news. Her mother always tiptoed gently when the mention of John's time in Vietnam came up. She knew it would send him into another night, another day, another week of depression.

She'd told Sara her father would be different when he returned from Vietnam. Sara soon found out what her mother meant by *different*. It frightened the young girl when her mother came to her bed in the middle of the night, crying and shaking, trying to escape the sounds of the nightmare her husband was having. She told Sara to never wake her dad when he was having a nightmare. The half-awake man would break anything he could grab before going to the kitchen to get his whiskey. John kept the nightmares to himself, never wanting to relive and talk about the experiences with his wife. He always treated his daughter with kindness, but when he drank, he had an edge Sara knew to stay away from.

Once, when John came out of the cabin and slammed the kitchen door so hard the glass shattered, Sara forgot and asked him why he was so mad. Her dad went for her. He grabbed her arm and turned her to spank her. The spanking stopped before it started.

And she never asked the question again.

THE SAME TWO METAL CHAIRS that had been her parents' spot to talk remained. In good weather, her parents ended the day in these cold metal things. Sara listened to her mom and dad talk about the large fish that got away, the local thief that got caught, and, by God, Washington politics that were never gonna change. She remembered her mother telling her about John doing a half-ass paint job on the chairs, so he could mark through the dreaded to-do list she'd kept taped to the front of the refrigerator.

Brushing the dirt off the seat of one of the metal chairs, Sara slumped onto it. The bourbon was just starting to hit her when John came out of the kitchen and plopped down beside her.

"Talk to me, Sara. Tell me what's going on."

"Like you talked to Mom about 'Nam? Shit."

"It's why I asked you to come here and stay with me."

"If you don't stop, I'll damn—"

"All right."

Getting up, she stomped into the kitchen and headed for the thirty-year-old faded front of the refrigerator, hoping against hope she would find ice cubes for her next drink. Instead, the ten-inch-deep freezer at the top was stuffed with aluminum foil packages of trout.

"Not a trout night." Sara leaned her head against the frozen packages. She needed another drink and the bottle was nearly empty.

John stood in the kitchen doorway. "What?"

"Old Man, can we go to town and get something to eat?"

"Are you up to town after today?"

"Yes, if you'll shut up about it. Get out of those clothes, they smell like fish. You've got time for a shower before I'm ready."

"Don't shower but once a week. Don't want to run the cistern dry."

"Always jokes, Dad? Turn on the river pump. You stink."

Sara went into her bedroom and took off her cap. She used her fingers to comb the wad of long black hair straight behind her back. She slipped her tee shirt over her head and then adjusted the black bra's edge over the healing wound in her left side. After sniffing her armpits, she dug for the deodorant in her army travel kit and promised herself to jump in the river later that night with a bar of soap.

The contents of her duffle bag offered little to wear for a trip to town. Only a white blouse and a pair of black slacks were clean. When she tried on the blouse over her black bra, she winced. It's the only bra she had. No one would notice. And now the hair, always the hair to worry with. She'd consider going back to the butch cut she had during the first tour, before he came along. She dug again into her travel kit and came up with the army-issued hairbrush. With the short bristles, the brush was more for a man. It had been a man's army all the way. Sara bent her head low and brushed her hair over the top of her head. She closed her eyes and smoothed the hair down flat across her face. After a minute of hard brushing, she spread her long locks over the bra to keep it hidden.

She reached into the bag again and took out the cream the nurses told her to use on the scar. It hurt when she rubbed it over the places where the stitches had been. The hurt brought back the morning memories of lying flat in the boat and screaming to kill men who weren't even there. Too bad there wasn't a cream to stop that shit from happening. Dressed in the white blouse and black slacks, she went to the cabin front room to wait for her dad.

"Good lord, Pops. Can't you ever get away from being a fishing guide?" She shook her head at him standing in the doorway dressed in a tan shirt and pants, the embroidery on the shirt read *"John Randolph, Fishing Guide."*

"Nope. Guess I'm stuck with it." He grinned.

"Come on. I'm buying tonight. Some place where I can get a drink." Sara led the way out the door. "You drive, Dad. I'm riding shotgun tonight."

John opened the passenger door to the Ford pickup to let her climb in. He stopped at the front of the truck and brushed the leaves off the hood, pausing to give her a smile. Sara only had a blank stare to return. She saw herself sitting in the seat of the Humvee she kept trying to forget. It frightened her, and she wondered if she would ever be safe again.

three

MOONLIGHT AND THE FLASH OF the *Open* sign lit the tops of more than a dozen pickups lined up in front of the black building as her dad turned down into the bar's steep driveway. The worked-hard bodies of the trucks sprouted rust and most of the rusting wounds broke through, leaving gaping holes to grace the bottoms of the door panels. The row of trucks was broken now and then by the long tops of vans with sliding panel doors below them. Sara knew there would be child seats strapped in the back of most of them. Off to the ends of the rows were the low car tops, muted by paint turned to chalk and starting to break away, letting the rust escape. A world so different from the vehicles Sara remembered. She still saw them— ordered rows of uniform camouflaged trucks and armored Humvees waiting for the call to battle.

When she read the tilted neon sign hanging over the door, *Bear's Bar and Grill,* it brought her quickly back to the present.

"This look okay?" John asked, his door already half open.

"Only if I can get a stiff shot of bourbon in there." She opened the truck door and slid to the ground.

"Maybe go easy after what happened on the river?"

"Stop, damn it." She slammed the truck door shut.

Sara went in first and stopped just inside the door of the bar to adjust to the dim light and the clammy smell of smoke and spilled beer. John stepped in alongside her and locked his arm in hers.

"Ready, gal? Will you be nervous around a crowd?"

"Maybe a little."

If the men and women at the bar had been talking, they weren't now. Silent heads with unfinished sentences turned to see the good-looking woman on John Randolph's arm. Sara saw the man first. He was seated at the bar wearing a black leather cut and a gold chain that could tow a truck. The sound of his Texas-style boots hitting the floor and sliding to turn him toward them put Sara on alert. She guessed what was coming when the man started walking toward them. John's grip tightened on her arm. The man stopped in front of them, eyeballing her.

"We're not going to walk around you, mister." John motioned with his hand toward the bar. "You need to get back over there."

Taking the toothpick out of the corner of his mouth and dropping it on the floor, the man said, "What you doing with this old prick, woman?"

Sara took a step forward. "You mean this old prick ex-Marine who's going to kick your fucking ass if you don't get out of our way?" She could feel the rush of blood to her face and the hair on her neck rise.

"I've got this," John said. "Last time. Get out of our way, mister."

"She looks just like the kind of piece of ass I'm looking for tonight." The man reached out to touch her arm.

She didn't hesitate. The echo of her slap brought the drinking crowd off their seats to watch.

"You, *bitch!*" He cocked his arm to take a swing at Sara.

John swung first.

The blow caught the man's jaw and twisted his head. The man shook his head twice, then he swung for John's stomach. The punch landed. John dropped to his knees.

"Semper Fi, John! Get up and get him!" someone yelled. "Somebody call the sheriff!"

Sara knelt by her dad. "Breathe, Dad." She rose and turned to the enemy facing her. "So, you think I'm the kind of woman you want?"

She ran her hand under the long drape of her black hair and tossed it over her shoulder. The man's eyes were glued on her black bra. It stood out like the white shirt wasn't even there. She caressed his arm. He backed away.

Sara followed. "Are you up for this?"

She pulled him roughly toward her, and when they were face to face, she slammed with every ounce of hurt she could get with her right knee. She enjoyed the feel of the crunch as it landed.

"Up for me now?"

"You... *whore!*" he sputtered, slumping to the floor.

"I'm going to kill this bastard."

She didn't stop. She kicked him twice in the face. Shoving him over, she dropped across his chest and slugged him in the mouth. When he turned trying to reach his groin, she came down hard on his throat with both hands in a death grip.

"Stop, *stop!* That's enough, Sara." John pulled his daughter off the groaning man. Sara didn't answer. Her mind was no longer in the bar.

She screamed, *"Kill* them. They're on top of the wall. RPG—"

Sara felt someone grab her arms and pull her backward out of the Humvee. Still she kicked with legs aimed for the snipers shooting at them.

"Goddamn it! Leave me with my men, Sarge."

"You're safe, Sara." He dragged her to a booth and pushed her into the seat.

He leaned over her, rubbing her back and telling her to just breath. She was home. It took a lot longer this time for her to return. It was more than ten minutes before she began to reason again.

"God. Twice in one day I've wanted to kill." Sara rubbed her sore hand.

"We're going home. I need to find a doctor that can help you with this."

"Hell, no. They'll try and pump me full of more meds. I'm not going through coming down again from that shit."

A waitress stood a table away from them. "My boss wants to know if you're okay, John? He said to tell you Ruiz is out there shouting he'll kill you both."

"It's all right, Mindy. We'll be okay." He stood and took Sara's arm to leave.

"Sit, Dad. Mindy, bring me a shot of bourbon with a beer chaser." She pushed her dad into the booth across from her.

"John, what's for you? Needin' something stronger than a beer?" the waitress asked.

"Reckon I do, Mindy. Same for me."

"Coming right up," Mindy turned and bumped into a man wearing a green uniform and a badge.

"Excuse me, Mindy."

He leaned over their table resting a hand on each side. "John, I heard about what happened when you came in. The sheriff's up north in the county, so they sent me. Do you want to file charges on him?"

"No, Luke, I think Sara took care of the problem."

"Heard he deserved what he got."

"Sara, this young fellow's a friend of mine. We've known each other for a while. He's with the Arkansas Conservation Police." John slid over and motioned for the agent to sit down.

He held out a hand to Sara. "Luke Matthews."

She took his warm hand and let it linger in hers. He sat down beside John before their hands separated.

"Someone said you really taught that guy a lesson."

"I... I, uh… think I may have gone overboard with that, sir."

Her response was slow. Her eyes stared at the gun on his belt and the badge on his shirt, then paused a long moment at the handsome face smiling at her. She looked again at the neat black holster and the Glock 9 mm there. She reached instinctively for her side where she had carried her own weapon. "Saw the badge and thought I might be in trouble."

"No trouble for you. That guy is bringing a lot of trouble down on this whole area. Be careful and watch your backs." The radio on his shoulder sounded a call. "Sorry, folks, looks like I'm wanted elsewhere. Nice meeting you, Sara. John."

He stood and quickly headed for the door.

"Do you see him often on the river, Dad?"

"Might be seeing him a lot more after tonight."

"Really?" She needed a little spot of happiness like that.

Mindy set the tray of drinks down on the table. "Boss said your drinks are on the house."

"Thanks, Mindy. I think we both need these." John tossed a ten-dollar bill on the tray. "For you."

"Ruiz and the couple guys with him left a few minutes ago. Be careful. He's a mean bastard. The town's afraid of them," Mindy picked up the ten and headed back to the bar.

"Here's to all the mean bastards in the world." Sara lifted the bourbon high above her head before downing it and the beer chaser. "Whoa. After today that felt really good."

"Here's to better days on the river." John tossed back his own drink. "We should take what Mindy said seriously."

"Can we start with that tomorrow?"

Tomorrow came quickly when they reached the parking lot. Both front tires on John's truck were flat and an eight-inch stiletto knife still hung from the side of one of the tires.

John helped Sara into the truck. "It'll be all right. I'll wake up a friend. He has a tire shop right near here."

Sara rolled up the truck window and rested her spinning head against it. The day had taken its toll on her.

four

THE ROBINS SINGING THEIR SONGS welcomed the light from the promising sunrise. Sara fluffed her pillow and wrapped it around her ears to try and block their sounds. Outside, the male robins led the choir with their sharp vocal tunes to their mates who were busy with the sides of their heads turned to the ground. The robins knew spring came early this year and had been waiting for more than a month for days like today when the worms would come up from the depths of winter.

Disappointment for the robins came early from the west. They quit feeding and took shelter when the sudden Midwest storm's frontal winds came to rake the ground and rattle the trees.

Sara stood at the window listening to the rain pelt the cabin's tin roof. The heavy rain quickly overflowed the cabin gutters, flooding the bare backyard and running down the riverbank in a rushing stream of mud and small tree branches. The rain washed away all the plans she'd made for the day.

She opened the back door and looked through the wet screen at the empty dock below. Dad must be somewhere upriver with the boat. He'd been hoping the rain would stop so he could take on the trip the trout dock had booked for him. Now the quiet of the cabin seemed to scream at her, *"You're all alone."*

She paced the hardwood floors, unsure of what to do with herself. Back n the Sandbox, the Army had places she could go for entertainment. So she'd never had to be alone. What the hell was she supposed to do now?

After ten minutes of trying to get the satellite television to work, she gave up. She started pacing again, picking up things and setting them right back down in the dust. Realizing she needed to do laundry, she took her dirty clothes from her bedroom and tossed them in her dad's old top-load washing machine, grateful for something to do. After starting the machine cycle, she lifted the soap jug, shook it, and then threw it on the floor. Empty. *What the hell, Dad?* Disgusted, she walked away, leaving the washing machine churning away without any soap. It became all too much to think about.

When she passed the only mirror in the cabin, she stopped and stared at her reflection in the glass. She didn't recognize the woman staring back at her.

"Who are you?" she whispered.

She turned her head and pulled her hair away to see the scar. How could she forget what she had done when she'd have this forever? Digging her fingernails across the scar, she scratched at it, searching for the blood of the soldier she wanted to punish. She put her finger in her mouth, tasted the blood. She had to escape the sounds of battle rattling the cabin's windows.

She covered her ears and screamed, *"They're all dead!"*

In a panic, she searched the most likely place—her dad's room. She opened the small table drawer by the bed to look, then peered under the edge of the mattress, and finally searched in his dresser where she found the things she looked for. She slid the faded cardboard cartridge box open.

What? Only one bullet?

Next to the box the pistol lay wrapped in an oily rag. Breaking the pistol's action open, she loaded the cartridge, closed it, and spun the cylinder to the firing position. She felt her heartbeat surge blood to the tips of her fingers. She slumped to the floor, pushed her back against the wall, and pulled her legs tight against her chest. Her shaking right hand pushed the barrel of the pistol against her right temple. She didn't pause. She squeezed the trigger. Her mind went blank when the pistol's hammer hit down.

Dazed, confused, and unsure of what happened, she stood up. The gun hung from the limp fingers of her right hand. Madness gripped her. Weapons have to *work.*

She flung the pistol across the room.

"This isn't over yet. Damn you," she whispered, desperate. She staggered across the floor, picked up the pistol and cursed it again.

Pointing the weapon at her head, she pulled the trigger again and again until her fingers got tired. It wouldn't fire. She dropped the gun and sat down on the floor with it in front of her. The men of her dead crew marched across her mind, burning footprints with each step they took.

Afraid her dad would find out what she'd done, she opened the pistol's action and spun the cylinder. Taking the single round out, she turned it over in the palm of her hand, then pressed the dull metal tip to her temple.

Why wasn't the damn thing sitting in the middle of her dead head right now? "Next time you've got to work."

She lifted the oily rag from the drawer and wrapped the handgun back the way she'd found it. The cardboard box sat empty in the drawer. She lifted it and slid the single cartridge back in the worn slot it must have come out of. With the dresser drawer closed on her secret, she went to the kitchen.

Passing the dining table, she picked up the truck keys her father had left there. Turning them in her hand, one of his old dogtags flattened against her palm. She rubbed her finger across the stamped letters of his name and serial number. And then reported for duty. "Sir, Corporal Sara Randolph, 495...." She dropped his key and dogtags like they were on fire and went to slump down into her dad's favorite chair. She felt totally wasted, and sleep came fast.

She didn't wake until she heard John coming up the steps from the dock.

"Did I catch you sleeping?"

"I was tired. The storm made me nervous this morning." Drained, she stood, zombie-like by his chair.

"Just give it time, Sara. You'll get to where you can relax."

"Yes, sir, general." She gave him a middle finger salute.

Yeah. Maybe she could relax and blow her fucking brains out next time.

five

IT WAS TWO DAYS LATER when Sara started to feel herself gaining some control over her desire to end her life. She had eaten very little since her breakdown and felt weak. When she checked the refrigerator and found nothing but trout, she went to the kitchen table and picked up the truck keys.

She paused, realizing she hadn't driven since Iraq.

Stopping at the sink, she turned on the faucet for the cistern, letting it run until it felt cold, then using it to splash her face. It stung like hell. She turned and tore off a paper towel and softly blotted the scar on the side of her face. When she finished, she brushed her hair over the scar to hide it from view. Slipping out of her thoughts about her deep and troubling past often left her thinking—*why? Why* was she torturing herself like this?

In a second it all came flashing back to her—she knew damn well why.

Headed again for the truck, she climbed in the driver's seat and sat, turning knobs and pushing buttons. When she realized she was stalling, she took a deep breath and turned the truck's key. The big V-8 engine roared to life. Sara liked the feel of being in control of something again.

She slipped the truck into gear and drove out of the yard onto the gravel road toward town. She pulled up at a flooded concrete branch crossing and got out to check the water level. Years ago, her dad told her to not cross if the water ran deeper than the tops of her ankles. The water had turned a muddy brown from the heavy rain. She knelt on the edge of the crossing and cupped both hands to toss the water into the air. The last time she tossed stuff in the air it was desert sand, and it came back in her face. She licked the droplets of water off her hands and smiled when she tasted it. She'd drunk a lot worse back on patrol in Iraq.

Back in the truck, she started over the crossing. She hadn't paid enough attention to how fast the water racing across the concrete was rising. Halfway across, her wet shoe slipped on the gas pedal, causing a heavy push. The truck's wheels spun on the slick concrete culvert and surprised her. The right rear wheel dropped off the low water crossing, and the truck leaned hard to the right. The rising water on the culvert was getting deeper. She wiped the sweat off her brow and reached to turn the four-wheel drive switch on the dash. Easing forward, the front wheels pulled the truck back on the concrete.

When she cleared the culvert, she took another deep breath. "I'm ready for this."

Two miles up the road, she changed her mind.

Having to share the narrow road with a wide dually pickup truck pulling a horse trailer caught her off guard. Without thinking, she took the ditch. The truck slid along a barbed wire fence before snapping two posts. The sudden stop against the fence post tossed her hard against the steering wheel.

She beat the steering wheel's rim.

"Dammit! I should have *known* it was too soon to drive." She held her side where her wound had just healed.

The dually and horse trailer skidded to a stop just past her.

Sara sat up and slowly turned her head. Someone was coming.

A woman wearing a Carhart cap and blue jeans cinched on by a belt with a buckle the size of a dinner plate ran toward the truck yelling. "Jeez Louise, are you bleeding? Are you hurt?"

Sara pinched herself to see if anything else had been hurt. "I'm just a little shaken. I'm Sara."

The woman leaned against the truck door. "Oh! I knew this truck belonged to John."

"I guess I'm a little rusty at driving." Sara reached to take off the seat belt she'd forgotten to fasten. When the woman stepped back, she opened the door and slid out of the truck's seat.

"Howdy, Sara. I'm Marty Johnson. I'm so glad to finally meet you. Your dad never stops talking about his army daughter. Sorry about running you off the road."

"No, no. It was my fault. My mind was somewhere else."

"My husband and I have been friends with your dad since we moved down here from up north. John said he had a beautiful daughter. Reckon he wasn't lying. Said you were fighting in Iraq. I'm sure he's happy you came to stay with him."

"Me, too, Marty."

"When did you get back?"

"I've been back about eight months now, I guess. I spent seven and a half of that in a veteran's hospital."

"You're okay, I hope?"

"A little patched up, but okay for sure." She lied. The wound on her side hurt from hitting the steering wheel. The pain didn't come close to matching the constant feeling of guilt and pain for losing her Humvee crew and leaving her unit in wartime.

She wished she could keep these thoughts at bay.

"Hey, I'm just taking my mare home from being bred. You're welcome to drop by my stable anytime. I'll saddle up a couple of my horses, and we can head up in the hills for an afternoon ride and see a beautiful view of the river."

"Thanks, Marty. I might just take you up on that."

"John's got our number on his fridge, so just call me. Want me to back the truck off the fence?"

"Would you? I think I've already done enough damage," Sara said, stepping away from the truck door.

Marty climbed in the truck, started it, and looked at Sara. "Got to really damn well mean it when trying to get out of this creek bottom mud."

She rocked the truck back and forth twice and then let it rip. Two of the fence wires caught on the bumper and popped. The truck came out of the ditch in a shower of mud and hunks of fence posts.

"Shit, if anything is busted on the truck, tell John that Marty did it."

"Do you know who owns the fence?"

"Don't worry about a couple fence posts. It's part of our back acres we don't use. I'll just add another honey-do to my husband's list to fix it."

"The least I can do is pay for any fence posts I broke." Sara reached back into the truck to get her billfold.

Marty patted her on the arm and chuckled. "Get on, girl, you can come help me clean stalls someday."

six

THE SMALL COUNTRY HOMETOWN SARA remembered was no longer there. The empty buildings lining the town's main street were separated by payday loan stores, dollar stores, and thrift shops. Yellow signs spread like welcome banners hung over the doorway of the payday loan store. Her Humvee crew in Iraq had shown her letters from their wives about payday lenders and tripling interest leading to bankruptcy. She pulled off the road and stopped in front of an empty store. She took a small notepad from her shirt pocket. When she opened it to the names of her crew, her tears dropped to the page. They mixed with the ink and blurred the names. Here friends were all gone. All of them. The memories were too much, she had to write some of this down. She flipped past the pages of notes she'd kept back then and started to write.

> *To my crew, I miss you all so much. Billy Link, you saved us so many times before with the .50 caliber. Travis, you sat there under the gun feeding the rounds to drive them off. I don't know why I made you stop, Johnson. Why in the fuck did I? I got you all blown to pieces. Why did I get out of it all alive? God damn. Why? I want to know.*

Sara reached for the 9mm she always carried when on duty. Her hand came up empty, and that brought more tears. She sat for more than an hour with her head against the steering wheel. At times she was asleep, then she would awaken scared and trying to catch her breath thinking she was still in the burning Humvee. She stumbled out of the truck, leaving it to walk along the street. After more than a half mile she felt sane again.

She realized that she was close to the little drive-in restaurant they would circle in their cars after school each day. The sight of it painted bright orange and yellow and green with a large sign calling it *Taco Ranch* was enough to tell her just how much things had changed in the town and in her life.

Drained, she plodded back to the truck.

Back in the truck and driving again, she watched the rows of closed stores flash by. A faded flashing window sign called out a tattoo artist's message of "*Get Ink.*" On another block, a big flashing "*E*" graced the front of the electronic cigarette store.

Sara hoped the farm store she was looking for would still be there on the edge of town. From a block away, she saw the rows of yellow machines butted against the edge of the highway right-of-way. Orange tractors, yellow tillers, and red scrapers all being watched over by a ten-foot-tall portable camouflaged hunting stand with openings on its four sides. The sight took her back to being watched over from a tower at the Bucca Prison. When she walked guard duty with her K-9 through the fence walkways, she always felt the men stationed in the towers were watching her instead of the prisoners they were supposed to be guarding. Sara parked the truck in the first available spot and got out. She walked quickly past the portable stand without looking up. She didn't want her memory to fill in the rifles and guards leaning over the rails leering at her.

Sara paused for a second in front of the store's automatic doors. When they opened, and she walked inside, the blanket of smells hit her, and her depression lightened. These were the scents of her hometown. She walked down the wide aisles and stopped to sort out the unique smell of each section of the store. She stopped and took a deeper breath. It brought a smile.

Her smile left as she hurried through the long aisles of insect sprays, rodent poisons, and garden fertilizer. The smell burnt her nose, and the memory of the stink of exploding shells rushed over her. She had to get away from the smell. She rushed toward the row of dressing rooms on the other side of the store. She tried two doors before finding the third one unoccupied. Sara locked the door and slumped to the seat and covered her face with her hands to muffle the sound of her sobbing. There it was fresh in her memory like it happened today rather than eight and half months ago. The burning Humvee and the horror of the shells hitting all around her surrounded her. For a few seconds she felt sorry for being alive, then her sorrow and grief became thoughts of her dead crew and their families. She flinched at the sudden knock on the dressing room door.

"Are you all right in there?" The sound of a woman's voice was calming.

"Yes. I'll be out in a minute."

The re-emergence of her memories were getting worse. She didn't know what to do to stop it, but she had to do *something*. Sara left the dressing room forcing herself to think about something else. She remembered the clothes she bought in the farm store years ago carried home an abundance of the sweet smells that stayed until the clothes were washed. The smell of the clothes made her feel at home.

She walked along the racks of blue jeans, trying to enjoy lifting and checking each new style. Some pockets on the rumps were trimmed with hearts and others with bright diamonds forming the shape of horseshoes. She chuckled, thinking anyone wearing those would look like they just got kicked in the ass by a mule. Humor didn't come easy at this point, but she tried. Stopping in front of a full-length mirror, she looked around to see if anyone was watching, then turned around to look at her butt. The thin, wasted body of the thirty-four-year-old in the mirror could not be her. Her time in the military hospital recovering from the wound in her side and the guilt from losing her crew had taken its toll on her once well-endowed five-foot-nine-inch frame. She made a mental note to self that getting something to eat in the cabin besides John's trout catches would be necessary.

Finally, she found a stack of jeans with the familiar straight stitch sewn across the top of both pockets and an X across the middle. With three pairs of jeans selected, she picked out two western style shirts and went to the fitting booth to try them on. The pearl snaps instead of buttons made trying on the shirts really necessary. When the snaps closed, she lifted the front of the shirt and realized she was wearing a tent.

After trying on the jeans that were too large, she went back and picked out two other pair that were two sizes smaller. They fit, but she still didn't fill them out. She would make them do.

Remembering the river and fishing with her dad, she gathered up a camo shirt and pants. Stopping at the western boot section, she took a pair from the shelf with all leather soles and sat down to try them on. When the price tag dropped out of the inside, she quickly slipped them back in the box. Filing for her partial disability could help with expenses, but this was her fault. She couldn't take that money. At checkout she had the lady include three eight-foot fence posts and then handed her John's credit card. The cashier read the name on the card and quickly entered the zip code into the register without asking. "How's that man doing out there all alone?"

"He's not alone any longer. I'm Sara, his daughter."

"He's always talkin' about you, honey. Welcome home, soldier. Go ahead and punch in his PIN."

"Oops, I forgot to ask him."

"I got 'em. He forgets them so often he had me memorize them," the woman said, leaning over the counter and punching in the numbers. "Drive over to the side. I'll have one of the boys load them fence posts for you."

"What's your name? I'll tell Dad I saw you."

"Just tell him it's the gal at the farm store that keeps trying to get him to take her to dinner more often. He'll know, sweetie."

Sara chuckled. "I'll tell him for sure, and thanks for your help."

With the fence posts loaded in the back of the truck, Sara headed for home. She slowed at the wrecked fence to unload the posts, but on second thought, decided to take them to Marty's barn.

She found Marty standing in front of the barn brushing a bay horse. She stopped brushing to wave a welcome.

"You're here just in time to help brush this old girl. She should be all shed off by now, but some things slow down with age," Marty said, motioning for Sara to come join her. "I'm sure there's a second brush over there in the bucket."

"I'd love to help." Sara picked up a brush and stood by the horse, not knowing where to start.

"Come on over here by me. I'll show you. Just start up on her hip and brush hard with the flow of her hair. Your brush will fill up with her shedding real quick."

"I went into town and picked up the new fence posts. I can dig them in."

"That's considerate of you, Sara, but my husband will do that."

"Are you sure? I broke the fence."

"I'm sure. I felt bad for you this morning. It seemed you weren't at ease driving the truck."

"The last time I drove was in Iraq."

"Your dad talked to us a lot about your service over there. He worried a lot about you and didn't mind telling us so."

"I tried to write him often and let him know I was okay."

"He came over to talk the day he said you were wounded. Were you driving then?"

"No, I was a team leader and riding shotgun when we got hit. My driver and crew were killed."

"I'm so sorry. Your dad didn't tell us what happened."

"I'm all right. This is the first time I've had a woman to talk to since getting out of the hospital. I hope you didn't mind me telling you what happened that day." She stood taking long strokes with the brush along the horse's hip.

"Nope. I get lonesome for someone to talk to out here. I'm alone a lot. My husband leaves to sell farm implements across the state. I end up talking to this old mare. You like to ride?"

"I've ridden some. Dad took me horseback riding often years ago, somewhere around here. I guess I've forgotten most of what I learned from him."

"It'll come back, dear. You'll be right at home on this old mare of mine. Hang on, I'll be right back."

She returned carrying a saddle over her shoulder and one in her hand. She saddled the mare for Sara and a gelding named Dusty for herself. Marty held the mare while Sara mounted.

"Sit tight, gal. I'm going to have to drop the stirrups for your long legs. How tall are you anyway?"

"Last time the army checked I was five-nine."

Marty made quick work of sliding the releases and pulling out five more inches of leather.

"There. Try that now." She held the wooden stirrup for Sara's foot. Sara caught the stirrup and slid her foot in. She followed getting her foot in the other stirrup. Marty let Sara's mare go and swung into the gelding's saddle on in one quick lift.

"It's a bit rough getting up the hills, but the beauty makes it worth it."

"I'm game."

Marty led the way when they left the barn and headed across the flat areas of the pasture.

"When it gets rough up ahead, just let the mare have her head."

"Her head?"

"I'm sorry, just loosen the reins. Let out about three inches on each side of her neck, and you'll do fine."

Sara let out an inch of the reins from her death grip. "Like this?"

"Maybe a little more."

Marty pointed to a rough patch of ground. "Wild pigs have been coming down out of the woods to find something to eat. They root and tear the hell out of things. Wrecked our garden last year."

"Might be time to have some ribs for barbeque."

Marty let out a big laugh. "Got to tell you my husband put a big spotlight on them, and I shot one of the son of a bitches. Bud had him hanging in the barn in a couple of hours. Turned out to be some of the best pork we ever had. Those hogs eat all-natural food in the woods, mostly acorns and pinecones. I've some pork chops in the freezer I'll send along with you when we get back."

"Thanks. We would love them. I am so tired of eating trout four or five times a week."

Fresh green shoots of willow trees had pushed up through the cattails along the far edge of Marty's pond. Tall and strong, they were more than ready to play host to the red-winged black birds looking to lure a mate to a waterfront property nest site. Marty led the way past the pleading male birds onto a cleared trail leading up a steep incline. Sara's mare followed with its nose almost on Dusty's tail as they climbed up the trail.

Marty turned in the saddle toward Sara. "There's a couple of rock outcroppings up ahead that get steep. Drop more slack in the reins, and she'll follow me and climb right up. Hold on to the saddle horn and lean forward when she lunges ahead over the rock ledges."

Sara gripped the saddle horn with both hands when her mare paused at the bottom of the first ledge. The savvy mare gathered her legs under it in a firm stance before lunging up the ledge.

The mares fast action caused Sara to fall forward, hard into the saddle horn. The wound in her side made her flinch and yell, "Wow! Shit!" She grabbed the horse's mane with both hands and slid back into position in her saddle.

"You've got it made now. Way to hang on, girl."

Sara felt like having a serious talk with herself about ever going horseback riding again. With her feet back in the stirrups, she straightened in the saddle.

"We're almost at the top. I think you'll like it up here. Bring the mare on up alongside me. Both of the horses like riding that way." They crossed out of the woods and onto a lush grass pasture. Marty pulled up some ways back from the edge of a bluff dropping to the river bottom below. "Bud and I like to ride up here to watch the sun come up. It's sort of like they do in the cowboy movies when they stand their horses and look across hundreds of acres filled with grass and cattle. At least we can look at a hundred and fifty acres sitting down there alongside the White River and know it's ours."

"It's truly beautiful, Marty. Even breathtaking."

"Bud and I sometimes just sit up here on horseback looking at it."

"I can remember a time when I would have walked a hundred miles to see a river valley like this. All we had to look at in Iraq were walls, windows, and dusty bare fields. The windows were the worst, shots meant to kill us came out of them. I'm sorry, Marty, for bringing it up. I don't want to burden with this."

"Sara, I'm a damn good listener."

"My mind goes back there way too often. I'm surprised it came out— talking about it with you, I mean."

"Maybe you just needed to share."

"It helps to have someone that listens. I try not to even bring it up around Dad. He still has all his demons from Vietnam."

"We've had dinner with John several times. He stays away from any talk about being in the war."

"I'm not surprised. I think he doesn't know what else to say to me. He really does try to help."

"I think he has been lonesome living there alone for so long."

"Don't say anything to him, but I found out he's got an admirer in town at the farm store."

"You know we went to dinner with them both a few months before you came home."

"Is it anything serious? I don't want to get in their way."

"Your dad can think for himself, Sara. I think he would tell you if it became a problem."

"Keep an ear to the ground, and let me know if you hear anything."

"I will. Come on there's a big stand of pine trees up here I want to show you."

Marty led off along a path cutting through the scrub brush. "I'll take you back to the barn an easier way. It'll take longer, but I think you'll love the pines."

Sara breathed a sigh of relief. "Can't wait."

When the trail wound through the deep green branches of the pines, Sara was wrapped in an unforgettable smell from her childhood. "Marty, you can just leave me here! I've needed this to really feel at home. My dad and mom took me camping in a grove of pines likes these when I was young. It's one of those times and smells I tried to think about when walking guard duty at night. It helped to push back the stink of the muck and filth in the prison."

"This is a good place to stop and get off. Bud and I dragged the log up here about a year ago so we could sit and enjoy the pine trees. We love to be here when there's a good breeze blowing through them. The smell and sounds of the moving branches are just overpowering."

"Do I need to tie the horse up?"

"Just drop the reins on the ground in front of the mare. She'll stand."

They both dismounted and walked to the log lying next to the trail. They sat and listened to the sound of the wind brushing the pines, lost in their own thoughts for more than a half hour before being reminded by squawking blue jays that the pines were their home, and company was no longer welcome.

BOTH HORSES PICKED UP THE pace going down the backside of the upper pasture area.

"We'll have to hold them back a bit, Sara. They like going home too much. I can tell when my husband has been riding this old horse. He just lets him have his head to go as fast as it wants."

When they reached the barn, Marty dismounted first.

"We won't have to walk them because they didn't break a sweat on the way back."

She loosened her saddle first and then showed Sara how to undo the cinch strap on her saddle. With the two saddles put away in the tack room and the saddle blankets hanging on a rack, Marty got out two brushes. Sara enjoyed brushing out the mare and watching the animal turn its head to rub against her side. With the two horses turned out in the stable lot, Marty showed Sara where to back the truck and unload the fence posts.

"Thank you, Marty. It's been good to have you to talk with. I really needed this today."

"You're welcome here anytime, honey. Don't run off. I'll get the pork chops out of the freezer for you." Marty rushed into the barn and returned with a big package of chops.

"Great. I know Dad's gonna love some home-cooked pork chops and taters! Thanks, Marty."

Marty gave Sara a big bear hug. "Honey, you're always welcome here. Tell John howdy for us."

"I will for sure." Sara left with a smile and a sense of new-found friendship. She needed a day to end well. Somehow she planned to cook one of the frozen pork chops as soon as she got to the cabin. She felt starved.

seven

SARA ROLLED OUT OF BED and stood to stretch her arms over her head. Her first step of the morning sent her down to her knees. She'd forgotten what riding a horse for over two hours would do to the thigh muscles of a green horn. She walked stiff legged around the kitchen, trying to relieve her cramping muscles. With a large glass of orange juice in her hand, she headed for John's lounge chair to watch the small nineteen-inch TV, thinking she was going to have to wait out the hurt before any more walking.

When the sun finally came out, it was midafternoon. Sara welcomed the chance to lay out and soak up some of its warmth. She slipped out of her clothes and put on an old robe she found in John's closet. The spot she picked behind the cabin would keep her sheltered from the fishing boats on the river and the country road to the west. She spread the robe on the grass and stretched out face up, relaxed and naked to the sun. When her sunglasses let in too much light, she pulled the robe over her face.

The barking of a neighbor's dog woke her, and she quickly sat up. Pulling her robe shut, she stood up and started toward the cabin. The sound of a car door shutting pushed her even faster to get inside the cabin. She stopped at the door when she heard a knock on the fence gate.

"Who are you looking for?" she asked the man standing halfway through the gate.

"I'm Pastor Blankenship."

The pastor was dressed in a black suit coat with sleeves that ended five inches from each hand and tan pants that hid all but the soles of his shoes. His hollow cheeks and gaunt body reminded Sara of the prisoners she'd watched back in Iraq trying to starve themselves into martyrdom.

She backed slowly behind the door screen. "I'm busy, Pastor."

The pastor took two more steps into the yard and didn't speak.

"Stop right there. Why are you staring at me?" Her back was against the cabin door.

"Folks in my church said John Randolph's got a woman living out here with him. Said she's gonna need savin'." The man reached into a leather bag hanging on a shoulder strap and took out a bible. He lifted the string bookmark and flattened the pages to read. "I came out here to pray for you. Bring you to God."

All the things she had thought about saying to God after she had gotten blown up in Iraq rushed to her mind. *Where were you, God, when my driver got his head blown off? How can you be so cruel?* She shook the thoughts off and opened the cabin door a crack behind her. She gave the preacher another reason she might need saving. She let the robe drop open and stood bare chested, pointing a hand and long finger at the man.

"Take your God and leave. I'm way, *way* past savin', preacher man."

She was sorry for saying it, even as it came out of her mouth. Sara knew deep inside God had nothing to do with what happened to her crew. *She had* killed them.

Backing in the door, she got a last look through her tears at the preacher leaning on one knee, head bowed, holding the bible in his outstretched hands out toward her. Sara wanted to go to him and ask for his and God's forgiveness, but she wasn't ready to face God. Maybe she never would be. The terror of battle flooded through her once again. Next, the guilt would come, pushing away all the progress she'd made. She shut the door and headed for the bread box and the bottle of booze there.

BEFORE HER DAD GOT BACK from fishing, she had three of Marty's pork chops with edges browned just enough to be crispy, sharing the top of the gas range with simmering sauerkraut flavored with strips of bacon, taters, and a big cut of onion. Her mom's cookbook, the one with the red and white faded cover, gave up her dad's favorite recipe for cornbread. The smell rising from the oven filled the whole cabin. She hoped this would make up for her run-in with the preacher. She lifted the coffee pot off the stove and topped off the last of the four cups she'd sucked down in hopes of ending her drunken afternoon.

"Sara, I'll be up in a couple minutes," John yelled from the dock.

"Hang on, Dad. Gotta get the cornbread out of the oven."

"Got four rainbows and a brown to clean for supper."

"Surprise! Supper is just about ready. Thought you might be a little tired of trout."

"Darn right I am. Be right up."

With two of the pork chops and half of the sauerkraut on a plate, she put a slice of buttered cornbread on top and started for the table. John stood in the doorway sniffing the air like a hound dog and then headed straight for the kitchen table.

"You go and wash that fish blood off your hands," Sara said, standing and holding her dad's plate off to her side.

"Ain't no need to tell me twice. I'm going."

John didn't waste much time washing his hands. Back at the table, he took one look at the dinner she'd set for him, smiled, and dug in. She joined him with the other pork chop and a big slice of cornbread with butter and honey. She'd found one of the jars of golden honey with a hunk of comb that John must've gathered last year. She remembered the shock of bumping into one of his beehives when she was six years old. Her mother had held her and put ice on the stings while she cried. Sara liked knowing that her dad rarely spoke when there was food on a plate in front of him. It would give her time to think about how to tell him about her afternoon.

John finished his dinner, leaned back in his chair, and rubbed his belly. "Minnow, it's been a long time since I've had a home cooked meal like this one. You did good on those wild hog pork chops, gal." He paused for a long belch. "Expect I need to get those trout cleaned."

"Just a minute, Daddy. A couple things happened today that I need to confess to."

"You're calling me Daddy? Did somebody die?"

"No. Nobody died."

"Then, hell, don't worry about having to confess anything to me. Besides, that damn preacher might stop coming out here and driving me crazy about coming to his rattlesnake-worshiping church."

"Holy shit. News spreads fast around here."

"Yep, don't need no internet when you've got a woman like Della over at the boat dock. That big scratch and dent on the right fender of the truck is okay, too."

Sara got up and gave him a full-arm bear hug. "I love you so much, always have, Daddy."

"You, too, Minnow." He patted her on the back, then took his dishes to the sink. After a moment, he returned to sit next to her at the table. "There's something else we need to talk about."

"Well, *that* sounds ominous."

"Sara, I've been waiting for the right time to talk with you about this. I know you went looking for my pistol. You were in my cabinet."

The urge to get flee suddenly became overwhelming. She stood up and backed away from the table. The scar on her face felt hot and raw.

"Don't go getting up and leaving when I'm trying to talk to you."

She stared hard at him for a moment, then sat back down, arms crossed in front of her.

"Remember what I'm going to tell you. I came home from 'Nam, and it didn't take long for the memories to get the best of me. I took that Smith & Wesson and a thirty-eight cartridge and went out back. I sat there for an hour or more looking at the shell 'fore I loaded it in the chamber. Set it to be the next one to fire and closed the cylinder. Then I look up and see your mother at the door, just staring at me. She knew what I was about to do. Told me to go ahead and do it, too, if that was what I wanted. She said it'd been coming for a long time. I was... I was out of my head. Thought I didn't have anything to live for. So I put that gun to the side of my head and pulled the trigger.

"Dad—"

"But you know what? The gun didn't fire. And in that moment, everything I would have missed raced through my mind. You. Your mother. *Everything.*"

"Dad, I—"

"No, *listen,* Sara. Your mother saved my life that day. After I calmed down, she told me that a week after I got home, she knew what I would end up doing. So she took the pistol out to the shed and filed the firing pin plum off the hammer so the gun wouldn't shoot."

Sara's face drained of blood and her heart dropped into her stomach.

Her mother had saved her life, too.

"I—"

"Let me finish. If you go and buy a new automatic to try this again, I promise you won't hear a *clunk.* That gun will kill you, and you won't get to think about all the good things that you'll miss. It'll just be over. The end. Hear me? Back then I didn't stop to think what killing myself would do to your mother. But believe me, I've thought about it a hell of a lot since." John reached up and gently wiped a tear off her cheek. "Don't do it. I don't want to lose you, Little Minnow. Thing *will* get better. *You'll* get better. I promise."

"I hope you're right, Daddy." She sniffled, thought again about her mother reaching out to protect her from beyond the grave. "I just can't see my way out yet."

eight

IT WAS EIGHT THIRTY IN the morning when they got to the dock. John carried a bait can he said was loaded for the big ones.

"Brought along some extra treats the browns will go after this time of year." He stepped in the boat and went to the motor at the back. "Just grab a rod you like."

"You forget? I still need a fishing license."

"We'll stop at the trout dock and get you fixed up. Don't want Luke coming along and arresting you."

"Well, now." She settled into the front seat of the jon boat.

"Sara. Behave! You ruined both our reputations yesterday."

He was smiling when he turned away.

WITH A FISHING LICENSE IN her pocket, Sara sat in the front of the jon boat and watched the other boats pass as her father motored about a mile upriver from the crowd of people fishing around the docks. John slowed the boat's motor to idle and lifted a float bottle and drag chain off the floor. Sara remembered his lesson on using a break-away chain. He liked to use the drag chain to keep the front of the boat pointed upstream as they drifted to fish. He told her how the chain could get caught on underwater logs, and if it didn't break away, how the boat could be drug under by the strong river current.

He handed her the chain. "Give it a pitch, and we can get to fishing."

Sara wound up and pitched it out into the current. It felt surprisingly good, being able to throw something without fear of breaking it. She grinned and sat back down.

Now he handed her a small fish from his cooler. "Now put this bait on the bigger rod. It has heavier line on it."

"What the hell is that thing?"

"It's a sculpin—a fish that lives on the bottom of the river. Big brown trout like to eat big bait. They can spend all day eating insects and never get full, so they go after sculpin in a big rush. Now, go ahead and put it on and hook, about an inch up from the tail."

"What makes you think I'm going to touch that?" Taking it from him, laughing, she hooked the sculpin through the tail. She'd just been yanking his chain. Hell, there were times on patrol back in the Sandbox when she was so hungry, she would have eaten the damn thing raw.

The boat drifted down river with the bow pointing upstream, the dragging chain keeping it straight for easy fishing toward the bank.

"Remember how to toss with a spinning rod?"

"Before I throw this bait out to exactly where I want it, Old Man let me tell you about fishing in Baghdad. The captain took my squad to spend a weekend by the lake Saddam put in by his mansion. I'm the only one who caught anything, and I fished that bastard's lake empty. We had crappie and bass to eat for days. So yes, I remember how to cast a spinning reel."

He chuckled. "Well, then, if you're so damn good, let's see you lay that bait over by the west bank, right on this side of the muddy water coming down the little branch."

She took on the tease of his challenge and didn't miss by far. The bait landed only about a foot into the muddy water. Lifting the rod tip, she cranked the bait into the clear water. She felt the heavy tug when the fish grabbed the sculpin. Sara hauled back on the rod.

"Easy, he's hooked good now. Gonna have to follow this big fellow. Hang on!"

He cranked the motor and started upstream.

"Just keep a little bend in the rod and take up some line if we gain on him."

The trout's pull on the line sent a shiver up her back. It was almost as good as sex.

Well, on second thought... maybe not.

"There's a big tree sunk in the middle of the river about twenty yards ahead. I'm pulling over toward the bank, and you're going to have to try and steer him away from the tree. Otherwise, he's going to be a goner. Lookin' like way more than a keeper. Stay on him."

"He's really working me, Dad! What do I have on here?" Sweat was already popping out on her forehead. She was enjoying the chase.

"Sure as hell not a minnow is it?"

Forty minutes passed before the bend in the rod lessened and the big fish tired. Sara's arms started to quiver from the strain. She did her best to keep tension on the line, cranking on the reel as the fish gave in to her steady pull. "He's coming up!"

"The net's ready. Bring him alongside." John dipped the net into the water.

She lifted the rod-tip high. "Get him quick, he's diving under the boat."

Sweeping the net forward and around the trout, he lifted the fish into the boat with a rebel yell.

"I'm looking forward to supper tonight," Sara said. "Oh, wow! That fish is *way* more than one supper."

John put the fish on his handheld scale, and they both looked to see what it weighed.

He whistled. "Twenty-two pounds. This old fellow's been in here for a long time. I'd feel sorry taking him away from his home. What's say, Sara? Toss him back? Let him father some more monsters? In a few more years, he's going to be up around the thirty-pound record fish caught on the White."

"Hell, no, Old Man. Not until you take my picture holding this whale." Sara reached into her back pocket for her phone. Clicking on the camera icon, she handed it over. "Just aim and touch the button, Dad. Think you can handle that?"

"At my advanced age?" He shook his head. "Are you sure you trust me?"

"Just take the damn picture, Old Man."

She lifted the trout out of the net, held it between her outstretched hands, and gave it a big kiss as John tapping the shutter button.

"Got it!"

Slipping her fingers in the trout's mouth, she cradled it with a hand under its tail and gently lowered it back into the river. It swam slowly alongside the drifting boat for a moment. Then, with a sweep of the it's tail and a resounding splash, it disappeared back into the depths.

Sara was proud of the catch. She tapped the smartphone screen and brought the picture up for her dad to see.

"How do I get a copy of that picture, Minnow?"

She laughed. "I'm going to get several prints made."

"Good. Let's get one blown up and framed. I want to put it in the living room over the mantle."

"Don't you think that's a bit much?"

"For my Minnow? Never."

The warm, contented feeling she'd longed for when she first came home had finally arrived.

nine

"SARA, I'M HEADING OVER TO Baxter today, so the boat's all yours."

"What's in Baxter?"

"I've been seeing a doc over there. He's a fishing customer of mine and, well, we're kind of friends."

"Have you been feeling bad? You haven't said anything."

"Naw, just regular stuff."

"As long as you're sure, Dad." She realized he had been too quick to get off the subject. She would question him more later.

"There's a fly rod in the closet behind the refrigerator. It was your mother's. Tie on one of the flies she left in her creel and give it a try."

"I forgot all about that closet. You built it to hide your guns."

"The guns are gone now. Your mom sold the whole lot."

Sara didn't need to be told twice to go fly fishing. Remembering her mother's lessons using an old wooden fly rod, Sara would whip the line back and forth over her head and then smoothly, so as not to scare the fish—that was the secret—let the fly drop to the water's surface.

It would be cool out on the water, so she put on a light sweater and pants, tucked her hair under a ball cap, and headed for the closet to find the fly rod.

She pushed the thirty-year-old fridge off to the side and stooped to get a grip on the door panel sunk into the rough wall of the cabin. It wouldn't move. Now, where did her dad keep a screwdriver? She found it right where she suspected, in the drawer divider next to the forks. Men.

With a little prying on the oak panel, it gave way, and the rusty hinges voiced their annoyance at someone intruding to find the hidden treasures. Sara reached into the dark hideaway and swept her hand across the back wall. The thump of the fly rod falling over woke up the mouse living in the closet. The mouse flew out of the darkness, landing belly button high on Sara's waist. Moving fast was the last thing she had intended to do this morning. Getting the mouse off became her new morning goal. She scooted backward to the middle of the room and yelled at it, but that didn't do much. The frightened mouse with ears the size of a rabbit's was caught in her sweater like it was Velcro. It stared hard at her face.

"Darn, you're cute." She caught her breath. She almost wanted to risk getting bit just to pet the mouse. The thought of one morning in Iraq when she awakened to find a scorpion sharing a pillow with her gave her reason to be leery of staring faces. The scorpion hadn't had cute ears, just one hell of a mean looking stinger at the end of its tail.

Sara stripped her sweater off, wadded it in a ball around the mouse, and took it to the porch. She opened the ball on the deck and laughed when the mouse ran out, slipped through a crack, and disappeared. Sure the mouse would beat her back to the closet, she headed to the kitchen cabinet to get a flashlight.

Her mother's fly rod had fallen behind a wooden box. Sara lifted the rod and slid it out on the floor behind her. She looked again and found her mother's fly-fishing creel neatly sitting to the left of the wooden box on the wide board. Sara remembered the board and the small vice on it that her mother used to tie flies for her dad's guide trips. Then she remembered the secret her mother told her. "These special flies in the little box in my creel are for you, Sara. Your dad doesn't know the secret way I tie them and how they will bring up even the biggest trout from the rock bottom of the river." That very morning her mother had taken her out on the river to fish with the new flies. She'd stopped the boat's engine and had Sara pick out the fly she wanted to use. Her mother carefully tied the small nymph on the line and handed Sara the fly rod. Then a sudden rain shower hit like someone had dumped a tub of water on them. Drenched and dripping, her mother sat at the back of the boat laughing and holding her sides. Sara joined the laughter after her mother promised they would come back out later after they got dried off and the rain stopped.

She opened the fishing creel and took out the tiny wooden box with her name carved into the top. She held it against her lips and took a deep breath. It wasn't a kiss. More of a reach to find a trace, a smell, a memory of the mother she'd lost. She opened the box and her eyes welled up. Her tears made it hard to see the tiny nymph fly treasures inside. She sighed. The cork bottom holding all the flies had broken. Sliding the pieces back in place, she carefully grasped a fly, backing it from the cork. Holding it to the light, she remembered the day her mother tied the tiny hook with the gatherings Sara had collected. Hair pulled from a red fox squirrel skin-wrapped hook for the body. Darker black hair from a skunk pelt for the head of the insect. Then, finally, some tiny feathers that Mom had her pull from Old Willy the rooster.

Sara returned the nymph to the cork and closed the box. More tears fell on the wood as she carefully placed it back into the creel. She took the board with the fly-tying vice and the wooden box from the closet and set it on her bedroom table. Her mom had shown her so much of this art.

Now it was her time to make treasures for herself.

GUIDING THE BOAT THROUGH THE thick morning fog made her feel halfway normal again. Her narrow path through the fog created the illusion of being cut off from the rest of the world, traveling in a space and world all her own. She hoped the journey would never end. Idling back the engine even more, she enjoyed the solitude for another mile before coming close to hitting a tree trunk sticking out of the water.

The fog lifted by the time she got to where Crooked Creek merged into the White River. She passed the waters her dad told her to fish and went on upstream. Another mile upriver and it would be time to put out the drag chain and drift back down to their cabin. Her dad had told her where the trout would be feeding this time of morning, and catching a few keepers would be easy with the dozen special dry flies she had just tied during the early morning hours. After passing a half-dozen boats drifting with the current, she slipped the engine out of gear, went to the bow and threw out the chain.

Pushing a strand of hair back under her camo cap, she leaned forward to grab her mother's old fly rod from the floor of the boat. Flexing the rod and tossing a dry fly out thirty feet from the drifting boat would take some of the stiffness out of her left side. She whipped the bamboo rod back and forth, spilling out the green line. The rod came from another time, when building a work of art ruled the fly-fishing world. The feel and sound of the rod working the heavy line reminded her of the days her mother took her to the river to fish and try out the masterful flies she dreamed up to mimic insects dropping to the water of the river.

She lifted the tip of the rod just before the fly reached the spot she'd aimed for. The fly dropped to the water first, the clear leader easing down on the surface behind. Good cast. She'd left the fly floating on top of the water. She moved the rod tip and the fly just a jiggle to entice the trout she could see below. Several small ones left the bottom and headed for the fly, but they weren't what she wanted to catch today. She reeled the fly from the water, ready to move to another place. Lifting the drag-chain, she motored downstream a half-mile before throwing it out again.

Another boat eased past and she got a friendly wave from the guide and the couple fishing with him.

"Doing any good drifting, miss?"

She waved back. "Not yet, but I'm hoping."

Getting paid to fish could be something to give some thought to. It was fun watching the guides share in the fishing, tossing their lines in right alongside paying customers.

With one nice rainbow trout in the cooler, she relaxed. Her fly-tying was paying off well. Restarting the motor, she headed back upstream to fish the same area again. As she went, she counted the new, expensive houses lining the east bank of the river. Launch ramps and new docks were starting to fill the riverbanks in this area. Out of the corner of her eye she noticed a black Dodge sedan sitting at the top of one of the ramps.

The car sat facing the river. That was a funny place to park.

A mile down the river, she saw the Dodge again. The car slowly followed the river on a side road, then turned off when she drifted by. She thought of the threat Ruiz had made a few days earlier and promised herself not to worry her dad with it.

She watched a dark green boat round the bend down river speeding toward her. It came on fast, not like the guide boats with small engines. As it got closer, it slowed to a crawl. She saw the Arkansas Conservation Commission sign on its side and the uniformed woman in green piloting the boat. The woman turned to the man sitting beside her and pointed at Sara's boat.

When the man waved, she realized it was Luke. The agents had two men sitting in the front of the boat, arms handcuffed behind their back. She waved back, glad they were getting some poachers off her river.

The fish count in the live well stood at two, so she stowed the fly rod, lifted the drag chain out of the water, and turned the boat downsteam. Time to call it a day.

When she pulled into the dock, John stood at the top of the steps and gave her a wave. "Welcome home, Minnow."

"Got a couple to clean. I'm going to run these over to Marty and her husband." Sara had reached the point where she would have driven a hundred miles to get trout off her menu.

AFTER A DINNER OF BACON and eggs, they sat in the living room with the television off. It was strange. John always had the six o'clock news on.

Sara cleared her throat. "You're really quiet tonight. Want me to turn the television on?"

"Doc gave me some things to think about today."

"Are you okay?"

"Thought so, until today. Doc wants to run some more tests."

"Stop it, Dad. Quit pitching out the doctor visits without telling me what's going on with you."

"I don't think it's going to be anything serious."

"You don't think? What's the testing for, Dad? Tell me."

"When I told him I get short of breath and dizzy once in a while, he wanted to run some stress tests on me."

"Dizzy? How often—"

"Damn it. Stop! Just why I never told your mother about things. She always got all worried up."

"Dad, don't you know she loved you? Mom and I both have a worry gene in our DNA."

"Quit the worry. I'll tell you what he finds out with the test. Okay, Little Minnow?"

"You had better, Old Man. I love you. I just—"

"You getting tired of too much fishing?"

Sara realized he was trying to change the subject, and she would go with that for now.

"Hell, no. Never get tired of the river, but we both know I'm going to have to find a job soon. I've got enough saved from my pay in Iraq to get a car and pay for a place to live. It's not right for me to keep living off of your savings and not paying you."

"Going to work right now might—"

"What do you mean, right now?" The back of her neck tightened up.

"You worry me when things go bad around you. I think you just need more time to unwind from Iraq. Besides, shouldn't you be getting your disability pay soon?"

"I'm not going to take that money. I fell for a trap. It was my fault what happened."

"It's hard to lay blame in a war."

She got up to leave.

"You've never really told me what happened your last day in Iraq."

She turned around and stood facing her dad. "What happened is I stopped our convoy and got my crew killed. It was my fault, Dad."

"Sara, you—"

"I know what you are going to say."

"I'll say it anyway. You should get some V.A. help."

"I'm tired of all the waiting crap that happens with the V.A. You should know about that."

"Your mother rode my ass about getting help. I'd best shut up. Right?"

"Right. Pick up a newspaper for me tomorrow so I can check the job ads. Please, Dad."

"Why don't you go to work for me?"

"For you?" She sat back down beside him.

"The morning trips up the river take a lot of time. Having you drive me and the boat up there would save a lot of hours on the water. Then you could pick us up here and take us back to the trout dock."

"I could do that. If you're sure it would help."

"Damn right it would. It would save me three hours a day at least."

She went to bed with a lot to think about. She knew helping her dad with the guide job would be a good thing for both of them. She turned over and pulled her third pillow tight against the scar on her left side, hoped it might help fend off the nightmares that would come just before dawn.

———————

SHE AWOKE TWO HOURS BEFORE dawn, turned on the lights, and went to her bedroom table. She slid her mother's wooden board and the fly-tying vice close under the lamp shade. Her mother's wooden box would have most of what she needed. She needed to try and tie the smallest of flies. Opening the box, she pushed the tanned animal hides and quail feathers aside until she found the package of tiny hooks. With one of the hooks secure in the vice, she sorted through the strings, yarn, and hides until she came to some stiff hair that had been bleached white. She leaned over the vice and hook with a long piece of thread and started to tie the hair to the hook. When her hand flinched and tightened up, she got up and paced the room shaking both hands to relax them.

She didn't sit back down until the tightness in her hands relaxed. She looked again in her mother's toolbox and found a tiny pair of tweezers. She gripped the string again and wrapped the white hair to the hook. She smiled, knowing she would work past sunup and avoid the nightmares this night.

ten

BY SEVEN O'CLOCK THE TRAILER was hooked up to the truck. Backing the boat out of the dock, John loaded it on the trailer, and with Sara driving, they started their first trip together to the trout dock.

"Hope I didn't forget anything you might need. Got the baits you wanted and all the rods in the boat. The dock called last night and said the customers like diet cola and would bring anything else they wanted for drinks. I loaded up three Zip-Lock bags with trail mix and a couple candy bars for you."

Sara winced as they passed the spot in the road where she hit the fence.

The look didn't escape him. "Boy, you did a number on those old fence posts, girl. Don't show much damage on the truck."

She grinned. "Did you look at the side of the truck in the daytime, Dad?"

"It wasn't the first dent this old fellow has had."

Turning off the main street of town, Sara drove down the steep hill into the large parking area at the edge of the White River.

"I'm going in the office to tell the Hineses we're here. You can take the driveway around the building and back the trailer down the ramp for me. Try not to hit any fence posts!" he said and then chuckled. "If you take the boat off, put it in the second slip in the dock."

She watched as he stepped on the porch of the trout dock office and said hello to the three men standing there. She guessed they were fishing guides waiting for clients to arrive. The office was in a red, single-story wood building that sat more than fifty feet above the river. The fishing docks and boats floated in a cove that protected them from the fast currents of the river.

She backed the trailer down the ramp into the river, then climbed into the boat, and started the motor. She backed the boat off the trailer and steered it into a slip. After she tied the boat, she went to the office to meet her dad. His customers still hadn't arrived.

"Hang on a minute. I want you to meet the owners, the ones that schedule my guide trips for us. This is George Hines and his wife, Barbara. Folks, this is my daughter, Sara. She just got back from her second tour in Iraq. Just about didn't get her back at all."

"I guess things could have been a lot worse. I'm home safe. Glad to meet you both. Dad talks quite fondly of you." Both the owners shook hands with Sara and thanked her for her service and for helping to get John back and forth on his guide trips.

"What time do I meet you this afternoon, Dad?"

"This is half a day, so around one o'clock at our dock."

"See you then." She headed out the door to the truck. She had pulled it up off the ramp but left it blocking anyone else trying to launch.

"Going to move that truck of yours anytime soon? You're blocking an official agent of the Arkansas Conservation Commission from getting to work," a lady in uniform said. She was sitting in a dark green official truck.

"I'm sorry. I'll get it moved from there right now."

"Had to say that to you, Sara. My working partner said to kid you up a bit. I can't get him to stop talking about meeting a good-looking Iraq army veteran. My name, by the way, is Gwen."

"It's nice to meet you, Gwen. Where's Luke? I saw you hauling those two guys up the river the other day. They sure didn't look too happy. I never seem to find Luke on dry land, he's always passing me when I'm fishing."

"Luke's around the other side of the dock. He went over there to check on a boat he didn't recognize. He'll check their trout tags and be back soon. Why don't you wait and say hello?"

"Maybe some other time. I've gotta run. Nice to meet you, and sorry I had you blocked from the boat ramp." Sara climbed in the truck and drove around the dock in time to see Luke coming up the steps. Luke waved and hurried toward the moving truck.

She rolled down the window the rest of the way and stopped by Luke's side.

Luke spoke first. "I saw you out on the river the other day. Sorry I wasn't able to stop."

"Running bad guys up the river must keep you pretty busy."

"Couple bad dudes, those fellows. Caught them trying to break in the fish hatchery with a net, they were going after the big breeding fish we milk for eggs. Gwen and I are going to be in court with them on Thursday."

"Be sure and send them up for a long time."

"The judge will probably order some jail time for stealing."

"Good, I'm glad. Hey, I have to get going. See you back on the river, Mister Lawman."

"Would you mind if I give you a call some time? You know, when you aren't fishing and I'm not arresting people? Your dad gave me your cell number."

"Oh! He did, did he?"

Luke smiled and said, "Well. Uh...."

"Relax, I like to tease a little."

"I asked him for it the day after we met."

Her cheeks got hot. "Oh, really! Crap."

They both smiled as she put the truck in gear. Luke reached out and touched her hand on the steering wheel.

"Promise I'll call soon." He stepped back from the truck.

"Later."

She wasn't sure how she felt about going on a date. The last times she spent time alone with a man it had been her CO in Iraq.

She realized now he had abused her for months.

SHE HAD JUST WALKED INTO the cabin when her cellphone buzzed.

She flipped the phone open. "Hello."

"Was this too soon to call? It's Luke."

"I'm glad you at least let me get home. Hello, Luke."

"If you watch out front, you will see us jet by in about a minute," Luke said

over the purr of the waterjet boat's engine. Sara went to the back deck and waved as the boat with Luke and his partner skimmed by.

"That boat is fast—really fast."

"I know. I have to admit Gwen's showing off. She's got the throttle wide open. I wanted to ask if you can get away this Saturday. There's someplace I'd like to take you. Fact is I never have a weekend day off, but I'm taking this as vacation."

"Where would we be going?" Sara wondered if she was ready for his "someplace," reply.

"Not far. About an hour south of here. A lot of the mountain folk are getting together for a celebration and a lot of old-time music. I play a little with them."

"What do you play?"

"Just the guitar."

"I really don't know you very well, Luke. Will we be coming back Saturday night?" Sara was trying to be coy with him and knew it was failing. She needed a night away with a man who didn't control every element of her life.

"It will be late Saturday night when we get back."

"What time will you pick me up?"

"Like to start down there early. Would seven o'clock in the morning be okay?"

"Guess I could do that." She gave a little laugh she kept from the phone.

"Good deal. Saturday it is, then."

The flood of memories about the last man she had been with rushed in. She didn't realize until it was too late what her company commander at Bucca Prison had in mind for her. He got close to her with talk and praise for her contributions to his command. The two promotions he rushed through for her had come quickly. After he told her he loved her a dozen times, it became easy for a young woman fresh from the back roads and small towns of Arkansas to give in to his abuse. She gave him what he wanted, despite the danger of getting caught. She regretted and hated that the danger of war had made the sex even more intense, even for her. There was something about him holding her in the darkness of night that took away all the terror of living near a thousand prisoners who wanted to do nothing more than cut her head off. She'd fallen for his abuse.

"Help me forget him, Luke." Sara spoke to an ended call and a quiet cabin.

She pushed the dark military thoughts away. She desperately needed something to wear for the date with Luke besides military clothes. Most things she liked turned out to be either too short, too loose, or just didn't fit. She felt tired of the constant camo uniforms and the one basic black outfit she had.

When she checked her dad's maps for the distance, she found would have to drive to find a store. It was too far to go before she had to meet her dad at the trout dock. She put it off until tomorrow.

SARA SAT IN THE TRUCK and watched her dad return from his guide trip. She could tell his clients were out of hand even before they reached the dock. John was yelling at them to sit the hell down and wait for him to stop. They weren't paying any attention. John skipped going in the dock slip and instead ran the front of the boat up on the edge of the bank. Both men fell between the chairs before jumping overboard in the shallow water and whipping them out to piss.

John stepped over the bow of the boat, and holding the tie rope for the boat, went to the waiting truck. Sara got out to join him.

"This ain't going to end well." John shook his head. "They both been drinking since we started this morning."

"Hey, John. You still going to charge us for this trip? All we got is them five little fish," one of the drunks yelled, still up to his knees in the river.

"Can we call someone to come and get them?" Sara asked. "Oh, crap, they're getting back in the boat."

John turned to look as the pair nearly tipped the little vessel over trying to crawl back in. Their getting out of the water was probably a good thing because Sara guessed her dad wanted to drown both of them right there alongside his dock.

What came next convinced her she had hit the nail on the head.

"Hot damn! Look at that. I'd give my left nut to lay next to that tall cup of tea," one spouted.

The other one stepped out of the boat and started pushing past John toward Sara. "Gonna have to take turns on that."

Sara picked up a paddle from the back of the truck, arched it over her head, and headed for the man. "Get in the fucking boat, you idiot."

He fell over the gunnel and back into the boat. She kept following ready to bash him.

John intervened. "Sara! Easy. You boys sit down in the chairs. I'm gonna show you one more fishin' spot we need to try."

Sara realized her dad was doing his best to head off what she was in the middle of.

"More fishing?" The man fell back into the boat's chair. "You stay right there, you pretty lady. I'll be back for ya!"

Rolling his eyes, John climbed back in and started the engine. He headed his boat upstream. "We'll be back in about half an hour, Sara."

After more than an hour passed, she began to wonder what he'd done with the men. She felt certain those guys were never going to make it back to the trout dock today.

———————————————

TWO HOURS LATER, JOHN PULLED into the cabin's dock with an empty boat. She noticed the smile creep on his face when he saw her.

"Took those drunks upriver, got about a hundred yards south from the trout dock, and pulled up on a sandbar. Told them we were going to cook the fish we had. I put their cooler on the bank, and they climbed out like little, dumb puppies. I thought they needed some time to sober up before driving."

"You really mean before I broke that paddle over their heads, right?"

"That, too. Backed the boat off the bar before they could get back in. Figured they would start to holler at me about then. Nope, they just sat down in the sand and took another beer out of their cooler."

She laughed hard at the tale. But her laughter faded quickly as her guilt slapped her in the face for being so very happy.

Then she wanted to punish herself.

"What're the trout dock folks going to say about this?"

"They don't mind clients drinking a bit, but being drunk doesn't sit well with them. They'll never be able to book another fishing trip here. I went by the dock and told them where to find them. They said they'd give them a couple hours to maybe sober up."

"Didn't they have a lot more beer to drink?"

"Well... that, too." He patted her on the shoulder and went up the steps to the cabin.

She hesitated, wishing she could talk to him about the guilt and grief that had just overcome her. "Wait up. Can we sit on the deck for a few minutes? I need to talk to with you."

"Come on up. I've saved Mom's favorite chair for you."

She gave the chair's seat a lick with the palm of her hand to brush off the dust. "There, Mom, it's all clean now."

"You sounded serious about wanting to talk. What's wrong?"

She sat down beside him. "Don't be mad for me bringing this up, okay? Mom said you led a squad of men that fought in the jungles."

"Are you sure you want me to talk about what I did, not about what happened to you instead?"

"Both, Dad." She stopped, trying to find her voice again. "Did some of those men you led die?"

"Yes. *Hell,* yes. You fucking know they died. Somebody I knew died every damn day we were out."

She slipped out of her chair and then down on her knees in front of him. Slapping a hand on the top of each of his knees, she gripped them with all her strength. Sara didn't understand what she was doing, really. She just knew that she needed to know someone else felt the way she did. She fought to get at what he had felt in battle all those years before.

"Sara!"

"My crew died because of me, Dad. They were blown apart all over the Humvee and all over—"

"Stop it. You were at war, Sara."

"I have to know how you felt when your men died."

He sighed. "At the end of it all, I only felt dead."

"I gave a command to stop our convoy. It should not have been given in the middle of a town filled with Al-Qaeda fighters."

"You made a mistake, Sara. Mistakes happen all the time—in life and in war. I made plenty myself."

"Mistakes kill people. I knew better than to stop."

"What caused you to give the command?"

"No more." She rubbed his knees. "I'm sorry if I hurt you."

She took the steps going down to the dock in twos. She needed the river now. She yearned for the quiet that came with just letting the boat drift. With the ropes on the boat untied she pushed away from the dock, out into the fast current of the river. She didn't start the engine. The boat made only a little squeak as it turned sideways and headed downstream. She sat on the floor with her back against the rear seat. She wanted to tell her Dad about the Iraqi child that ran in front of her Humvee and caused her to stop the convoy. She was afraid he'd think she was making excuses, though. It would have to come later. It was another two hours before she even thought about starting the engine to take her back upstream.

CERTAIN SHE WASN'T HUNGRY, SHE still fixed pancakes and sausage for John's supper. She sat with him long enough to have a cup of coffee before explaining she needed to put away some of her military clothes. She went to her room and unloaded all the military clothes she brought with her on the bed. She sat with her uniform in her lap, turning it, and then holding the shirt to her chest. Twice, she threw the uniform into the corner of the closet only to go get it and sit, staring at it. She ran her hand over the combat ribbons and removed them, clutching them in her hand.

"Hey, gal, I'm heading to bed. We need to get an early start for tomorrow's charter...."

Sara wasn't hearing him. Drinking what was left of her bottle of bourbon, she'd gone someplace she didn't want to be. She had fought to stay positive, but despite being on the river she loved, black depression still came and went like the rising and falling of the water.

She pointed the gun she didn't have at her right temple. "Bang."

Then she cried herself to sleep.

———————————

JOHN ALREADY HAD THE BOAT on the trailer and the truck idling the next morning when he woke her. "Let's go, sleepyhead."

She jumped out of bed and hurried to the bathroom to splash cold water on her face. Brushed her teeth with a couple of quick strokes of the toothbrush, she tied her hair in a ponytail with a rubber band. Yesterday's jeans and shirt would have to do. She pulled them on and ran out of the cabin to jump in the truck.

When he'd turned out onto the road, she cleared her throat. "Luke asked me out for this Saturday. We're going to a folk music celebration."

"Has to be down at Mountain View." John slapped his leg. "Yea-*haw*, girl."

"I've got to get something to wear. Army camo or jeans won't do, will it?"

"Oh, hell. The place'll be full of locals and folks coming from out of the mountains to play some tunes. Saddle up and head up to the country store in town. Good fittin' pair of Levi's and a cowgirl shirt will set you up just right."

"You sure? I've got a couple shirts and some Levi's."

"Oh, yes. Your mom and I used to go down there several times a year before you were born. We would take our lawn chairs and just sit around the pickin' and singin' groups on the courthouse lawn and over in the city park. She loved to listen to the fiddles playing the old, slow waltzes. We would get up and waltz right there on the lawn. What time are you going? Maybe I'll join you." John chuckled just a bit.

"He said around—oh, stop that, Old Man. Sure hope you still have a guide job after yesterday."

"Been thinking it might be about time for me to retire and stop guiding, anyway. Ain't getting no damn younger. Can't hardly put up with the kinds of bullshit we had yesterday anymore."

"Stop that. Is it your health? You still have the stress test to take, right?"

"Been thinkin' of putting that off. Dizziness gone away."

"No! Darn it, Old Man. Go for those tests. Better to know, isn't it?"

"Stop it. You're dogging' me again."

"I'll stop, but.... Okay, well now I hate to ask you but...."

"But, *what?*"

"Will you mind my taking the day off Saturday?"

"Just go, girl. You deserve time for a little happy in your life." He gave her an affectionate push on the cheek.

eleven

SATURDAY MORNING FOUND SARA DRESSED and ready an hour early. She washed the new jeans the night before and found them uncomfortably tight after wearing all her loosely fitting army uniforms for years.

She slipped on the short, tan leather jacket she found at a thrift store over her blue and white western shirt and stood before the mirror on the kitchen door. "You know, girl, this body may still have some life in it."

"Good outfit, Sara. It's good seeing you in something besides camo."

"Don't get used to it, Dad. It'll be back to camo tomorrow."

"You look great, girl. See you tonight."

She paced the kitchen, nervously dipping her hand into a box of Cheerios each time she went by. For the second time, she went to the kitchen mirror and stood looking at the scar she'd tried to cover with makeup. After another swipe of powder, she brushed her hair forward a bit to hide the fresh scratches she punished herself with. A check of her watch showed it was now seven thirty, and Luke was late. By seven forty-five, she felt sure she'd been stood up, by a man she barely knew. The thought that maybe it was for the best went away quickly when she heard a car pull in the cabin driveway. She stood looking through the window when her first smile about the date happened. Luke was driving an open top Jeep Wrangler. She went outside to greet him.

"Sorry I'm late, Sara. We had a late night on the river. We had to rescue a man and his wife off a sandbar. The motor quit on their boat."

"Oh, driving a Jeep makes up for you being late! I'm glad it's open sky time."

"Glad you don't mind the wind."

"Mountain View here we come, right?"

"I thought you or your dad would figure that out."

It was a beautiful morning for a drive, and Sara enjoyed Luke telling her the history of the small towns along the way. At the town of Calico Rock, he stopped before crossing the bridge over the White River.

"My family has a lot of history in Calico Rock. Hope we can come back here when we have time to go through the museum. Some of our family treasures are there."

"We were here several times when I was little. My mother liked to shop in the stores along Main Street."

The rest of the drive to Mountain View went quickly. Luke suggested a stop for a late breakfast and pulled into a local restaurant. "We often stop in here when we work down south on the river. They have some of the best country ham around."

"Country ham! I haven't had any since I was a kid. Once in a while, my Dad would buy a ham from a farmer that had a smoke house."

"Well, hope the old salty taste will bring back some good memories."

"Let's go for it."

She let Luke order for both of them. Two eggs scrambled, crispy hash browns, and a big slice of his favorite country ham. Luke poured her coffee from the pot the waitress left on the table and then poured his. They sat looking at the coffee and stirring it with their spoons.

She glanced up first and laughed. "Now what do we say?"

Luke chuckled. "The quiet came on quick, didn't it?"

"Yes, it did."

"Well—"

"Why? Why did you ask me out, Luke?"

"You interest me a lot, Sara. John told me about your Military Police background and how you love the river and the outdoors. Well... we have things in common, I guess."

"You're not dating anyone? Dad said you always have ladies waiting in line."

"A couple movie dates, about all. John does tend to stretch the truth a bit, Sara. He didn't stretch it when he told me how beautiful you were."

A blush spread across her cheeks.

The waitress set two of the best-looking breakfasts Sara had seen in a long time on their table and then refilled both of their coffee cups from the pot on the table.

Luke thanked the waitress and handed Sara one of the serrated knives that came with the tough country ham. Wasting no time, he cut the big slice on his plate, offering the first bite of his slice to Sara.

"Here, try this," Luke said, trying to hurry her into tasting the ham.

Sara let Luke put the bite of ham in her mouth. She bit down on the salty cured delight that Luke liked so well and chewed away. Memories of her mom smoking up the kitchen cooking big slices of ham came along with the delight of having the salty treat once again.

"Catch the waitress's eye. I'm going to need a big glass of water."

With both their plates clean, Luke motioned for the check and handed the waitress a ten-dollar tip. "Come on lady, we need to get down to the Courthouse Square. There's lots of pickin' going on about now."

FOR MORE THAN A HUNDRED years, the hand-laid stone courthouse sat in the middle of the town. Today, no one in the town even thought about the real purpose of the court room, the sheriff's office, or the meeting room when the county board met and gave its blessing for the huge event taking place. The courthouse was surrounded by pickers and music lovers. Loud mandolin licks competing with the sharp crackle of a banjo took control of the courthouse's west side. A short walk away on the north side, Sara could hear the chords and rhythm of two guitars melted into the words and music of a small choir of six singing the last words of "Amazing Grace."
On the front steps of the courthouse, four microphones stood ready on their stands. Four young girls stood behind them, waiting to perform. The big guitars hanging on straps over their shoulders seemed to dwarf the performers.

Sara held Luke's hand, holding him back just a bit. "Can we wait. I think they are just about to take the stage."

"Sure, we can. They're the Cooper Family. The youngest is Jenney, and she's just eight."

Luke stood by Sara's side, his guitar case pressing against his other side. Sara noticed the little fidget Luke made when the girls started their second song.

"Come on, Music Man. Let's get you playing."

"My pickers are probably over in the park, just up the street."

The first group playing on the east edge of the park waved to greet Luke. A banjo led the folk song they were playing. When the song ended, Sara and Luke watched as a schoolgirl no more than twelve joined the group with a fiddle. After a couple tweaks of the tuning knobs, she bowed each of the strings, listening for their pitch, and then struck a beautiful lick leading into a fiddle tune. Luke smiled, whispering to Sara that he first saw the girl play when she was five years old.

When the little girl started a waltz, Luke gently took both of Sara's hands, holding them as she leaned back, and he turned her to the music's tempo. The music and dance comforted her. Getting a little dizzy, Sara leaned against Luke. They turned slowly with arms around each other, her head on his shoulder. She felt Luke could be the down-home boy she had longed for while Captain Bartlett controlled her.

The banjo player called, "Luke, Luke! Let that lady rest and get that guitar out. We need you to play lead on the next one, your favorite."

Luke kept Sara in his arms until the fiddle whispered the last note of the waltz before letting her go to pick up his guitar case. He set the case on the ground behind the mandolin player, opened it, and lifted the guitar out. He took a flannel cloth out of the case and carefully wiped the top of the guitar body and then the strings and finally the peghead of the instrument.

"It's a really old Martin, got a few scratches, but sounds better than the new ones. Belonged to my grandfather. He gave it to me just before he died."

"It's a beautiful instrument," Sara said, touching the "Martin" name at the top of the peghead with her finger.

"Stays in tune really well." He gave a couple small turns on the tuning pegs and then left her. He slid onto a bench beside the mandolin player.

"Give us a count, Luke," said the banjo player.

Luke started the count, "One, two—"

"Hang on, Luke." The banjo player pointed to a fellow carrying a large bass fiddle across the street. "Hey, Jimbo, get your bass over here and join us. We need you, boy! Now we gonna have some music, folks."

Sara listened as Luke again counted down the start of the old mountain song. He played the lead and took the song up a couple notches in tempo before he nodded to the mandolin player to grab the lead from him. Sara began to feel at home with the people and music of the mountains of Arkansas. She found an empty bench just across from the group and settled in to listen and spend the morning. It was more than an hour before Luke took a break and came to sit by her.

"I can pack up the Martin if you would like to walk around the park area."

"Stay and play. I'll go over to the craft booth and find something to take home to Dad."

"If you're sure you don't mind. I'll stay for a couple more songs."

She stood long enough to hear Luke start another song and then headed toward the courthouse south yard. She stopped in front of the courthouse stage to watch the performers. More than a hundred people were gathered in front of the stage. Some brought their own lawn chairs, while others sat on the rock wall separating the yard from the street. The three performers welcomed a half-dozen folks up to dance on the wooden platform on the courthouse lawn. The fiddle player led the group, playing an old mountain jig. Sara marveled at the ancient man who rose with a cane and joined the dancers. He turned slowly, barely lifting his feet. Still, he tapped the rhythm of the mountain jig with his hand-carved cane. The other dancers quickly moved to the back of the floor to watch the old man. They stood clapping their hands and stomping their feet to the beat of the jig.

"Well, there, he's showing all those young folks up," the band's singer said, clapping her hands. Sara joined in, clapping to the rhythm of the music. She tapped her foot, then lifted both her feet, finding the steps of the jig the old man was doing. She felt happy and so at home with the crowd around her. When the song ended, she gave her loudest whistle for the old man. She left the crowd and crossed the yard to the roped-off street filled with tents and booths.

It was difficult to find just the right thing to take home from so many choices of mountain art and treasures for sale. The shelf of birdhouses in the second booth drew her attention. When the old man sitting at the rear of the booth looked her way, she said, "Is this birdhouse made for bluebirds?" She lifted the birdhouse from the shelf.

"Nope, not that one. Bluebird is 'ticular about makin' a home. One over there at the top of shelve would be it."

"They both look the same."

"Bluebird house got a long back for mounting on fence posts down low in the pasture," said the old man. "What's a good-lookin' uptown woman like you doing down here in these mountains?"

She ignored him and reached for the bird house on the top shelve.

"Being ninety-five years old, what you thinkin' sometimes just runs out your mouth."

"I took it as a compliment, old man. Seems you're still lookin' even at ninety-five."

"Yes, 'um. I'll stop lookin' when I'm done dead."

Sara laughed and promised she would be back to buy the bluebird house before she left.

Walking back across the courthouse yard, she saw Luke coming to meet her.

"Thought you might be getting hungry."

"Let's see, it's been three hours since that mountainous feeding you took me to," she replied.

"Come on, girl, gotta try the ham and beans cooking over there in the park. Big black kettle's been on the fire for hours."

"Let's go, Music Man."

Sara loved the smell of the steam coming off the black kettles of boiling ham and beans. When her mother cooked beans, she would always add the almost bare ham bone the butcher gave her. Sara watched the men dip their long wooden paddles into the kettles and bring up the large chunks of pink ham from the bottom. Her stomach growled. She was starting to get hungry again.

Luke set the guitar case against the closest picnic table, and both of them got in line. The lady serving overflowed their two bowls with the savory smelling ham and beans and pointed out the table of fixins. Luke led the way to the table and loaded his bowl with chopped onions.

Sara grabbed his arm. "Luke, your guitar's gone!" They both set their bowls on an empty table.

"Crap. Things have always been safe here!"

"Which way should we look?"

"Whoever took it is either going to head up by the courthouse or to the parking lot."

"I've got the courthouse," Sara yelled, already running in that direction. She saw three people in front of her carrying instrument cases, two of them had guitars. She remembered the big Martin decal on Luke's case and noticed that one of the men carried a case with that decal. When she got three steps behind the man she yelled, "Stop!" The man didn't turn. He took off running in a different direction with Sara on his heels. He headed right for Luke.

The man was fast, but Sara was gaining on him. Luke came around a car in front of the man, grabbed the guitar case with one hand, and hit the man in the face with the other.

"It's one thing to be a little stupid, mister. It's another to be real stupid and steal a guitar from a cop." Luke had the man down on his face holding one of his arms while he reached for the hand cuffs he carried behind his pistol case. He snapped them on the thief's arm, then reached for the other to restrain it also.

"Glad you came, officer. That crazy, tall bitch was chasing me," the handcuffed man said.

"Oh, you mean *this* crazy bitch?" Sara said, cocking her foot for a field goal try.

Luke scooted in front of her.

"It's okay, Sara. I've got this one. You're lucky she didn't catch you, asshole."

The local sheriff's car pulled up, and two officers got out. "Luke, why the hell are you doing our work?"

"He's kidding, Luke. Too much of a smartass," the Sheriff said. "Wouldn't want you to lose that old Martin your dad and granddad used to play here."

"Sara saw him first after he grabbed it from our table. She's the one that ran him down here."

"That damn bitch was going to kick me," the man tried again. "Keep her away from me!"

"Too bad she didn't kick some of that bad out of you," the Sheriff said. "We'll take him from here, Luke." He pointed for his deputy to get the man off the ground. "Swap out the cuffs with Luke."

"Thanks, Sheriff."

"Sara. It was nice meeting you. If you ever want a job, I could use another deputy on our force. Your dad's told us you were with the Military Police in Iraq."

"Thank you, Sheriff. I've thought about it. You really think the military training would transfer over to law enforcement?"

"No doubt at all. Be sure and come see me first. Oh—saw you dancing with Luke a little while back, glad to see he has a girlfriend. He spends too much time down on that river."

"Not *too* much. That's where I get to see him the most. He passes my dad's place often." Having Luke pass the cabin and always wave had made her rush out to the top of the steps coming up from the dock to wave back. It made her feel good that he might care about her.

"Bet it's a lot more now that he's met you." The Sheriff swapped out the cuffs. "Stand up, idiot. You came to the wrong town to steal a guitar."

By the time Sara and Luke got back to the bean cooking kettles, they were sold out, and their bowls were nowhere to be found.

"Looks like we're going to have to settle for hotdogs instead of beans and cornbread."

"That's okay. Running that thief down wore me out. I think it means less fishing and more endurance training."

"I spend so much time on the river the same may be good for me too. Let's head back up north. There's a place in Calico Rock I would like to show you. Belongs to my mom and dad."

"Let's make one more stop at the booths. I promised a ninety-five-year-old I would be back to get a bluebird house." Sara led the way.

twelve

LUKE PULLED OVER AND STOPPED in the river bottoms a half mile before the bridge that crossed the White River and led up into the town of Calico Rock. The lush green pastures of the bottoms stretched for miles in each direction. A split rail fence separated the road's turnoff from the grass and provided a turnoff cars had used for years to view the scenic panorama of the bluffs.

High above the bottoms they could see the two-story rock buildings perched along sheer bluffs way above the river and the floods the river would bring in the Spring.

"My dad would stop here on our Sunday drives. He liked to point out the colors of the river bluff rocks—the red, orange, and blue like calico cloth. Then, he would tell us to look out to the west of town at the big pine tree that stands out on top of the bluff. He said we'd build a house there some day. We're headed up there."

"I see the pine tree. It would be a beautiful place for a home. I remember my dad took us to the old part of town years ago to show us a rock wall jail. My mother wouldn't let me get out. She said it was part of the ghost town."

"There's lots of legends about the old town. It was built when the steamboats stopped here in the 1800s. There was a lot of moonshine traded in these parts."

"My dad took Mom and me through there once. A long time ago."

"Maybe I can show you around. I happen to know a lot of the old moonshiner tales."

"Really? That would be fun."

"For now, let's head up to the bluff."

"The bluffs seem to surround the whole area." She tightened her seatbelt, and suddenly she wasn't in Arkansas any longer.

The starter on the Humvee rumbled, and Sara pointed at the top of the concrete walls surrounding them. She slapped her driver on the arm. "RPG! Get us out of here, Johnston!" She stomped on the driver's foot, shoving it to the floor. "Go, go, go, God damn it!"

The Humvee lunged ahead.

"What the hell!" Johnston shouted. He pushed her leg and foot away and slid the vehicle to a stop.

"Don't touch me, Sarge!" She lunged out of the vehicle and stumbled toward the wall.

The engine grew quiet, and the sound of footsteps grew closer behind here. She leaned on a split rail fence post, sobbing and holding her hand out behind her to keep him away.

"My crew's all shot to hell. They're dead, Sarge. All of them!"

He reached for her arm. "It's Luke, Sara. Who's dead? What happened?"

She let him touch her.

"I'm sorry...." Her sobbing slowed, and she looked up. "I couldn't stop it. Couldn't stop them all from dying."

"You scared me."

"Shit.... It all came back."

"*What,* came back? What can I do?"

She reached for him and collapsed against him. "Just give me a minute."

The comfort of his arms brought her back. She stayed there for as long as she dared, then moved only a short distance away. She looked across the blowing grasses of the mile-long pasture toward the calico bluffs. The colors of the cliffs were getting clearer as her tears slowed. Colors of home and colors of memories shared with her family helped her push out the colors of terror, grey dirt walls, and patches of blood in the sand.

"Johnston was my driver. I saw him again. He died that day in Iraq."

"I'm so sorry, Sara. Do you want me to take you home?"

"No. I don't want to ruin our day." She turned to face him.

"It's not ruined. I just want to help."

"Can we just go into town and find a place to sit and have coffee?"

Back in the Jeep, Luke paused before starting it. "Are you ready?"

"Go ahead, my flashbacks don't last very long. It's just that I'm having them more often." She gripped the edge of seat as he started the Jeep.

"Are you okay?"

"Take us across the bridge, and let's see what's in town."

Luke drove them into Calico Rock and parked across from a small coffee shop sitting three tiers of steps above the road. He was around the Jeep with his hand out before Sara had a leg out.

"May I, Miss Sara?"

She didn't answer, only took his warm hand and held onto it. They walked the sidewalks on both sides of the street, stopping when Sara would point out an antique item in store windows and asking if he knew what the heck it would have been used for. When they reached the coffee shop, Luke opened the door, and they went in and took a seat at the window overlooking the street below. Luke left and went to the counter to order their coffee. It gave Sara a moment alone to think of having him take her home, ending the day with him before evening. Telling him about some of the dark terror and memories that haunted her made her afraid he'd want nothing more to do with her.

Luke returned and set the two cups of coffee on the table. She watched the steam rise off her cup and twisted her index finger in the warm tendrils.

He took a careful sip of the hot coffee. "Feeling better?"

"My mind goes nuts sometimes. I don't know how to explain it. I don't know it's coming. It just hits me upside the head, and I'm back there when my squad got hit."

"Does talking about it help?"

"No.... Well, I'm not sure. It's not fair putting you through this." She laid her hand gently on his arm.

"It's all right. Coffee first. Then we can talk okay?"

They sat quietly sipping the coffee. She felt Luke was afraid to start a conversation after what she had said. So, she would have to do it.

"I didn't want to stay at Walter Reed any longer after they patched me up physically. I didn't think my going zappo crazy a few times a week would be something that would last. I was so damn fucking wrong. It's been way more often. Any little thing can trigger me into something like you saw out there in the bottoms."

"Have you thought about going back for some help with it?"

"Dad has started telling me I should ask the V.A. for help. I thought that being home here on the river would be all that I needed to get well."

"I wish I knew how to relate to what happens, Sara. It just seemed to steal you away in a second."

"You don't want to relate to this shit. I would understand if you just wanted to stay away from me."

"Don't, Sara. I want to listen. Don't be afraid to tell me what's happening."

"I'll talk to you, Luke, but don't tell Dad. He doesn't know how bad it's getting, and I'm not sure if he isn't having health problems himself."

"He hasn't said anything to me. Are you sure?"

"I'm not. He's mostly closed mouth with me like he was with my mother."

Sara had reached the limit of things she wanted to tell her new friend— it was time to go. Besides, she really needed a double shot of bourbon in her coffee.

"Come on, let's go see your place on the bluff."

"Are you sure?"

"Yes. If you still want to take me." She started to get up from the table. Luke was quick to follow. "Let's go."

THE DRIVE ON BLACKTOP LASTED only two miles before Luke turned off onto a gravel road.

"Road gets rough from here on. The Jeep comes in handy."

The steep rises and falls of the gravel road felt a lot like a roller coaster ride to Sara. In the valley the road wound along several small creeks that caught her attention. She made plans to come back someday and fly fish them. At the top of a long rise, Luke pulled off the road and stopped at a wire fence gate.

"Sit tight. I'll get this." Sara jumped out of the Jeep and took down the two wires. When Luke pulled through the gap, she closed it and hopped back in the vehicle. Luke drove across the pasture of natural grasses and flowers before he stopped at the edge of a thick grove of trees.

"We've got to walk the rest of the way." With the guitar case in one hand, he led the way around a patch of blackberry brambles and along a narrow path.

Nestled in a grove of sheltering cedar trees, the back wall of the cabin was dwarfed by the chimney crafted of colorful bluff stones. Ledges of moss oozed from between the planks on the cabin side walls and reached to join hands across the boards, painting a pale green portrait of the cabin's age. The front of the cabin and the porch were set in the perfect direction to enjoy both special times of the day when the sun commanded, "Watch me."

They stood arm in arm and watched the last breath of sunlight. Only a narrow sliver of the brilliant light remained. It came through the cloud layers to the west and decorated the sky with a changing pallet of bright reds, pinks, and oranges.

"Thanks for bringing me. It's really beautiful here. What a place for a dream house."

"For now, it's just a one-room cabin with a huge fireplace and a sleeping loft to climb into. Come help. We'll get a fire started."

"Do you have a striker and some flint?"

"No, I do it the old Boy Scout way, with a leather strap and a board. Let's carry in some split wood from the side pile."

Sara found the stash of firewood before Luke got around the house. She reached for the two logs that had rolled off the stack.

"Wait! That's a gathering place for our local copperhead clan." Luke stepped in front of her and started kicking the logs.

"Our camp in the Sandbox had its share of snakes. We had to be careful walking in the sand because of this one nasty horned viper. They'd burrow in and disappear. Leave their little horns and eyes sticking up, that's it. Then they'd burst out and bite your boot. Hell of a scare."

"I've had to carry off four or five copperheads. Took them way down to the bottom of the bluff."

"We never killed the vipers in Iraq, either. Just took them to the edge of the fence and tossed them over where we thought the bad guys would be."

With the talk of snakes over and a small pile of kindling burning the bottoms of four logs, Luke opened a locked cabinet and took out a bottle of Cabernet Sauvignon.

"Wine?"

"Yes, please. Want me to pour?"

"Got it." He turned the corkscrew in and pulled the cork. Using a paper towel to wipe two of the dusty glasses sitting on the cabin shelf, he poured the first glass for her.

She took it and lifted it in a toast. "Here's to the fire that I hope will get started soon. It's gotten dark as hell up here."

"I promise it will. Wait, I have two lanterns." He opened a side cabinet and took out the two kerosene lamps. Lifting the mantels off both, he struck a match to light the wicks. When he got them both glowing, he set one on each side of the cabin.

"Thanks for putting a little light on the subject. How often do you get to come here?"

"Not often. River's got me too busy. I like coming when I can borrow my dad's Jeep, though." He sat down beside her on the couch with his glass of wine.

"Tell me about your life carrying a badge and gun?"

"I'll tell you if you promise to tell me about signing up to go fight a war."

They found that getting to know each other would take a lot longer than the four logs, which were now only glowing ashes. Luke stoked the ashes and laid three more split pieces of wood on to burn. The second bottle of wine vanished when Sara let the last few drops fall in the back of her throat. It wasn't the bourbon she had thought about, but it sure was doing the job getting the relaxation she craved.

The growing familiarity, the wine, and ease of telling and asking about life lessons brought them to soft voices and closeness. Luke lifted Sara's hair, which had fallen across the scar and down over her lips. He pushed it back with his hand, his fingers wrapping around the back of her neck in a soft, gentle urging.

Sara was way beyond needing urging. She turned her head and pressed against his lips, seeking his tongue. She gathered him in, lying on her side across his lap and into his arms. One arm wrapped behind his head while her other hand pressed against the side of his cheek, begging for more of the embrace. She dropped her arm from behind his head and lifted his hand, pressing it hard against her breast. Luke slipped down flat on to the couch, and she followed over him, pressing with her hips on the spot she felt his need. Both of his hands joined the rhythm, pulling on the back of her hips. Sara slowed and then paused with her head over his face, teasing with a thousand tiny fingers of her hair tickling back and forth across his nose. She should have known the sneeze would be inevitable.

"Oh, God. That didn't really happen. Did it? Sara don't pay any attention, but I've got to look at my watch."

"What?"

"I promised your ex-Marine dad I would have you back before midnight."

"You're drunk Luke, you shouldn't make promises you know we weren't going to keep."

"It's only a quarter after eight. Now shut up and kiss me."

"Don't you mean quarter after twelve?" She leaned in to kiss him again.

LUKE PULLED INTO JOHN'S DRIVE just as the sun kissed the eastern skyline. "So much for promises."

"Just don't make any more." She reached across the console and pulled him over to meet her lips. hSe softly bit his lower lip. "Just keep the one about taking me back to Calico Rock."

Sara went to the cabin door and turned to wave goodbye. Then she remembered the birdhouse in the back of the Jeep. It brought a smile to her face. Hopefully he'd bring it back soon.

She went in quietly, closing the door behind her.

"Sara, go back to sleep. I'm taking the day off. Don't have any trips scheduled. You didn't have to get up so early," John yelled.

It took all she had not to fall to the floor laughing.

thirteen

WITH HER DAD GONE EARLY, she dressed in her camo outfit and laid down for a short nap. After a small bowl of cereal and a cup of warmed-over coffee, it was time to try out some new tennis shoes. With a smile on her face as she thought of Luke, she went out the back of the cabin and headed up the road for a late morning jog. The sun felt good on her back, and the green of the valley sparkled from the dampness of the morning dew.

She saw a black car parked on a trail cut in the trees, two hundred yards away. As she jogged by, the sun's reflection caught her eye.

It had to be the glass on a rifle scope.

She dropped to the ditch when she heard the hiss of the bullets plow into the dirt on both sides of her. "Sarge, get the fifties opened up, there's a sniper at one o'clock. Somebody take him out." She pointed at the trees and reaching for the weapons she no longer carried. "You're going to die. We're going to kill all of you bastards."

She spun at the sound of a horse whinnying. The rider stood in the stirrups looking at the trees where Sara had been pointing.

"Sara? It's Marty. What's wrong? Who's going to die?"

"Them." She pointed at the black Dodge now pulling out of the trees on the hill. "They shot at me."

Marty slid off the side of her horse, dropping the reins. "They shot at you?"

"Yes! The bullets hit the bank." She stood in the road and pointed at the side of the ditch.

Marty just looked confused.

"But Sara... I just rode up when you yelled to someone named Sarge. I didn't hear a gunshot."

"You had to see the dirt fly from the bullets," Sara insisted.

"No, I didn't see any dirt fly. My horse would still be running if someone had shot down here." Marty walked to her and put an arm around her shoulder.

"Did you see that car leave? They've been watching me. I saw them along the river following me."

"I saw the car. Who was that? I'm worried. Who's watching you?"

She saw Marty's face and knew she had scared her. "I'm sorry, Marty. I lost it, and you had to see it."

Sara turned away.

"Look at me, Sara. Stop talking that way."

"I'm sorry."

"Come on. I'll just walk along with you. We can take this old horse over to the barn. I've got coffee on."

The older woman looped the reins over the mare's head and the saddle horn, then loosened the horse's girth. "This old horse will just follow us along to the barn."

At the barn, the horse left their side and walked in the open double doors. Marty followed, dropping the bridle off the horse and replacing it with a halter. "If you'll open the door over on the right, I'll get the saddle off and stowed."

Sara opened the door marked with a tack room sign and looked for the light switch. "They'll come on by themselves. Another honey-do I got done." Marty slipped the saddle onto an empty rack. "I think the table is clean so have a seat."

"Marty, do you have a cigarette? I don't smoke often, but right now it needs to be either a cigarette or a shot of Jim Beam. I would really like to have them both."

"Sit. I've got the bourbon covered. The cigarette would have to be away from the barn."

Marty set the bottle of Old Kentucky on the table along with a pair of glasses. "It's a little too early for me, but after what just happened back there, I'll say this can be an exception."

Sara didn't sip the bourbon, she downed it. Warmth spread down her throat and across her belly. She liked it and wanted to ask for more. Too embarrassed, she started talking. "Do you spend all your time out here in the barn?"

"We do. This is our tack room and kitchen. Our bedroom is up the stairs. We put all of our money into building this barn and riding arena. If it pays off, we may get to build the log home we want some day."

"I'm sorry you heard me out there on the road. The black car on the hill has been following me. I panicked when I saw the reflection off of a piece of glass and thought a rifle was aimed at me. I got confused. When things scare me, I go all nuts."

"I didn't retire from any high-thinking job where I could offer you help, but I can sure listen."

"I'm ashamed to say this, but the Walter Reed doctors were offering me help while I was there. I didn't think I needed anyone's help, and then I convinced myself they just wanted to get me gone."

"I hate to relate what's happening to you to a horse, but I have a two-year-old gelding that got turned over in a trailer. He got up shaking and scared. After that we were riding in the forest and surprised a couple feral pigs. When they snorted, the horse whirled and took off for home. A bunch of quail did the same thing to him out in the pasture. He was too much for us to handle, so we sent him to a professional trainer. He's back now, a different horse. I still wouldn't put kids on him, but he's fine for us to ride."

"You're inferring I should get some help, right?"

"I'm just about saying it straight out. Isn't there someone you can call and get help?"

She bit her lip rather than admit there was a captain that once said he loved her.

SARA SPENT THE NEXT FEW days thinking of Captain Bartlett and all the pain he'd caused her. She knew her odds of getting into the V.A.'s psychological care without his help were slim. He'd used her, then put her in a convoy to another command. He'd sent her away. Yet the bastard was still her only option even now. It made her sick to her stomach to think he still held such power over her. But she had to try.

She wrote the letter asking for his help.

fourteen

SARA TIGHTENED HER SEATBELT AND sat stiff-legged against the seat in front of her. The flight from Little Rock had gone smoothly until they got near the East Coast. The rough air quickly convinced her she wanted to go home—the thought of what would come in the V.A.'s Mental Health Recovery Program was even more convincing. After the plane made a rough touch down, she found herself one of the last to leave the plane and enter the terminal. Just past the security gate she saw a soldier holding a sign. As she got closer, she saw it read, *Corporal Randolph.*

It surprised her. Someone had rolled out the carpet for her. With nothing more than a quick greeting and a stop to get her luggage, the soldier led the way to an official Army van and driver waiting for them. After they were seated, she began to realize the van wasn't from the V.A. She sat quietly until the young soldier spoke to her again. "I understand you served with our captain while in Iraq."

"Who would that be?" But she already knew.

"Captain Bartlett. The driver and I are both in his command here."

"Did he send you to pick me up?" This felt way too close to Bartlett for her to be comfortable.

"No, Ma'am. It was First Sergeant O'Dell that sent us."

Hearing O'Dell's name, and that he was still in the command, meant so much to her. Sara had missed O'Dell. A First Sergeant that always tried to look out for her in Iraq. It gave her a good feeling of what would come in the next few days and weeks.

June 12, 2009

Dear Dad,

I'm sorry I didn't give you much of a warning that I was leaving. I'm sure they will let me out of here in no time. Would you please let Luke know I'm not locked up in the nuthouse? Could you send me his address, too? I would like to send him a note later on.

I had to leave quickly. I hated to ask Captain Bartlett for his help. I didn't leave there on good terms with him. But I did anyway, since there was no one else I knew that would help me get in the VA quickly. Bartlett went overboard in cutting through tons of red tape to get me into the VA's Mental Health Center. The wait time for this place is generally up to a year.

I don't know if my getting mad and wanting to kill someone means I will. Sooner or later, it could happen. My outbursts frightened me, and I'm sure you, too. I shared a lot of what happened with Marty and got a lot of down-home logic from her. Got me to realize that just living and fishing wasn't going to fix me. I wrote a lot of letters to myself when I was here the first time, at least when I sat writing them it got me thinking about the good times in Iraq. Yes, there were good times in spite of the bad things I have nightmares about. You remember my squad fishing trip we talked about? Those are the kind of things I need to think about, not just the damn incoming.

I've been thinking about Mom and the patience she had, to sit with her little tweezers, tying hair and feathers on to the tiny hooks. A while back, it got me started watching the stages of the insects that light on the water and doing a little of my own secret fly-tying. Look under the steps in the closet, and you will find the ones I left for you to test for me. I must have a lot of Mom's blood, because fly fishing is growing on me.

I hope you will tell me what your doctor says about your health. You *like to act like everything's fine, but I'm worried about you, anyway. I won't be here long, and they don't keep the doors locked if you need me home.*

Love,
Sara

———————————

June 12, 2009

Captain Bartlett,
 As you know, I'm here at the VA Mental Health Center.
 I can't stop seeing and reliving what happened when the rockets hit us. I stopped the convoy because of a child, and it got my crew killed. I'll never get over the loss of my men. I'm to blame for this.
 The only other thing I can say to you, is thank you for helping me. Do not try and see me while I'm here.

Sara

———————————

June 16, 2009

Dear Sara,
 There isn't a day goes by without thinking of being with you that evening and watching the beautiful sunset from the bluff. I miss seeing you fishing on the river, and even Gwen asked if you were on a trip somewhere. I hope you don't mind I told her you had gone to the VA Hospital for some therapy for your wounds. Really, it's not so far from the truth is it? I kept hounding your dad till I got the hospital address. I hope my writing you doesn't disturb the daily therapy I'm sure they have you busy with.

I want so much to see you. Do you have weekends that you can leave the hospital? I would fly up there in a heartbeat if you said you wanted me to come. I know we really just had the one date, but to me it was life changing, and I hope that's true for you also. Sorry, guess I'm wanting to assume way too much. Write or email me when you can. badge2035luke@gmail.com

Missing you,
Luke

6/16/2009 8:05 PM
From: randolphsara2019@gmail.com
To: badge2035luke@gmail.com
Subject: Missing you also.

Your letter came at just the right time. I was feeling my home and you were so far away. I wanted to hear from you. I'm not sure you realize, but what happened in the bottoms at Calico Rock and our talk over coffee got me closer to realizing I needed help with this. The wine we drank and the evening of the long talk we had made me want oh so much to just be normal for you. I'm not ruling out the love making either for helping me feel normal. Thank you for being gentle, kind, and giving to a person that had gone nuts on you earlier in the day.

I must tell you I have no shame in having PTSD. If it bothers you, please tell me. If anyone asks, tell them the truth about me. I'm here because I go nearly crazy when the attacks hit me. Tell them that, I'm not ashamed. If you are, then I'm really the wrong woman for you.

I'm sorry, Luke, but please don't try and come out here. I'm staying in on the weekends and working on the writing therapy the doctors want us to do. I hope you understand. I do want to see you, but it's just that I want to be the normal person that you deserve. I haven't forgotten the

*promise you made to take me back to the cabin and Calico Rock. I check
for email several times a day. Looking forward to your fast update on
river life and how my dad is doing. Sara.*

————————————

*6/16/2009 8:23 PM
From: badge2035luke@gmail.com
To: randolphsara2019@gmail.com
Subject: New updates*

*I'm sorry if I overstepped talking to Gwen. I only wanted to protect your
privacy but realize now there should never be any shame in having or
suffering from PTSD. I know this is sudden, but I think you are so much
the woman for me. I promise many trips back to the cabin on the bluff
for many sunsets and sunrises if you permit me. Now on the river, we've
had too much rain, and the flood gates have been running a lot of water.
As you know it makes it dangerous on the river for people fishing in
their own boats. Some have never fished water so swift and drag chains
get caught and suck the front of their boats under. I saw your father at
the trout dock yesterday and talked to him for a few. He's missing his
Minnow, he told me. He looks good and headed out with three clients.
Luke*

————————————

June 20, 2009

Dad,
     *They have me spend much of the day writing about my life in Iraq.
They want all the good thoughts I can come up with to be in writing.
Soon, they are going to have me write about the nightmare day my crew
was killed. They want me to write it as I remember it happening. Each*

little detail, each sound, each smell, each fear I felt. Each pain I felt. I really don't understand how this is going to help. I've been writing these things for weeks now. They keep saying I should write more about the day my crew was lost and how it all went down. I can't. I just can't, and I won't yet.

After a lot of convincing on the doctor's part, I agreed to take one of their drugs, prazosin. It has stopped my nightmares, and now I can at least get a goodnight's sleep. I keep watching to see if the darn stuff dulls my senses. So far, I don't think it has.

Some of the men here are getting Virtual Reality therapy, wearing computer goggles that show battle scenes and cause them to rethink what happened to them. I'm not looking forward to doing that.

P.S. I had a letter from Luke this week. I really miss the talks I was starting to have with him. I'm not sure he understands what you and I have been through in war, but he tries, and that's what really counts. For having such a short time with him, I miss him. I bet that makes you smile.

Love you,
Sara

———————————

6/24/2009 2:23 PM
From:randolphsara2019@gmail.com
To:badge2035luke@gmail.com
Subject: Been buried in homework

I thought email would be great for us. I'm sorry it's been a few days since I've written you. I feel totally drained, Luke. They put me through a visual simulation of an attack. It was almost like the one I went through, the RPGs come at you hissing and exploding in the air. Sound systems make it so damn real, I just wanted to die. They had me sit down with a psychotherapist before the simulation. He put me through a deep breathing exercise and pushed me on how to get away from the simulation effects coming at me. They have you hooked up to a heart rate and breathing monitor while in the simulation. He said my heart rate stayed down for about 30 seconds, then went crazy. I wanted to come home. I still do, Luke. Get me the hell out of here.

———————————

From:randolphsara2019@gmail.com
To:badge2035luke@gmail.com
Subject: Sorry for the rant
6/24/2009 3:45 PM

No, Luke. Don't do anything. The doctor came to my room after I stormed out of the test area and made me promise to stick out another two days of the testing. He hadn't told me that the exercise probably wouldn't help the first day. I need this. I'm going back to letters after this, it gives me more time to think what I want to say. Sorry for other email. Sara.

———————————

From:badge2035luke@gmail.com
To:randolphsara2019@gmail.com
Subject: New updates
6/24/2009 8:23 PM

I'm glad I read your second email today first. I'm not kidding about flying out and getting you or just coming to spend a dinner or Sunday afternoon with you. I'm sure you're tired, so I won't go on much longer here. If I can help, please email right then and I'll be back to you same day. Thinking of you, Luke

-----

July 24, 2009

Captain Bartlett

They tell me you have been here twice to see me in the last two weeks. Stop trying to see me. I do not want to see you. I really have nothing to say to you. Except, thank you and goodbye. Please.

Corporal Sara Randolph

July 28, 2009

Dear Luke,

Day three of the simulation has come and gone. They tell me I did great. Maybe it will take a few days for the great to come to my mind. Anyway, as they thought on the third day, my pulse and breathing only increased by a small amount. I was able to think about other things while it went on. I picked the sunset view from the bluff with you at Calico Rock. I've got to go back there and soon, Lawman. Please don't tell Dad about the simulations and what I went through. It will make him relive some of his own horror from 'Nam. They tell me I will be released in August. They have taught me how to counteract the flashbacks that I had been having. I need more time to practice what they taught me. Time will always tell! Right?

Can't wait to see you.
Sara.

July 28, 2009

Dad

    Today in this letter, I'm going to write and finally tell you all of what happened on my last day in Iraq. It isn't pretty, Dad. The day started with twelve in our squad standing at ease and listening to Captain Bartlett giving us our orders for transporting Aziz—a bad ass terrorist and a bomb maker—out of Camp Bucca prison. I knew the CIA wanted him put in some dark hole for more interrogations. I helped torture him beyond anything a human being should have to endure. I'm not proud of what the CIA ordered me to do They had the prisoner tied up naked against a wire cage, then they sent me in with my K-9, Tank, to try and scare the hell of him. They told me to let the dog rush at him, if it bit him that was even better. I hated the CIA and Bartlett for making me do it. I don't think Aziz even flinched when the dog went at him. What I did would cause any man to hate me and our country. After that Bartlett told us we had to get him delivered five miles west of town for a helicopter pickup. He was sending me with the prisoner. I knew he just wanted me gone.

    After releasing the other troops to the Humvees, Bartlett wanted a word with me. I was Andrew Bartlett's secret lover in our prison camp—a relationship I was pressured into. It wasn't something I wanted. I think word got back to his wife about what he was doing. Now he wanted nothing more than to get rid of me. I was speaking up about the prisoner torture, and he felt sure it would come back to ruin his career. He told me the bullshit that I was needed to go with the prisoner to question him, and the CIA felt sure the prisoner's hate for me would cause him to spill out valuable information.

    I unloaded on Bartlett for all that he had put me through. Telling a captain to go screw himself felt just so damn good. My crew watched as I turned halfway back to my Humvee and gave the captain a middle finger salute.

    I gave my crew last minute instructions to stay alert going through the streets of Bucca. I told Link, my fifty cal gunner, to be sure he was ready at all times. His loader, Travis, who sat under him in the Humvee, was good at having the ammo unfurled and ready. My driver, Johnston, had the engine running when our Platoon Sergeant, O'Dell, radioed to move out.

My team responded with, "We're ready, Heat." I liked the name they gave me as their team leader. I felt that I earned it more than once in the last year.

A half mile out from the prison, O'Dell called for us to tighten up on his Humvee. The three-story walls full of windows on both sides of the road had me worried. I told Link to stay on it watching the tops of the buildings. I told them, "Don't anybody think we're going to stop in this hornet's nest." The dust from Sarge's vehicle just about smothered us. Still he called for us to close up on him even more. He yelled on the radio for me to tell Johnston to step on the damn gas pedal or do it myself if I had to.

I remember seeing the small figure come out of a side street and run in front of us. I slapped the dash and yelled, "Brake!" to Johnston. He slid the Humvee to a stop. The little girl stood smiling at us when the first RPG hit Link's gun shield on top. His body fell into the Humvee on top of Travis and my K-9. I don't think I heard the second shell hit. I only heard a buzz and a hissing sound, and then I felt pieces of Johnston's body slap across my face and chest. Someone opened the door by me, and I fell out. Sarge was dragging me. I yelled for him to get my crew out first. He told me to shut up. They were all dead. I wanted him to leave me. "God Damn it. Get away from me! I killed them," I kept screaming. I felt the shock when the round hit him. He dropped my arms. I don't remember anything else until I woke up in the hospital. They said I had been there four days.

Don't hate me for being weak, Dad. I killed my crew....

Sara.

August 10, 2009

Dear Daughter,

Oh! I wish you had told me all that happened when you were here with me. In no way do I think you are weak, sweetheart. I would have slammed on the brakes myself.

I'm so damn mad about how you were used by the CIA and the Captain Bartlett you talk about in your letter. I guess relationships at war happened, and I don't blame either of you for trying to escape the nightmares around you. The CIA is another matter. Damn them and damn the Captain for letting someone he was having an affair with be used that way. Did you ever report what had happened? I want to call the son of a bitch.

You said the guilt for losing your crew was almost too much for you to bear. After reading your letter, it's clear that you were set up that day. The girl was forced out there in the street. They knew anyone driving would stop and not hit her. So don't blame yourself, Minnow. Have you heard any more about what happened after the attack? The Captain hasn't written you about it?

I hope we can talk about all this when you are home again.

Love,
Dad.

August 20, 2009

Dear Sara,

I've cooled down a little since writing you last week. What happened was a lot for me to take in and realize that my daughter had to endure it all. I'm so sorry for what you went through, Sara. Now I have to change the subject, knowing we will sit and talk about it all when you are home.

I took that look in the closet under the steps and found the two boxes of flies. You had written my name on one, your mother had written Sara on the other. I had to steal a look at the flies she always called "her secret flies for Sara," and funny not one of them matched anything she had ever tied for me to use on guide trips. I had watched her go out at different times of the day on the river with her butterfly net and collect the insects from the water. She would bring them back and sit at the kitchen table looking at them and going through all the hides and feathers she had collected to match the colors and shape of the bugs. She was really quite an artist and tied flies for some of my best catches.

I have watched you when we fish, how you watch and remember where the trout spend the day as the sun moves. I've wondered why you would change baits before I had even thought about it and then bring in a brown trout bigger than anything else I caught that day. So, I'm heading out this morning with the flies you tied for me and Martha's bamboo fly rod to try them out. I think her old rod will still hold up under the pullin' the big 'uns gonna do.

I hope you feel the time at the V.A. has been worth it. It may have been better for me when I got back if I would have sought out some therapy early on in a private setting. The two dozen visits to the veteran's center doctors were scattered over too long a time to help much. Seeing four different doctors just meant starting over each time and each of them finally telling me to just suck it up.

There are some things with the guide business I want to talk over with you when you get back. Don't get alarmed, I'm feeling fine, and my doctor has given me a thumbs up on whatever I feel like doing. So, I don't plan on quitting for a while.

Dad

Dear Dad,

It's been weeks since I got here, and I think the writing they had me do here at the hospital helped a lot. I wrote about the good things I saw and felt while in the prison camps and Iraq. I tore most of what I wrote up when the writing was finished, but just thinking about it again while away from Iraq helped.

On a pass out of here this weekend, I got a tattoo. Just a small minnow on the wrist of my right hand. It has a very special meaning for me. When I look at it, I know I'm past a lot of the bad thinking I was going through. If I ever fall back into that trap, my tattoo of a little minnow will be right where it needs to be to make me think of you. You saved my life when you told me your story of deep despair and lost hope.

What about the guide business, Dad? You mentioned that in your letter. You're not thinking of quitting, are you?

Love,
L.M.

P.S. I should be released from here on Friday next week. I'll take the bus to town from the airport. Please have someone pick me up. I'll let you know what time.

fifteen

THE BLUE HERON STOOD AND watched from the water's edge, waiting for a telltale ripple to signal it was time to go after a morning catch. When the ripple came, the heron flapped its wings and flew to the center of the river currents. Diving through the surface of the water with its beak open, it caught the fish it had been watching. Back at the bank, the heron tossed the hapless fish into the air, letting it fall into the back of its mouth. Gone in a flash. Sara watched, amazed. The heron left the flooding bank and flew across the river, landing in a tree high above the rising water.

She had promised herself that going easy for a few days would be the best prescription, but like the river in front of her that was rising fast, she realized slowing down just didn't go with the deck of cards she was playing.

Her dad stood with his hand gently resting in the middle of her back. "I'm glad to have you home"

"I'm home this time, Dad. *Really* home!" She leaned her head on his shoulder. At times things between them hadn't allowed the closeness they now shared. After her mom died, fighting with him got to be normal. She had learned quickly that standing her ground would be the only way she would become the strong woman she wanted to be. He lost the battle when they argued over her joining the National Guard on the eve of the second Iraq War. After that he started letting it be known his daughter thought for herself, and by damn, he was proud of her.

"I guess I got used to being here alone for the years you were in the service. Then you came home after the hospital stay for your wounds, and my life sort of woke up. After that, having you gone for the last months have been like hell for me, Minnow. I'm glad you're home this time."

"Thanks, Daddy. You know Luke's going to try and steal me away from you."

"Are you going to let him?"

"Never. I think we're on a kind of a roller coaster ride right now. I do like him a lot. We'll just have to see how my heart feels. Right, Dad?"

"Hate to change the subject when we're on such a 'love' discussion, but that old river came up a bunch last night. I'm going to call the Corp of Engineers and see if they are going to open more gates on the dam. We could be in for a washout if they do," John said as he headed down the steps to the dock. "Give me a hand, we need to get some more cable ties on the dock. Otherwise, it might be headed down the river."

"Wouldn't it be a better idea to go ahead and get the boat out and on the trailer before it comes up anymore?" she asked, following him down the steps.

"Yep, back the trailer down the ramp, and we'll load it up."

With the boat and the dock secure, Sara and her dad relaxed on his favorite rusty white lawn chairs he kept under the trees outside the cabin. Sara remembered coming home and finding her mother sitting in the same place with her dad, both watching the rising White River. Her dad told them the river never rose high enough to get into their home high on the river's bank. Today, she hoped he had been right.

"Your last letter worried me. Want to tell me what the doctor had to say?"

"I'm tired, Sara, and in spite of my doc saying I'm fine, I feel like taking a few months off to rest up."

"Tired? You're never tired. Tell me, damn it. What did the doctor tell you?"

"That's all he said, Minnow. Don't worry so much about me."

"It's a daughter thing, Old Man. I'm going with you on the next doctor visit. Say it."

"All right, woman! You're going with me."

"Was that so hard?"

Anxious to change the subject, her dad said, "I told you I wanted to talk about the guide business, right?"

"Yeah? You're not planning on just giving up a lifetime business, are you?"

"I'm not giving up, Sara, just passing it on to you."

"Me! Why do you think I can do this?"

"You know this river as well as most of the guides I know."

"There's lots of problems. First off, I don't have a license to guide. Are there really any women guides on the river?"

"There have been a few, and most of them have quit after a while because of the pressure from the men guides."

"Really? What kind of pressure are you talking about?"

"The men didn't really take nicely to having women taking their clients. They shot some holes in one woman's boat. She quit right after that."

"Are you just saying that to challenge me?"

"I figured it would get your hackles twitching, woman."

"They're twitching. Dad, you've been responsible for building up the fishing business around this area. People come for miles just to fish with you."

"Damn, Sara. You just need to brush up on all the things your mother and I taught you about the White."

"Stop it, Dad. My mind is spinning right now. I've got a lot of questions."

"Well, go ahead. Ask them."

"What do I do about a license? Do I have to study and get tested for that?"

"Well, tomorrow we're going to head up to the Fish and Game office at Calico Rock. I've got an old friend there that I fish with, and I'm sure he'll help us."

She shook her head. "If I have to pass a test, I'll do it on the legit, Dad."

"Got your telephone?"

"The black one with the push buttons on it or the big wooden box that hung on the wall when I was a kid?"

"I'm hearing a little bit of the smart-ass kid I remember, Minnow. Pull out that computer thing and look up the Arkansas Game Commission." Sara's fingers got busy on the keys. "Tell me what it says about the guide license." He leaned back in the rusty chair until it gave a snap. "Oh, crap. This is going to need fixin'." Sara ignored the chair snapping. Her head was in the phone.

"Damn you, Dad. It says I can put down twenty-five dollars and walk out with a guide license."

"Really?" John chuckled.

s i x t e e n

SARA AND HER DAD WERE back at the cabin before noon. Sara held the twenty-five-dollar guide license and wondered what the heck did she do now?

"Dad, will I be the only female guide on the river?" Sara asked, turning the permit over in her hand to read the backside.

"No, you won't. There are still two up toward the dam area that guide when the docks get busy. Won't be no better one than you, counting the men and all. We'll go up tomorrow and tell the dock owners. They won't be surprised. I mentioned it last week."

"You were that sure I would go for this?"

"Didn't hurt for me to think that you would. Looks like since the river's not rising any more, they must have started shutting some of the gates on the dam. Tomorrow will be a good day to fish for a record brown trout. I've been seeing big 'uns in the catch and release area just waiting for us."

"You go, Dad. I've got a heck of a lot of things to do to even think about taking a guide trip."

They stood up and turned toward the back of the house when they heard a car pull in. "I'll go, Dad. That sounded like a Jeep I remember."

Sara headed around the corner of the house. Luke got out of the Jeep and held his arms out to give her a hug. Sara returned the hug and the kiss on the cheek he gave her.

"It's been way too long, Sara. God I'm glad to see you. You look great, lady."

"Well, I don't know about the great part, but I feel a hell of a lot better about myself."

"Hang on a minute. I've got something of yours in the Jeep."

Luke went to the Jeep came up with the bluebird house in his hand. "I've been keeping this in my apartment."

"Dad's gonna love it. Thanks. Got something to show you." She took the birdhouse and handed the guide license to him.

"What's this? Did you finally get a fishing license?"

"Hey, you jerk."

He turned the license over in his hand. "Oh!"

"Dad surprised me. He's backing off guiding and wants me to take over his guide trips."

"I hope he's told you what you're in for."

"Can you explain that, please?"

"Being a woman and dealing with the assholes we get out here on the river will be tough."

She grabbed the license out of his hand. "Being a woman! Really? What kind of man crap is that?"

He got very red in the face. "I want to make sure you're safe."

"I don't need a man to keep me safe. I spent two years guarding Iraqi terrorists. That taught me how to take care of myself."

"I didn't mean it that—"

"Hell, you didn't." She turned and walked away, leaving him with a look of bewilderment on his face.

She heard the Jeep start and pull out of the driveway as she handed the birdhouse to her dad and then slumped into the chair next to him.

"Bluebird house. Where did you get this?" John turned the house around and tapped on the wood sides. "This one's made by a craftsman. You bought it for me?"

"Luke just stopped by to drop it off. I got it for you months ago when we went to Mountain View. A ninety-five-year-old built it."

"Thanks, Sara. I love them bluebirds. This is going up on a fence post tomorrow. Where's Luke?"

"He's gone."

Damn, she didn't expect this kind of crap of from Luke.

"He's coming back, isn't he?"

"Hell, no."

"What happened?"

"He said something that told me a lot about his beliefs about women. Just forget it, Dad."

"Whoa, girl. Did you get a little too worldly for us country folks?"

"Shut up. Life's too complicated right now."

She sat questioning herself, her left hand pressed against the little minnow tattoo on her right wrist. *You were supposed to bring me good luck.*

SARA LEFT HER DAD SITTING in the yard. She was sure he was trying to figure out what she meant by *complicated*. She didn't plan on explaining—at least not to him. The short walk to Marty's ranch took only fifteen minutes. She wanted to thank the woman who encouraged her to make the call and get help. Sara found her with a manure fork in her hand and an overflowing wheelbarrow.

"Hi, Marty. Where do I dump this?" Sara lifted the handles of the wheelbarrow.

"Hey, girl, thank goodness you came along. Perfect timing! Thanks." She pointed to the large pile of manure just out the backdoor. "Just over to the side of the pile will be fine."

Sara wheeled the heavy load out the backdoor and dumped the wheelbarrow. The wheelbarrow twisted to the side, but her strength had it back upright quickly. Marty met her back by the tack room door with two glasses of iced tea.

"Come on. I'm sure we have bunches to talk about," Marty said, leading the way out of the barn to a bench in the shade. "Tell me about your V.A. stay."

"I came to thank you for giving me a kick in the butt. The V.A. helped me. I'm grateful for that. The fear is still in my head."

"Is it fear of what happened in Iraq?"

"Yes, they told me that fear might never go away. They taught me ways to think through things that happen and cause me to feel like I'm being overcome."

"Like when the black car we saw frightened you?"

"Next time I see the car, I'll do something about it. I beat up a fellow in a bar that was attacking my dad. It turned out he's a Mexican drug runner. He could have it in for me and having me followed."

"Good Lord, girl. Have you called the sheriff? You might have set yourself up for all kinds of trouble. Be careful."

"You're right. I'll call his office today. Thanks for caring, Marty."

"Isn't this what friends are for?"

"Yes, it's just—I have to learn more about relationships and where life's gonna take me while I'm still carrying all this baggage. I'm almost ashamed to admit how much it's bothering me."

"How are you and your dad getting along? I sure do love that old man." Marty set her empty glass on the ground by the side of the bench.

"Did you know Dad's letting me take over his guide business?"

"He mentioned he wanted to quit guiding. How's his health, Sara? We've been worried."

"He told me his stress tests came out fine. I think he may be doing this to get me busy."

"Good for him. You said relation*ships*. Is there another?

"There is. I had a date to Mountain View with Luke Matthews."

"That good-looking man can arrest me anytime he likes. Way to go, girl."

"I don't know if it's just him or all men. He got under my skin when I told him I was taking over Dad's guide business."

"How's that?" Marty asked, she had a surprised look on her face.

"He turned on his worried side and said things might be tough for a woman competing with the men guides."

"Straighten him out now, Sara. Worked for me."

"I sort of cut him off at the knees and left him standing in the yard earlier this afternoon."

"Good for you. If he's worth his salt, he'll be back, honey."

"I hope so."

seventeen

JOHN TOOK A SEAT AT the breakfast table. "Why don't we spend the next week with you as my guide, Sara? You run the show and get the boat ready,"

"Great idea." She finished a bowl of cereal and headed for the dock and the storage shed. An hour later, she yelled for her dad to get aboard the jon boat.

"Okay, let's shove off." Playing the part of the guide, she starting to back the boat away from the dock. "This morning we're going to fish the river drifting from Cotter back down to the takeout place at the cabin."

"Which rod do I use? Where's the bait?"

"We have a few miles to go to get to the best fishing."

The engine burped, then kicked out a couple more spasms, and stopped. Sara was puzzled but quickly tried to restart with the starter rope. She got only a cough out of the motor.

"Darn, we have a slight problem here, sir."

John sat quietly in the front of the boat. Sara pulled the starter rope more than a dozen times, trying to start the engine. Giving up, she picked up the paddle and began steering the boat. "Looks like we're going to drift back to the cabin, sir."

John didn't stir.

"This current is strong. I might need some help getting it back into the dock, Dad."

John smiled. Sara knew that smile well. He wasn't going to help. She began digging the paddle deeper in the water, hoping she could avoid crashing into the dock. When she realized the boat was going to hit hard, she went to the front and shoved it away from the dock. The boat turned and slid along the dock's side. She paddled hard and steered the boat toward the concrete ramp. With the boat still three feet from the bank, she grabbed the boat's tie rope and jumped into the water on the edge of the ramp. She looped the rope around her hand and braced her feet on the slimy concrete to pull. The boat turned and scraped to a stop.

"There, that wasn't so bad, now was it, sir?" She climbed halfway up the ramp and tied the boat to a small tree.

"When do we start fishing, Miss?"

"Fishing! Shit." Sara headed toward the cabin. "Darn engine is worn out."

"Did you check the gas tank this morning?" John yelled. "I think it's 'worn out' of gas."

Sara slumped in the metal lawn chair, waiting for her dad and the ass-chewing he would no doubt be giving her. John filled the small metal gas tank and shepherded the jon boat back into the dock slip before he came to sit beside Sara.

"Go ahead, chew me out. That was really a stupid thing for me to do, I can't do this shit."

"Too many things to remember at first, Minnow. We'll try again. This time make a checklist and use it every time."

"You're not giving up on me?"

"Never knew you to give up on yourself."

"Okay. First on the list, be sure the damn gas tank is filled after each time we go out."

They spent the rest of the morning sitting on the bank high over the river, working on the checklist.

"Good list. I wish I could tell you what to expect with the people you guide. Some need a babysitter, others just want you to put them on the right spot for a big one. I think you can handle them all."

"Let's start again after I fix us some lunch. This time you be the instructor and tell me what I'll need to be doing on a guide trip."

For the next week, morning and afternoon, John took Sara to every section of the river she would be fishing. He showed her the dangers of underwater boulders and sunken trees and warned her to be careful when the upstream dam opened a lot of gates, which would cause the river to rise rapidly. The final thing he covered was what to do with the few problem people she might have to deal with. He warned that if she didn't like the feel of fishing with someone to call it off early and head back to the trout dock. Sara's building confidence started to tell her that with her military training she could handle whatever came her way. She knew she would be ready when her first guide trip came. With her dad's training complete, she settled in getting her fishing gear ready and to wait for the trout dock to call with a trip.

IT WAS WEEK LATER WHEN John took the call from the dock. "Sara, the dock called and said they have a trip for you tomorrow."

"Let's go check in at the dock. We'll see what I need to get ready." She was already in the driver's seat of the truck when her dad got there.

"I haven't seen you this excited for a long time, Little Minnow."

"I'm starting to feel a lot more like my old self, Dad."

"I've been hoping to hear you say that."

eighteen

SARA RUMMAGED THROUGH THE MORE than two dozen ballcaps her dad had stashed in his closet and finally picked an old Bass Pro cap to wear with her camo shirt and pants. When fishing with her dad, she never wore makeup. Today, she thought about covering the scar on the side of her face but remembered John telling her to wear the scar with pride. With her aviator sunglasses in place, she checked her reflection in the mirror and gave herself a thumbs-up. She was ready for the trip upriver to pick up her first clients.

Sara arrived an hour early and well prepared for the float trip. She picked one of the middle slips in the trout dock and motored the old jon boat in. With the boat securely tied, she went to the dock office to get the snacks and drinks they had ready for her.

Barbara greeted her with a smile. "Hi, Sara. Are you ready?"

"I am! Who's fishing with me today?"

"It's a man and his wife from St. Louis. They've fished here a couple times in the past with your dad. They think he's the best guide on the river."

"Oh, boy, I've got Dad to live up to. You know I'm proud to do just that."

"I'll put the snacks in the boat and bait up the lines. I'll be waiting there by the boat."

Four other guide boats had pulled into the open docks around Sara's boat. The fifth guide boat idled just out from the slip where hers was docked. The dirty red beard on the man in the boat met his chest right at the top of his overalls. His eyes were sunken back in his skull so far his facial hair all but hid the buckshot pupils.

When he saw Sara, he slammed a railroader's cap against the back of one of the chairs in his boat. "You've got your goddamn boat in my spot. Get it out. We don't allow no bitches in here."

"Hey, is your name on this slip? Here, let me look. This bitch don't see a Dirty Red sign anywhere here." Her middle finger was about to go up, but she thought better of it.

She stepped into her boat and turned away from the man. Choking and laughing came from two of the boats tied up alongside her. The man she called Dirty Red cussed and gave her a gloved fist pointed at her face.

"Nobody's put old Red down that good for quite a time, lady." One of the older guides gave Sara a thumbs-up. "You're Sara, aren't you? Red heard you were starting to guide. Last thing that old redneck wanted to see was a woman guide on the river."

"I am, but you can just call me 'Heat.'" She hadn't meant for it to, but it just slipped out. Conflict still brought out the soldier in her.

"Okay. 'Heat.' Welcome to the trout dock. John told me about you and that he hoped you would be here someday fishing in his old boat."

"Thanks, sir. And what's your name?"

"It's Bob. I stopped being a 'sir' when I took off my suit and came down here to guide on the White. If Red gives you any more trouble, just holler. 'Spect you won't be needin' any help."

The intercom on the dock crackled to life. *"Sara! There's a lady up here from the flower shop for you."*

Crap, Dad was going to embarrass her again. All she needed to get along with this group of rednecks was a bunch of flowers for them to ride her about. She stepped out of the boat and rushed up the steps.

"Are you Sara Randolph?" the lady at the flower van asked.

"Umm…. Yes, I'm Sara."

"These flowers are for you. The card is on the inside of the box."

"Thanks, I'm sure they're beautiful." Sara turned and carried the box of flowers into the trout dock office. "Would you please hide these someplace? I'll pick them up when we get back."

"Sure, but aren't you going to check them out first?"

"Well, let's do it later."

Barbara flashed a knowing smile as she said, "Anyway, your customers are just pulling up. Their name is Campbell. Darren and Judith."

"Thanks, Barbara, I'll get out there." Sara rushed out letting the office door slam behind her.

SHE HAD HER HAND OUT to Mr. Campbell while she was still five feet away. "Mister and Missus Campbell, welcome to the Cotter Trout Dock. I'm Sara Randolph. I told Dad you were coming, and he sent a big howdy."

Mr. Campbell greeted her with a smile. "We fished with that old boy a lot of times. How's he doing?"

"He's fine. Always has some project going around the cabin." Sara reached out to shake hands with Mrs. Campbell.

Mrs. Campbell took her hand and covered it with a second one. "So, you're the Sara we've heard so much about. Between catching fish, you were all your dad talked about. Thank you for your service to our country, soldier."

"Thank you both for signing up for me to guide for you." She had a slight blush from the warm thank you.

"Let me carry your cooler, and we can head down to the boat. Some of the other guides are saying they're biting this morning."

After stowing their small cooler, she helped them step aboard. "The dock folks fixed drinks and some snacks for you both. Is there anything else I can get for you before we hit the fishing?"

Darren shook his head. "I think we're good to go, Sara."

"Great. The river is a little high, and we always wear life vests." Sara turned to put hers on. Her guests followed her lead. "We're going to head upstream about a hundred yards."

She took the boat up close to the west bank, which was a favorite fishing hole she had found. She didn't tell the Campbells the rainbow trout there would be feeding like hogs in a trough. She was certain they would love the fun of catching a fish with almost every cast.

"Darren, would you mind tossing out the chain up there in front? It'll drag the bottom and help keep us parallel with the bank. The lines are baited, so go ahead and cast out in the current toward the bank."

As the boat drifted downstream, Darren and his wife tossed the lines Sara had baited for them. Sara saw the small bump and flex of Judith's rod before the woman realized she had a bite.

"Fish. Judith, give it a light tap with the rod, and it'll be hooked."

Sara reached for the net with the long handle. The lady wasn't an expert at catching trout but did just fine in bringing the twelve-inch rainbow alongside the boat.

"Way to go. That's a nice keeper."

Sara netted the trout and carefully took out the hook before dropping the fish in the live-well.

"Darren! Watch your rod."

"What the hell is on here?" Darren started to crank hard against the heavy pull of the fish.

"That's a big brown trout you've hooked." Sara started the outboard to follow the fish.

"Damn, he's gone. My line just broke."

"I'm so sorry. It's my fault for not getting the outboard started sooner."

"You have nothing to be sorry for. Just feeling that fish take the line was worth our whole trip."

"Okay, then. Hand me the end of the broken line, and I'll get you baited back up. Maybe another brown out there." With a new hook on the line and three salmon eggs threaded on, she tossed the line over the edge of the boat. "You're ready, Darren. Let's try for some more excitement."

Darren's cast had just hit the top of the water. "It's hit twice and then let off. There he is, got him this time," Darren had a big smile on his face. He worked the lightweight rod and line to bring the small trout alongside for Sara to net.

"Good job, folks. Sit tight for a minute. I'm going to start the boat up and head back up there. We'll make another pass drifting over that hot spot." With fish in the live-well and two happy clients, Sara was enjoying being a teacher and the boss of her boat. In position for a big catch, she cut the boat's engine.

She smiled at the sound of loud Latino booming music rolling out across the water from somewhere along the shore. She had started to roll her hips when she saw the black Dodge drive out from behind a stand of cedars on the north road along the river.

Her joy suddenly became anger.

Her heartbeat quickened when she thought of the man that had threated to kill her. Ruiz?

The car slowly followed them as they moved downstream. She turned the boat toward the bank but then realized the time for that would have to come later. The Dodge sped out of sight.

THE CAMPBELLS HAD CAUGHT AND released more than twenty trout by the time their float trip neared the end after drifting more than five miles to near John's cabin and dock.

"I hope you don't mind, we've gone about an hour over your trip time. My dad's got the trailer in the water and the truck ready for me to drive you back to the Cotter Trout Dock."

Judith shook her head. "We don't mind at all. I'm so glad Darren brought me along."

Sara counted the fish in the live-wells and told them they could each keep one more to make up the limit of five per person.

"Do you guys have time for fishing one more spot that's close by?"

"Let's go!"

She asked Darren to pull in the drag chain and motored the boat to a fast-moving rock rapids near the bank. "Cast up just to the edge of the rocks and let the bait drop."

Both of the customers' rods bent when the two rainbows hit. Darren's trout came to the top and danced across the water on its tail. He reeled the fish in as his wife fought against a rainbow that had gone downstream.

"What a way to end the day," Darren said.

With the limits in the live wells now filled, she took the boat and the happy customers to the takeout ramp. Her dad already had the trailer backed in the water, and he stood waiting for them.

"Hey, hello to the Campbells. Saw all the action out there. Looks like she didn't disappoint you."

Darren pointed to one of the live wells. "Lots of fish. Maybe even more than you put us on the last time we were here."

"You can be proud of this one, John." Judith stood to get out of the boat.

Sara helped the Campbells out of the boat and put the fish into a carry cooler for the trip back to the dock. After they told her dad goodbye, Sara drove them back to the Cotter Trout Dock.

At the trout dock, she took them in to settle up for the trip while she cleaned the fish. The cleaning table at the dock's edge wasn't busy, so Sara quickly had the trout bagged and packed on ice for the couple to take home.

"Thank you both for fishing with me. I hope you had fun. It's sure been fun for me. I loved watching both your faces on those last catches." Sara handed the cooler over to Darren.

"Fun for us, too, Sara. Here's a little extra thank you for taking us on a great float." Darren's wife handed Sara an envelope.

"Thank you both." Sara walked with the Campbells to their car and thanked them again. "Hope to see you again."

She waved goodbye and then went into the trout dock office to get the flowers from her dad. Seated back in the truck, she opened the box to see roses and quickly realized these were not from her ex-marine father. She opened the small envelope. *I'm sorry, I was really stupid, Luke.*

She lifted the bundle of roses to her nose. The fragrance of the deep red flowers caught her off guard. She suddenly longed to wrap her arms around Luke, kiss him, and thank him for topping off her great day. When her mind came back to reality, she opened the envelope the Campbells had given her and found another surprise, a hundred-dollar bill. She waved the bill in the air and then put it in her wallet. She was wearing a smile from ear to ear.

nineteen

WITH NO NEW FISHING TRIPS to guide, Sara was anxious to get back on the river. When her dad talked about catching smallmouth bass on the Buffalo River, she jumped at the opportunity for a new adventure. She thanked him for the fishing tip and loaded up the boat with her fishing gear and headed downstream to where the Buffalo joined the White River. The small town of Buffalo City sat on the west bank and provided a good spot for a much-needed bathroom break. She beached the jon boat at the fishing resort and headed for their tackle shop. As she went through the door, her phone vibrated. Luke. She flipped the phone open and put it to her ear without speaking.

"*Sara? Are you there?*"

She still didn't speak.

"*What do you want me to say? I'm really sorry? I've missed you an awful lot.*"

Sara backed out the door while he was talking and let it go shut before saying anything. "You can stop now, Luke. I forgive you. The flowers were beautiful and made me want to thank you with a kiss."

The phone fell silent again but only for a few seconds then, "*You really had me sweating there. Can I get a promise I'll still get the kiss?*"

"I promise you will."

"*Are you close?*"

"Not now. I'm going after smallmouth bass down on the Buffalo River."

"*But I'm not that far from there!*"

"I'm sure Gwen would just love to follow you down here for you to get my kiss." She ended the call and realized she was smiling a lot more these days. She went back through the door and into the office. The man sweeping the floor looked up.

"Hello, what brings you to Buffalo City, Miss?" He set the broom and the dustpan he was using against the side wall.

"Mind if I use your restroom, sir?"

"The door is just around the back."

"Thanks."

When she got back inside the tackle shop, she leaned over the glass countertop to check out their selection of baits.

"Anything I can help you with?"

"I came down from Cotter to try the smallmouth fishing. Your guides say anything about what they're biting on?"

"That's the last thing the guides down here would talk about." The man smiled. "However, I can tell you what baits they buy a lot of. By the way, my name is Ron Brady."

"Hi, Ron. We do the same up at Cotter, try to keep all our secrets, secret," Sara said and smiled.

"Cotter. Would you be Sara Randolph, the guide?"

"Well, yes, I would. Why would you know my name?"

"Word is getting around about some of the big fish you and your dad have caught. Any close to the state record?"

"Oh, yes! The one that got away yesterday. It was, well, right on the state record," Sara kidded. "How about you, Ron. Do you guide on the Buffalo?"

"No, running this place is about all I can manage since I lost my wife two years ago. It's been hard keeping the place going. Finally got in the black last year. If I don't get flooded out again, I should be fine."

"I'm so sorry about your wife."

"She drowned when the big washout flood hit down through here."

"That's terrible. I missed that flood. I was in Iraq."

"One of my guides was in Iraq. He's told me some real horror stories."

"All of us that served there have some of those stories. Was your wife out in a boat when the storm hit?"

"No. Jenny had ran back down to the dock to get our dog. I left our Sheltie in the boat house when we got back from fishing early that morning. I watched her holding onto the side of the dock when it turned against the bank and broke apart. Then she was gone."

Sara wondered how the man could talk about losing a loved one so casually. It always tore at her gut when she talked about her crew. They were a team that was supposed to look out for each other.

She thought about telling him about her horror and how the nightmare plagued her for so long, but his story felt too close to home for Sara. She needed to move on. With some hesitation but wanting to change the subject she said, "Why don't you show me those baits the guides are buying?"

With four of the baits bagged and paid for, Sara started for the door.

"Miss Randolph, if you ever decide to guide on the Buffalo, please come see me."

With a firm and friendly handshake, she nodded. "I will. By the way, just call me Sara."

A QUARTER MILE UP THE Buffalo, Sara guided the boat to what she thought would be the deeper side of a fast-moving section of the river. The keel of her outboard engine dragged bottom twice before she beached the jon boat and walked to a narrow section of the stream. John had told her to look for unlikely places to fish for the smallmouth bass because they liked to hide when the sun was out. She carried the bass rod her dad had told her to take up to the start of the small rapids and cast out a few feet to let the bait roll along with the current. A strike came before she expected it, and she gave the hard jerk her dad had told her to use to set the hook for smallmouth bass. It was too much. The wayward rainbow trout came flying out of the water and right over Sara's head, landing on the sand behind her. She doubled over laughing.

There was a loud grunt that turned into a growl behind her. She spun around and instinctively reached for her service weapon.

The weapon wasn't there.

The black bear standing a few yards away grunted again and stomped the ground. Sara stood still, not sure if she should run. Moving her hands slowly, she cranked on the fishing reel and took up the slack line holding the fish. When the fish moved a few inches, the bear limped toward it. Two more cranks of the reel, two more steps by the bear toward the fish.

"Oh, my, you look kind of beat up, bear."

Thinking she needed to do something quick to get out of the situation, she jerked the line hard and pulled the fish to her. With the hook out of the fish's mouth, she quickly threw it within reach of the bear. Making only a grunt, the bear grabbed it with its teeth. It sat back on its haunches and quickly ate the trout. Sara felt bad for the lame bear. When it had picked up the trout, she saw it was missing an ear and had a large scar running across the top of its head.

Wanting the bear to leave, she waved her hands in the air and shouted, "Get, bear!"

When the bear held its ground, she guessed it was staying for another fish. She figured the guides on the river must have been feeding it with fish guts and skins. Sara slowly backed to her boat and pushed off the sandbar. Waving to the waiting bear, she realized seeing the animal had given her a high she had actually enjoyed.

"Goodbye, Old One Ear. I'll look for you again."

A quarter mile more upstream, she went back to fishing for smallmouth bass. Casting in the waters so close to the White River brought nothing but a few strikes from small rainbow trout, so she walked the jon boat through the shallow water before setting the engine down and heading up stream to deeper water. Her dad had told her that when she left the White, there would be more than twenty miles of what he called "wild country." When she came to a horseshoe bend in the river, she noticed a sweeping sandbar pushed out into the water. Fishing the sandbar on the way downstream would be first on her list of places the bass might go to feed in the evening. She had traveled more than five miles before she slowed, turning the boat and letting it drift with the current.

Sara loved the beauty of the mountain ridges that rose from the river and were covered with cedar, spruce, and tall oaks. Her dad was right, this river was surrounded by some wild country.

She was starting to get impatient after two hours of getting nothing but small bluegill nibbles on her line. Where were the smallmouth? She watched the clear water and watched the sun perch leave their hiding places and head for the drifting bait. A minute later, the smallmouth strike came so hard and suddenly, she almost dropped the rod. Slow on the recovery, she struck back with a hookset jerk, but it was way too late.

Had that been real? She'd fished on the big Arkansas lakes a number of times for smallmouth but never had a strike that felt like this one. The largemouth bass of the big lakes hit hard and fought hard, but smallmouth bass, well, this was something different. Natural river bred fish had a whole different attitude about not wanting to get caught.

She cast back in the same deep hole and got ready for the strike she hoped for. This time her hookset jerk worked. The smallmouth bent the rod as it swam sideways against the pull of the line, and then it headed toward a large tree trunk sticking up from the riverbed.

Oh, no you don't, fish!

The smallmouth pulled hard, stripping line from the reel. Sara tightened the reel's drag a full turn. With every four cranks on the handle, she inched the fighting fish toward the boat. Her eyes opened wide when she saw the size of the bass pulling her line straight for the back of the boat and the motor's propeller. Standing above the boat's engine, she worked it around the prop and back out into the open. With the fish alongside the boat, she quickly brought it onboard with the dip net.

She dropped it into the boat's live well and turned on the aerator to keep it alive. "Shit! This one's going home to show the boys."

With the risk of losing another fish on the sharp edges of the boat's propeller, she beached the boat on the bank and walked upstream along the steep bank and rock cliff. After a half hour of casting along the bank, and not getting another bite, she headed back. She stood for a moment and watched the sun starting to dip behind the Ozark mountain ridge. When she felt lonely for home in Iraq, she tried to remember the colors and warmth of the day's end sunlight highlighting the outline of the trees. There had been so many days when she thought she might never see this sight again.

Pushing the boat off the bank, she lifted the lid on the live well to have another look at her lucky catch of the day.

The fish was gone.

What the hell?

She started the engine and ran the boat back up on the bank. Looking again in the live-well to be sure the fish was gone, she hopped into the knee-deep water. She finally spotted it in the short sand strip along the water's edge—a footprint.

Sara stooped and opened her fingers to span the small print.

A kid had stolen her fish.

Everything she had been told about the more than twenty miles of wild country along this section of the Buffalo River came rushing to her mind. They said no one lived within miles of this section of river. Sara looked the bank area over until she found the deep imprint where the child had jumped off the boat. A snapped branch of a small tree showed the start of the tracks going up the hill. She pushed the heavy growth of poison ivy aside and went looking for other signs of the thief's tracks.

Memories of her K-9 partner in Iraq—his name was Tank—came to mind. She wished he were with her now to help track this kid. She paused, trying to remember the last time she'd seen the dog.

The back of the Humvee, bloody and dead.

Stop. I can't go there, not now.

One after another, she followed the signs left in the trail—a turned leaf, a disturbed rock, and a bent branch lead her up the steep incline. The trail winding up a steep mountain side surprised her. She couldn't imagine where a kid would be headed in this wilderness.

Three-fourths of the way up the mountain, a sheer wall of rock ledges blocked the way. An animal trail led in both directions along the foot of the rock ledges. There was a choice to make. Which way did the child go? She chose the trail to the east. Soon the rock ledges opened up into a cave. Stooping, she stepped under the top of the cave and looked for signs of the kid. Nothing stood out, and then she saw a small trimmed tree branch laying along the side of the cave. Sara picked it up and realized she had found someone's fishing pole and line. The pole was strung with a strand of dark fishing line and tied to the end was a lure that would be a favorite for the smallmouth of the Buffalo. She tested the line and quickly realized it was a very expensive type of line a fisherman must have lost on the river. She went back in the cave but found nothing more. She backed out and returned along the trail to the point where she'd came up the hill. Looking back up the mountain she saw only a tiny sliver of the sun was left in the treeline. It was then she saw the dark outline of a small boy standing there watching her.

"Who are you?"

No answer came, and the boy vanished as quickly as he'd appeared.

She started up the hill, but stopped. It was too late, and it would be dark soon. She had to head back to the cabin.

The mystery of the child would have to wait for another day.

WITH THE JON BOAT ENGINE running smoothly, and the night closing in from all sides, she motored for the cabin hoping to talk with her dad about the child in the wilderness. She reached to check her rod in the sideboard rack only to realize it was gone.

The little shit had doubled back on her and stolen her rod, too.

Just as she reached the White River, her phone rang. Luke was still trying to get her to answer.

"Hello, Lawman. Hard for you to take a hint that I'm busy."

"It seems I had a couple of things to apologize for, and I'm really sorry."

"Okay, you've apologized. What's next? Can you take me to dinner tomorrow? I've been up on the Buffalo and can't wait to talk about something odd that has happened."

"Really? What happened? I've heard some crazy things about that stretch of the river."

"There was a kid that came down the mountain and stole my fish and rod."

"A kid? How old was he?"

"I only saw his footprint in the sand."

"Maybe he had a boat hid pulled up in the woods."

"I don't think so. Looked like he might be staying in a cave. I'll tell you all about it at dinner."

"Can't wait to hear. I'll pick you up early tomorrow around four o'clock. Don't forget the kiss!"

She killed the connection and shook her head. "Men."

twenty

SARA HEARD THE JEEP IN the driveway before she was ready. She yelled for her dad to keep Luke busy for five minutes. "Dad, ask him where we're going? I'm not sure what to wear."

"He says he's taking you to a fishing lodge with an airport."

"Where?" She leaned out the door of her room to wait for the response.

"You'll love it! You've been there with me and your mom. The restaurant sits up on the bank and overlooks the river. Your mom always liked watching the hummingbirds that came to the feeders in the windows."

Sara never liked rushing, it always made it hard for her to think. "We were there? Crap, I'm not ready yet."

She tossed the slim pickings of what she had to wear on the bed. Despite all the washings, her white blouse still had a small bloodstain on its side from the beating she'd given Ruiz. In a rush, she put it on, anyway, and covered it with a leather jacket. The jeans she bought at the farm store made up the rest of her outfit. With a quick goodbye to her dad, she slipped into the seat of Luke's Jeep.

"Ready to take me for a 'ride in your airship,' dear sir," She remembered the words of a song she had liked on their trip to Mountain View.

"'Away we go to visit the man in the moon.' You remembered!"

"Words to that song sort of stuck in my head."

"Well, I don't have an airship, but I *am* taking you to a little airport with a lodge. A great place to have dinner."

When they turned into the Gaston's drive, Sara remembered being there. "I came here with Mom and Dad. Dad had a real busy month of guiding on the river and wanted to celebrate by taking us to a special place."

"They have a couple miles of nature trail and a real beautiful path down along the river and then up into the hills." Luke walked around and opened the door for her. "There's still several hours before dark, so after we eat, we can take a walk over past the peacock pens."

"I would love that. I heard one scream when we drove in. Right now, this girl is starving. I somehow missed eating lunch today." She took his arm. "Okay, which way to the food?"

"In the lodge, the dining room sits up above their dock and the river."

"Can't wait."

The hostess greeted them and asked if they would like a window seat overlooking the river. Sara started to say a quiet booth would be better, but followed the waitress to the window seats. Luke held the chair for Sara.

"Thank you, sir. Look, the bird feeders are covered with hummers." The view from high above the river was breathtaking.

"Those are the ruby-throated we have so many of."

"My mom liked to get close to hummingbirds. She'd have them flying around her and even taking liquid out of this hand-held feeder she made. They were beautiful. So much fun to watch when they sparred for a place at the feeders."

When the hostess pointed out the large buffet spread across the center of the room, Sara was the first to rise. "Come on, Agent Matthews. We can do nature after we finish dinner!"

After Luke returned from his third trip to the buffet table with a huge slice of cherry cheesecake, she finished her coffee, sat her napkin on the table, and waited impatiently for him to devour the cheesecake.

"What do you know about there being a kid out in that wild area?"

"I don't think anyone lives anywhere near that area of the river. Are you sure someone didn't slip in on your boat from the river?"

"Yes, I'm sure. Absolutely certain, in fact Some kid went up the mountain with my fish, then came back down and stole my best bass fishing rod from right under my nose."

"I haven't heard any notices of missing children, but I promise to check first thing in the morning and give you a call."

"You better—I'm heading back up there to find that kid. Call me before I'm out of cell range."

"That's really weird. There may be someone up there with him. I should go with you."

"I've got this. Don't worry about me."

"Still, I think I should go. I'll check the computers and all you around eight, okay? If that's early enough?"

"I'll just be heading out. Oh, something else." She chuckled. "I met a beat-up black bear up there on the Buffalo. It wanted a trout I caught a whole lot more than I did."

He shook his head and laughed. "That old lame bear, he's a legend with the fishermen on the river. He seems to know just when to show up to steal a fish. I'm surprised someone hasn't shot him yet."

"After he got my fish, he just sat there waiting for more."

"We probably need to catch him and take him deeper in the wilderness before he gets into some real trouble."

"Don't, Luke. He's not bad. He's hurt and needs all the fish the guides leave for him to eat."

"OH, MY, I REALLY NEED to walk that buffet off. I ate way too much, but, dang, it was good." Sara led the way out of the lodge. Luke stopped her at the gift shop to show her some of the art from the locals. They walked through the display of paintings and carvings, pointing out the pieces they liked the most. Sara put her hand under a carved hummingbird house and lifted it to look inside.

"I've never seen a hummingbird house." She checked the price tag and "I'm getting this. It may never see a nesting hummingbird, but I'll see it every day when I wake up in the morning, and it will remind me of how happy the long-beaked birds seem to be."

He reached out to take it from her. "I'm getting that for you, then."

"No. I want to remember getting something I don't need for myself. I haven't done that, for—well, since before Iraq," Sara turned away and headed for the cashier. "Can you put it in a box for us, please?"

With the hummingbird house safely in the Jeep, Luke took Sara's hand, and they walked to the large cage areas filled with peacocks and turkeys. A half-dozen of the birds walked around the outside of the cages and stopped to watch the two visitors before flying to the top of the structures. Sara snapped a half-dozen pictures before turning her cell phone off and slipping it in her jacket pocket. At the edge of the grass airstrip, they watched the purple martins gathered on the supports holding the gleaming white gourd birdhouses.

"The birds are gathering before heading south for the winter. The cold can be deadly to them. Birdwatchers claim they even bunch up, ten or more in the gourds to keep warm."

She moved closer. "Maybe we need to bunch up a little more for this hike." Enjoying being with the tall, handsome outdoorsman had gotten her thinking that maybe there would be a place in her heart for another man. She felt ready for more than just a close friendship with Luke.

After topping the ridge, they headed back toward the lodge on the lower trail along the river. She pulled on his arm. "We need to go down there." She pointed to a boulder sticking out into the river and then led the way to climb out onto the rock's flat surface.

Sara laughed and sat, pulling on his hand to join her. "Come on, don't be a sissy. It's only a little wet down here." When Luke laid back on the rock, she moved against him, her leg across his hips, pressing tightly against his body. Her head hung over his, rubbing her nose against his lips to caress and tease. The river's swift current plowed against the side of the mammoth rock, showering the couple on top. Neither of them felt the splashing of the cold water.

twenty-one

THE NEXT MORNING IT WAS warm under the cloudy sky as Sara steered the jon boat onto the Buffalo River, retracing her route from her previous trip.

The tall pine forest to the east, the mountains to the west, and the cloud covered sky above gave her a feeling of being closed in as she motored up the narrow river channel. She remembered sounds of men trapped while standing in coffin-like boxes. Tortured by CIA agents seeking to extract the last of the secrets the men kept locked away in the name of their Allah. But claustrophobia torture methods rarely gained the secrets the CIA sought. Instead, it had only increased the raging hate the prisoners shouted. It made her sick then and now.

Her claustrophobia closed in.

Remembering the training her doctors had repeated over and over for her, she repeated it to herself silently—*replace the bad thoughts with brighter thoughts of things around you.*

Today, her good thoughts would be about finding the child. She was not about to let the mystery of a child alone in the wild area of the river go unsolved. Luke's call had come at eight and offered no clue to any missing child, only an offer to go with her. Once again, she'd told him no.

This was *her* mystery and challenge to solve.

She turned on the trail camera she had mounted by the boat's gas tank before she pulled up on the narrow sand ledge along the mountain side of the river. She came better equipped for the woods today—a long-sleeved shirt to keep out the poison ivy, ten-inch-tall boots to shield from snakebites, and a 9mm Berretta pistol strapped on her side. She had kept the new pistol as her secret. She felt armed and ready for whatever she might find on the mountain.

She dropped her cell phone in the thigh pocket on her khakis and climbed the steep slope to the rock ledges. Again, she took the trail to the east. Fifty yards along the trail, she took advantage of a cleft in the rocks and hid to watch her path up the slope from her boat at the river's edge.

After half an hour of sitting, she got impatient, broke from hiding, and backtracked to the animal trail heading off to the west. The trail was easy for a half mile, but then she reached a place where it was blocked by a section of the cliff that had fallen. She would have to climb it to get past it.

The first fallen ledge only reached her waist, so scaling it was easy. The second part of her climb was a lot harder. She reached high to get a handhold and then pulled herself up, stopping for a moment to rest. The next ledge was taller and impossible for her to see the top. She jumped for it, getting her right hand over the top and gripping the edge.

The sharp crack of the buzzing rattlesnake shook her.

Shit! Moving her hand would spook the rattler to strike. Her fingers felt numb. She moved a little finger, trying to ease the tingle.

It came again, the warning voice of the snake.

No matter what she did, she was about to get bit by a rattlesnake.

Trying to think of something funny—where in the hell was that rattlesnake lovin' preacher when she actually needed him?—didn't help. She thought of going for the Berretta with one hand and blasting the hell out of the top of the ledge with it. Just before she moved her hand, though, the hissing viper went flying over her head, wrapped in a coil like a bullwhip about to crack.

What the—

There was someone on the ledge above her. She struggled to pull herself up. Her fingers gave way, and she fell back. Hellbent on seeing who was above her, she lunged at the ledge, just getting her head over the edge.

A long-haired young boy saw her, turned, and ran back up the mountain.

"Hey, wait, kid!" He disappeared into the underbrush. She blew out a frustrated breath. "Come back and help me up here."

No use.

She lunged again at the ledge and got a grip to pull herself up and over. Just past the lip, she found a well-worn path leading toward the top of the mountain. And on the backside of the large boulder there, she found the stolen fishing rod sitting across her path.

One mystery solved.

She didn't think about turning back. She searched the heavily timbered area for more than two hours, calling often for the boy to come out, before giving up on trying to find him. She picked up her fishing rod and climbed back over the fallen rock ledges to the trail leading down the steep slope.

The image of the long-haired kid stuck in her mind and raised all sorts of new questions for her. Could it have been a girl? How did the kid end up in the mountains all alone? Where was he—or *she*—getting food, besides stealing her fish?

She stopped in her tracks.

This child needed this fishing rod more than she did. She turned down the trail to the east until she got back to the cave she'd found earlier. She set her tackle on the cave floor next to the homemade pole the boy must have been using. Back at the river's edge, she took the lunch she'd prepared and all that remained of her trail mix and left it at the edge of the timber. She hoped this would feed the child until she came back. And she *would* be back.

Back on the river with a strong cell signal, she called Luke.

"Hey, are you near the Buffalo River?"

"Hello. You okay? You sound funny."

"I'm fine." In reality, she could barely catch her breath. "Where are you? Something strange as hell just happened on the mountain."

"What happened? I'm not close. We had a feral hog call, and I'm up north."

"A boy saved me from getting rattlesnake bit. He ran away, and I've been trying for hours to find him. He wouldn't come out when I called."

"We'll be back around noon tomorrow. I'll get off, and we can look for him."

"Can you keep checking the computers in the meantime?"

"I checked, but I haven't heard back from our sheriff. I'll call as soon as I'm back in my truck."

"Call me in the morning. Whatever you find out."

"Sara, don't go back up there alone. You've got me worried."

"I've got this, Luke. Stop your worrying. I'm not some porcelain princess you have to protect all the damn time."

twenty-two

SARA WAS BACK THE NEXT morning hunting for the child who had saved her from the rattlesnake on the mountain. The V.A. therapy sessions had taught her to dig into mental challenges and not let them overcome her. She'd bought heavily into the V.A. training and pushed mental and physical challenges to the top of her priority list of things to get done.

Today she ran on a heavy dose of curiosity and determination. After finding an old map of the river in her dad's things, she marked the county road that would be just west of the horseshoe bend in the river.

She drove along the gravel road looking for a place to park and then hike to the top of the mountain where she'd last seen the child. Twice she drove past an opening in the heavy underbrush along the road before stopping and getting out to check if it was an easy way up the ridge. When she walked through the cleft in the brush, she found the start of an old dirt track headed up the mountain. Back in the truck and risking getting scratches on the sides, she drove through the brush and onto the road's steep climb.

She shifted the truck into four-wheel drive to keep from spinning the rear wheels. Certain the sound of the truck would warn of her approach, she pulled over after only a short distance and parked in the timber. She'd talked to Luke again about seeing the child. He told her this time he might be on to some news about a missing boy, but he was from an area miles away. He asked again for her to wait for him to go with her to look for the boy. Again, she had told him no. She had made it her mission to do alone.

Filling her pockets with high protein bars for the kid, Sara strapped on her water jug and slipped on her camo cap. Climbing the backside of the mountain would have been easier if she'd stayed on the logging road. Instead she worked her way up through the woods twenty yards to the north. At the top crest overlooking the bluff, she found a place where she would have a good view of the river and the trail leading to the cave where she'd left the fishing rod. She spread the thick green branches of a cedar tree and slipped under its camouflage to watch for the boy.

After an hour of sitting still, the strong odor of the cedar branches and limbs got to be too much for her. Her instincts were pushing her to search for the child instead of sitting here waiting for him. She climbed out from under the cedar branches and walked to the edge of the bluff, looking for signs of someone being there. A gathering of old branches and limbs broken into short lengths and stacked ready to burn was the first clue to the child being on the mountain top. She knelt and picked up a rock on the ground beside the wood. A flint. Striking it with the back of her hunting knife, she got the sparks she expected. When she looked again at the stacked wood, she saw a hunting knife lying in the leaves alongside the pile. The cut wood chips and slivers of bark under the pile felt soaking wet.

The boy's attempt to start a fire had been rained out.

The size of the stack of wood surprised her. It was way more than would be needed for a cooking fire. Maybe it had been a signal fire, instead?

A sudden noise in the leaves behind her caused her to turn quickly, hand instinctively reaching for her Beretta.

She smiled when she saw the dog. There it sat maybe twenty feet away staring at her. Thin, ragged, and standing taller than her German Shepherd, Tank, who had died when her convoy had been struck.

"Hey, boy. What ya doing up here, old hound?" There it was—the feeling against her side of her K-9 lightly pressing against her. Then the touch of dog was gone, leaving only thoughts of her dead Humvee crew. She pushed back against the ever-returning memories.

"Come here. Come." She wiped away the tears caressing her cheeks.

The dog didn't move toward her. Instead, it lifted its muzzle and let out the most mournful bawl she'd ever heard.

It then turned quickly and headed down the bluff trail.

"Wait!"

She ran after the animal, certain it would lead her to the child. At the bottom of the rock wall she found it again, its long tail wagging, waiting for her where the trail forked.

Waiting for her.

Seeing her again, the dog turned and trotted off along the rock wall edge. Sara followed, an odd sense of foreboding nagging at her brain. Then suddenly, the hound disappeared.

She turned and looked around. No way. It was *gone.*

How—?

Then she remembered the cave. Rushing ahead through the undergrowth, she heard the heavy sound of labored breathing before she rounded the corner to the front of the cave. The boy was lying on his back in the middle of the dirt floor. The hound stood on the opposite side of the boy, wagging its tail and whimpering. The foreboding exploded into full-blown worry.

Sara dropped to the boy's side and looked for trauma. One leg of the boy's threadbare jeans bulged outward over a swollen mass. Turning the boy's head to face her, she slapped his cheeks gently. "Snakebite?"

He didn't reply. Shit.

Her military training on snakebites had been intense, but it all called for immediate action after the bite occurred. This one must be hours old. The boy's forehead felt like it was on fire, and his breathing was short and gasping.

She cut away the pant leg and saw the bruising and discoloration of his leg. The fang marks stood out and looked deep and wide. One hell of a big snake had gotten him.

She shook the boy again "What kind of snake?"

God, what a stupid question. She had seen the rattlesnake that must have bitten him fly over her damn head.

The boy reached toward the water bottle on her side.

"I can't give you any. Not with a bite like this." She wet the edge of her bandana from her water bottle and rubbed it across the boy's lips. "I'm sorry, that's all I can do. I've got to get you out of here."

Rushing to the mouth of the cave, she tried her cell phone for a signal. There was none. Back in the cave, she took off her flannel shirt and tied the arms in a knot. She lifted the boy to a sitting position and slipped the shirt over his head and down under his arms. Slipping the sleeves over her head, she pulled the boy up on her back. His arms hung over her shoulders.

Lifting him felt easy, he weighed less than the backpack she'd carried in Iraq. She knew that getting back to the top of the mountain with the boy on her back would be a challenge. The tall ledge where he'd saved her from the rattlesnake was the most difficult. She took the boy off her back and balancing him between her hands, she lifted and rolled him onto the top of the ledge. She followed with a lunge and a jump that got half her body over the ledge. Pulling herself the rest of the way, she slid the boy back in her homemade carry sling and rushed up the last of the trail to the top. The dog had come around the ledge and was waiting at the top.

"Get out of the way, hound."

She pushed by it. Stopping to catch her breath was not an option. She was sure the boy was close to death. With the top of the mountain cleared, she paused and punched 911 on her cell phone. With the phone's speaker on, she ran with the boy on her back down the logging trail.

"I need help. I'm carrying a snake-bitten boy off the Boston Mountain on the backside of the Buffalo River horseshoe bend. My truck is on the gravel road 2840 west at the base of the mountain."

"*Where again, miss?*"

"Just listen. Ping my cell for my location if you have to. I'm taking him to Cotter, so get someone out here with oxygen to meet me. He's really bad off. Been snake bit for more than twenty-four hours. I'm leaving my cell on, so you can hear me." She started running, knowing her truck was close.

She draped the boy across the passenger seat of the truck and almost slammed the door on the hound climbing in by the boy. Without another thought, she started the truck, turned, and raced down the logging trail to the road.

Five miles from Cotter, she saw the lights of the ambulance coming down the blacktop. Pulling over, she jumped out and waved them down. Sara had the boy in her arms and was climbing in the back of the ambulance before either of them got out.

"Somebody drive. Right now!

"Not the dog!" one of the crew yelled.

"Bullshit!" Sara hissed at the driver. "He's already in here. Drive!"

"We're taking him to the Medical Center in Cotter." The paramedic moved to the boy's side and slipped an oxygen mask over his face.

"I'm starting an IV. Do you know what kind of snake bit him?"

"No. He couldn't tell me, but I would guess it was a rattlesnake. He saved me from getting bit yesterday. He must have taken the bite himself."

"They didn't want us to start the anti-venom until they see him because his breathing is so labored. What's his name?"

"I don't know his name or where he came from. I saw him up on that mountain a day ago and went back today to look for him. His dog led me to him."

She untied her shirt and gently slipped it out from under the boy and put it back on over her military sport bra.

"Sorry for being shirtless."

"Been too busy to notice, miss. Besides, using your shirt for a sling was a smart idea. Dog's licking my arm. Must know we're trying to help his friend."

SARA SAW LUKE WAITING FOR HER as the ambulance pulled into the medical center emergency lane. He ran out to help the medics when they opened the backdoor. Sara took his hand as she stepped down from the vehicle. The paramedics unloaded the gurney and headed for the ER door.

"Somebody keep the dog out of here," one of them shouted.

No one was listening. Sara and Luke and the dog followed close behind.

Luke tried to keep up with Sara's and the dog's pace. "Did he tell you anything when you found him?"

"Nothing at all. It was awful. It was the hound led me to him. The boy could barely breath."

A waiting nurse wrapped a stethoscope around the dog's neck and was leading him off before Sara stopped her.

"Put him somewhere safe. He saved the boy's life."

They stood at the examination table as the doctor examined the wound and ordered anti- enom. "Are you his parents?" the doctor asked.

"No. I found him and brought him here. I'm sure a rattlesnake bit him."

"How did he get the burns on his hands?"

"I didn't see the burns. I was rushing to get him here."

"Giving anti-venom can be very dangerous. He's got a big load of venom from that snake, and he could lose his leg before we get the internal bleeding stopped," the doctor said. "Can you contact his parents for their consent to give the anti-venom?"

Luke spoke up. "I think his parents may have been killed a few months ago."

"Then I'm going to start the anti-venom in a smaller dose at first and build up the dose size as I see the results. Right now, he's bleeding internally from the snake's venom, and his blood pressure is dropping. You both need to step out and let us do our job. I promise we're going to do our best to save this child."

Reluctantly, Sara allowed Luke to lead her to the waiting room.

"I know you wanted to stay with the boy, but...."

"Did you find out anything about the boy from Ponca?"

"Yes. He's eleven years old, and his parents were killed by an explosion and a fire. They had a trailer miles away on the east part of the Buffalo River, near Ponca. Sheriff said they were cooking meth."

"How the hell did he end up on that mountain, then? Do you think this is the same boy?" She pulled her bandana off and wiped her forehead.

"He must have floated downstream on a raft to get to where you found him."

Convinced there was nothing else she could do right now for the boy, Sara settled beside Luke on the couch. After telling him her account of getting the boy off the mountain, she told him she would stay at the hospital until the boy woke up. Luke promised her to take the boy's dog and come back after work.

Sara paced the waiting room. After an hour, she went to check on the boy's condition.

She stopped at the nurse's station. "The boy that came in with a snake bite, how's he doing?"

"The doctor is still in with him. I'll see if I can find out when he comes out of the ER. They were pretty worried about him when I last checked," the nurse told her. "You carried him off that mountain, didn't you?"

"Yes. I was afraid I wouldn't get him here in time to save him."

"He's one lucky boy. The doctor said he would have been dead in just a few hours."

"I'll check back." She headed back to the waiting room where she found her dad waiting. "He's in bad shape, Dad. I should have found him yesterday when I went back up there. It just got so late."

"You found him today and carried him off that mountain on your back. Mighty proud of you, Minnow."

"I was afraid he could stop breathing anytime. He was so weak."

"You must have found him just in time. He's a lucky boy."

"Only if they can keep him alive."

"It's hard to do sometimes. I saw a man get snakebit in 'Nam. Must have been a cobra got him. They couldn't save him."

"They've got to save this boy. He took a snakebite meant for me. It could have been on my face." She ran her index finger around the outline of the minnow tattoo, hoping it would bring the boy good luck.

"That rattlesnake was that close to your face?"

"My hand was over the edge of the rocks, and I had started to pull my head up."

"You would have been eyeball-to-eyeball with the damn thing."

"Stop, Dad. You're scaring me all over again."

"I've got to thank that boy when he wakes up."

"We both do, Dad."

"Let me take you home, Sara. Ambulance crew said your truck is sitting a few miles out of town. We can go by and get it."

"Go on home, Dad. The truck will be okay out there until I can get it."

"I'll get someone to go with me and pick it up. It'll be in the parking lot when you're ready to leave."

"Okay. Thanks, Dad. Love you."

––––––––––––

MORNING FOUND SARA IN THE medical center cafeteria pouring a cup of coffee for herself. She recognized the boy's doctor when he entered the cafeteria. She stood and went to meet him.

"How is the boy, doctor?" Sara asked, setting her coffee cup on the counter.

"We have him stable now. I had to put him on a respirator right after he came in. His breathing is stronger now, so we took him off the respirator, but his leg is in bad shape. We might not be able to save it. You know you saved his life, don't you? He's in room 202 if you want to see him."

"Yes. Thank you, Doc."

She rushed down the hallway, unsure of what she could say to a boy who might lose his leg and didn't know her. She found him with his eyes shut, and his breathing made a wheezing sound that frightened her. A transfusion bag full of blood hung just beside the bed. She settled in a chair pulled to his bed side to wait. Twice during the morning, the boy seemed to be awake, turning and twisting in the bed and staring at the ceiling. Sara stood by the bedside and wiped the boy's forehead with a cold cloth a nurse had brought. When she tried to ask the boy a question, there was no response. The burns on the back of the boy's hands reminded her of the flash burns she had seen on the wounded brought in from the battlefield in Iraq. She knew the boy had been through some kind of hell. Her hand felt for her own scar, and she fought to push against being overcome by the memory of that last day she spent in her own battle zone. She needed to get away from the bedside and the hospital smell. She left telling the nurses if the boy awoke to call her, and she would come back.

twenty-three

AFTER FINDING HER TRUCK IN the parking lot and going by Luke's to get the dog, she thanked him for taking care of the dog and headed home. The hound sat erect in the passenger seat with its head full out the window into the wind. There had always been something special for her about being alone with a dog. A simple call could bring undivided attention when she needed it most. She smiled at the flaps of skin on the dog's muzzle being pushed and buckled by the sixty mile an hour wind in his face. The slobber coming out of his mouth made a bubbling sound, and when the dog turned to look at her, drops of slime would splat on the back of the seat. It brought a much needed laugh.

Sara pulled into the driveway of the cabin, shut down the truck's engine, and opened the door. The dog sprinted across her lap and hit the grass of the yard. He was running back and forth and smelling his new hunting grounds. Sara followed, sliding off her truck seat to the driveway, and gave a wave to her dad coming out of the cabin's door. He knelt on one knee and called the dog. It looked up and then trotted to his side.

"He looks like quite a hunter. What's the boy call him?"

"He hasn't said a word, Dad. He's still pretty much out of it."

"Sorry to hear that."

"The snakebite and then the burns on his hands? The kid's been through hell."

"Is there anything I can do? Maybe go sit with him?"

"Not now, Dad. They have him on morphine to make him rest."

"Well, we can take good care of his blue tick hound for him. Let's just call him Blue. Luke told me what he knew about the boy. He said it's been a couple months since his folks were killed. How's he been livin' up there on the mountain all that time?"

The dog stood with one paw on John's knee, stretching out and trying to lick his face.

"Hard to tell. He must have trapped rabbits and caught fish on a stick rod he made before he stole my fishing rod two days ago. I'm going to take this hound for a little boat ride. I think we both need some river time."

She called the dog and headed down the steps toward the dock. "I'm gonna have to get you a collar, boy. Come on, we're going to take a boat ride!"

Her hand rubbed the top of the dog's head and scratched his ears while they walked. Halfway down the steps she stopped and sat down. Pulling the dog tight against her, she put her head against his chest, and all the good memories of her nights with her dog, Tank, came rushing back. The German Shepherd had been so loyal, unlike any relationship she'd ever had with a human friend, man or woman. Now Tank was gone. Dead because of the stupid call she'd made. The thoughts of losing her crew flooded her mind once again. She fought against them. She decided that a dose of being alone on the river with the dog would help.

"Come on, Old Hound Blue."

John stood at the top of the steps. He called out, "Going back to the hospital tonight?"

"Did they call?"

"No. I just knew you were worried about the boy and thought—"

"Tomorrow! They said the morphine will keep him asleep."

Blue jumped in the boat and went to sit straddling the Little Minnow carving in the front of the boat. He watched Sara start the engine and then turned to watch the water as the boat tapped the waves going up stream. His long blue-gray hound ears flapped back against his neck as the boat gained speed. When two ducks lifted off the water just in front of the boat, it brought Blue to his feet barking. When Sara slowed the engine, the dog settled back on the wooden seat. She slid the engine out of gear and then shut it down to let the boat drift.

"Okay, Blue. Come here."

Blue was still watching the ducks now fifty yards in front of the boat, their wings flared for landing back on the water.

"Blue!" Her call got the dog to turn his head and glance at her for a second. "Boy, we've got a long way to go with you, dog. Come here!"

Blue turned and crossed halfway to her before stopping and watching her. His mouth was open from panting, from the excitement of seeing the ducks. His pink tongue, longer than her hand, hung from the side of his mouth dripping and bouncing with each pant.

"Okay, now. Let's try sit. Blue, sit!" The dog continued to stare at her and finally dropped completely to the floor of the boat. "This is all going over your head isn't it, boy?"

She reached her hand out for the dog, and Blue raised off the boat's floor and came to her, dropping to sit by her side.

"It's all right, Blue. I just need to feel you here next to me, so I know this is all real and I'm home."

The hound looked at Sara when she spoke. She realized something was missing. The head tilt, the ears at full attention, and the stare, were all the things she missed about the companion she lost in Iraq.

"It's all right, old dog. I know you're listening. I've got to tell you about Tank, my guard dog in the war." She pulled the hound close with her arms around its shoulder. "Now look here," she commanded. Sara spent the next half-hour talking and telling how Tank would protect her when they walked guard duty or when she helped move prisoners in the compound. It didn't take long for the bluetick to drop down and rest its head on the top of its front legs. Sara was so happy to be talking to a friend. She didn't realize Blue was asleep.

The edges of the trees along the west side of the river were outlined in vivid red. The sun hung low, and only a small arch of its brilliance still remained. Sara was quiet now counting to herself the seconds left for the top of the sun to set. The swift water lapping the boat got her attention and reminded her the dock was still a few minutes away. Sara reluctantly started the boat's engine to head for the dock. She realized that again, the river had brought her back away from the precipice of her war memories.

twenty-four

AFTER SPENDING MOST OF THE night awake thinking about the boy, Sara convinced her dad to take her guide trip for the day. She wanted the time to spend at the hospital. It bothered her when she tried to imagine what he had been through—it brought back so many memories of her last day in Iraq. Wanting to help him became overpowering. She left the cabin early without breakfast and drove to the hospital. During a stop at the nurse's station she was told the boy wouldn't speak to anyone. She rushed down the hallway. Not at all sure what to say to the boy who might lose his leg. She found him with his eyes shut—his breathing still made a wheezing sound that frightened her. She pulled a chair to his side to wait.

"I heard you come in. I'm not asleep. Just don't want to look at my leg."

"Does it hurt?" She reached over to take the boy's hand. He pulled away from her touch. His eyes were open now and looking at her.

"I hoped you'd come back," he said in a weak, broken voice.

"I stayed with you for a while yesterday when you were asleep."

"I was in the creek when I heard them get blow'd up. They had sent me away 'cause—"

"Your mom and dad?"

"Them." He reached and tried to pull at the tape on the IV needle in his arm. Sara touched his hand, and he moved it away again.

"I'm so sorry."

"He come out of the house all his clothes and skin was burnin'."

Her memories came quickly, but she wanted to stay strong for the boy.

She knew that the doctors had trained her to shift her focus when the war memories came. Right now, she had to help the boy face his own memories and focus on him.

"I heard my mom screamin'."

She hadn't heard any screams. They were just blown to bits. She stopped the trembling of her left hand fingers as she tightened them on her minnow tattoo until it hurt. She would win this—it had to be about the boy.

"She told him his cookin' gonna get us all killed."

"The burns on your hands, you must have tried to help them."

"It was too late. He had stopped screaming when I got to him."

"Oh! That's—"

"I couldn't get through the burnin' to my mom."

"You were so brave to try and save your mother." She relaxed her grip on the tattoo, the trembling had stopped.

"I saw her standing inside waving her arms and yelling for me to stop and get away. She had fire all over her."

"Look at me. There wasn't anything you could have done to save her." It came out of her mouth before she realized what she was going to say. Then quickly she realized it wasn't true for her. She could have saved her crew, but she didn't. She changed her focus.

"Why don't you tell me your name?" She took a deep breath and realized what had just happened. The skills she had learned at the V.A. to handle her PTSD flashbacks had helped her. She had embraced the present, and her present situation dominated.

"My name is Jimmy, Miss Sara. I heard them talkin' about you bringing me down the mountain."

"Well, Jimmy, it's nice to meet you."

"Did somebody let my grandma know you found me?"

"I don't think anyone knew who you were or where you came from."

"I came a long way in an old boat. It sank when it hit a tree."

"What's your grandmother's name, Jimmy? We have to let her know you're all right."

"My mother called her Sally." He had covered his eyes with his arm.

Sara leaned over the boy and touched his shoulder and said softly, "Don't cry, Jimmy. We'll get word to her you're here and safe."

"Don't let them cut my leg off, Miss Sara."

"I'm sure the doctor is doing all he can to save your leg, Jimmy. I'll talk to him for you. Can you tell me your grandmother's last name?"

"Wilmore. She's being taken care of after she fell."

"Do you know where?"

"It was a place not far from where she lived."

"Let me go send word to her. I'll come right back."

"I gotta' go back up on that mountain."

"I'll be right back, Jimmy, and you can tell me why." She rushed to the hospital office and gave them the news about Jimmy's grandmother and then called Luke.

"Luke, Jimmy just told me the name of his grandmother and that she's probably in a nursing home near where she lived."

"Is her name Wilmore?"

"Yes."

"Word just came the sheriff over at Ponca had tracked her down. They let her know he's here. She's his legal guardian and told them to take care of him for now because she's unable."

"Good. I feel better now. Thanks for finding that out. Call me later, okay, good looking?"

She went quickly back to Jimmy's room and to the boy's side.

"They got word to you grandmother. She knows you're safe."

"Can you help me get back up the mountain?

"Why, Jimmy?"

"I have to find my dog. I love him. He stayed with me from home."

"He's safe, Jimmy. We have him. I know about loving dogs. I'll take good care of him for you." She leaned back in her chair and smiled.

"I still got to go back up where you found me?"

"Why?"

"I dropped my knife trying to build a fire."

"Was it a special knife? I think I saw it by a wood pile."

"'Bout the only thing I had when I left home, except my dog. My dad made it special for me. He scratched my name right on it."

"You keep getting well, Jimmy. Follow the doctor's orders. I'll be sure you get that knife back, even if I have to go back up there and get it for you."

After a promise to Jimmy she would check on him tomorrow and with the doctor's assurance they were doing all that could be done to save the boy and his leg, Sara left the hospital and headed for the mountain.

SHE PARKED HER TRUCK, GRABBED a couple water bottles, and strapped on her 9mm. She didn't relish going back up the snake-infested mountain, but she knew finding the knife and having it for the boy when he got better would be important to him. The sun had peaked overhead when she reached the site of the would-be campfire. The brush and rotten logs the boy had stacked together were still there. Leaves covered the ground around the stack, and Sara didn't intend sticking her hands in them to search for the boy's knife. One of the boy's fishing poles lay just off to the side of the path. Her first sweep of the leaves alongside the stack with the pole brought a hair-raising rattle from underneath. Sara slowly backed away from the firewood stack. Killing the snake was her first thought, then the thought of Luke and his efforts to protect wildlife took ahold of her.

The six-foot limb she found was just the thing. Reaching out she upset the whole pile of logs on the snake. The snake's head came out from under the pile, smelling the air with its pulsating tongue and then headed right for her. Shocked at the aggressive snake, she backed up, tripped, and fell backward.

"To hell with conservation." She pulled her pistol and emptied it into the oncoming snake. Damn. That thing had been *pissed*.

She took a couple minutes to brush the leaves and dirt off her rear, then dragged the dead rattlesnake off to the side and started her search for the boy's knife. Her second pass with the pole through the leaves struck pay dirt. She pushed it away from the pile of logs and picked it up to wipe it clean on her pants. She found the boy's name etched on the steel blade. "Jim." She knew how much it would mean to the boy. Giving it to him would have to wait until he got out of the hospital. With one last thing she wanted to do, she pushed the snake again to be sure it was dead, then used the boy's knife to cut off the snake's rattle.

Oh, yes, her dad would have this thing tied on the front of his hat.

twenty-five

A CANCELED GUIDE TRIP A week later gave Sara a morning to spend at the hospital for a visit with Jimmy. The talks she had been having with Jimmy were starting to raise questions in her mind if she could really help him get better. Jimmy would tell her stories about the outdoor things he did. Like the one where he had set on the edge of a wooden bridge with a pole and a long line dangling a red cloth and hook in front of a huge bull frog. The frog grabbed the cloth and hook. Jimmy got excited telling her the frog jumped way out into the creek, then hung there caught, fighting to get away. When he finally got the frog pulled up on the bridge, he took the hook out and got a firm grip on it to carry it home to show his mother. When he got to the door of the trailer, the frog got away and jumped right into the open door at his mother's feet.

The break in his story-telling came quickly with a scream and then crying. Sara felt certain the memory of his mother there in the door of the trailer had triggered the boy's PTSD and the day he saw her standing in the burning trailer. For a moment she thought of trying some of the types of therapy the psychologists had used to help her. She had stopped, knowing Jimmy would need the help of an expert.

Since Jimmy had been transferred to the Physical Therapy ward of the hospital, she had gotten permission to take him for short outings. The nurses had told her Jimmy was excited and couldn't wait for her visits—he loved the time out of the hospital.

Getting Jimmy to walk on his sore leg was easy. After she signed him out at the desk, she pointed out her truck and watched him hobble to get to the truck before her. He had mentioned wanting to see where the river went through town, so their first outing was to the town's city park and riverfront. More than two dozen kids were swimming and rope swinging into the natural spring pool in the park. Sara parked just across from the pool.

"Looks like half the town kids are swimming in the spring, Jimmy." She got out and went to open the door for the boy. He didn't get out right away.

"Is it free to swim in the spring?"

"Yeah, it's free, but it's also cold as heck. They say the water comes up from way underground."

"We had a spring-fed crick down the hill from our house."

"Did you get to play in it?"

"I was too little, but the water was great to drink. I could take you there sometime if you want."

"I'd like that, Jimmy. Come on, let's walk down to the river." She turned away from the truck trying to encourage Jimmy to follow.

He pointed at the kids playing and said, "Will them kids laugh at me when I walk?"

"Come on. They're too busy playing to even notice. Let me help you down." Her offer to help him out of the truck seat was enough. Jimmy quickly slid down the edge of the seat and stood at the edge of the truck's running board. He took a step down and turned and shut the door. They both started across the parking lot to the river.

"I'm going to walk good, Miss Sara. You just watch me." His first steps showed no sign of his trauma to his leg. Sara could tell from the grimace on his face his effort to not show his limp was going to be too much. Jimmy's sore leg gave out, and he went down to his knees. He pushed away her hand when she tried to take his arm, and then he struggled to his feet by himself.

"We got to go back now." Jimmy limped back to the truck and reached for the door latch.

Sara gave in to the boy's embarrassment from the fall. "Go ahead and get in, Jimmy. We can drive around town for a while before I take you back." Sara got in the truck, and with both seat belts in place, she left the park. She wanted to cheer the boy up, so her next stop would be the drug store with the old-fashion soda fountain and hand dipped ice cream. Going hungry on the mountain had taken a toll on the boy—he was tan but still sickly looking. She didn't say anything when she pulled up in front of the drug store, just got out and went to open the passenger door.

"Come on, Peg-Leg. We're getting ice cream." She was sorry that name slipped out of her mouth.

Jimmy laughed. "I like that name. It's funny." He slid out of the truck seat to join Sara on the sidewalk.

"But don't let nobody hear you call me that name. I'll never get rid of it if you do."

Sara chuckled and promised.

"How come it's a drugstore if we're going to get ice cream in there?" Jimmy asked, limping ahead of her.

"It's called a drugstore because people get their prescriptions and other medical stuff here. Like band aids and aspirins."

"My mother bought a lot of cold medicine in drugstores I guess."

Sara didn't answer. She knew where those kind of drugs would have gone. Jimmy opened the store's door for her.

"Well thank you, sir. You are quite a gentleman."

"That's something else I don't want to be called."

"Okay, I've got it now."

Sara felt certain the boy had never seen a soda fountain. They both were seated on the tall wire back chairs that were along the fountain's counter. Jimmy leaned forward starting to reach for one of the black handles on the fountain's spritzer taps. The young woman behind the counter had her hand on the black handle before Jimmy reached it.

In a rather stern voice she said, "May I help you, sir?"

"Huh."

Sara saw the blush on Jimmy's cheek. He pulled back quickly and got his hand away from the counter. He sat staring at the chalk board on the wall with a hand-written list of flavors.

"Can we get chocolate?"

"Of course. We'll have two chocolate shakes please, Miss."

The girl turned and reached for two stainless containers, then flopped open one of the black covers and started to fill the containers with vanilla ice cream. Jimmy sat forward in his chair while leaning over the counter to watch the ice cream drop into the container.

"Do you want to help?" the girl asked. Jimmy quickly sat back. She finished with the ice cream and held the containers under a nozzle while pushing the handle for four long pumps of dark chocolate in each one. She finished the loading with a shot of white milk, then turned and put both containers on an electric mixer. Jimmy leaned to the right to try and watch the mixer and the girl in action.

He whispered to Sara, "What is she doing twisting them around?"

"The ice cream is heavy, and it won't mix up if she doesn't help it."

"I wish she would hurry with them shakes."

The girl turned around with the two stainless containers in her hand and set them in front of Sara and the boy. Both steel containers were already covered with condensation, and Jimmy was writing letters in the liquid. The girl quickly set two glasses and straws on the counter and poured both shakes in the glasses.

Sara knew all of this was brand new to the boy. She felt glad that she had found something that excited him. She was halfway through her own milkshake when Jimmy began making loud sucking noises trying to clean up the bottom of his glass.

"Boy, that was good."

"Glad you liked it. We have to do this again."

"Yep." He was grinning from ear to ear.

She handed Jimmy a ten-dollar bill, "Pay her please. I want to look for something." Jimmy took the ten and slipped off his stool and paused. Sara knew he must be feeling embarrassed about talking to the girl. He limped down the counter to where she was standing and handed her the ten without saying anything.

"I'll get your change," she said, turning toward the cash register.

Jimmy stood waiting and took the four one-dollar bills from the girl. He went quickly to Sara and handed her the change.

Sara handed all four of the bills back to the boy. "Jimmy, please give the lady two of these dollars for a tip. The other two are for you to keep."

"But, Miss Sara, any money I ever got was working for my dad."

"It's all right, Jimmy. You might need a dollar now and then when you get out of the hospital ward."

Jimmy walked back across the room, and while looking at the floor, he handed the two dollars to the girl.

"Here."

"Thank you," the girl said. "Be sure and come back some time."

Her remark must have surprised Jimmy. He turned and quickly went to stand looking at the drug store shelves.

Sara finished shopping and bought some skin cream and thanked the pharmacist for helping her find it.

"Ready, Jimmy? Jimmy!" When she turned to look, the boy was staring at a display of pseudoephedrine cartons on the pharmacy shelf.

"Did you need something, Jimmy?" A minute later she realized what the boy had been staring at, certain the boy knew his father had used the chemical when he cooked meth. She went to his side.

"It's all right. I know what you are thinking."

"My dad made us go buy it for him. Can we go now? I want to get out of here."

Jimmy followed her silently out the door and got in the truck. He didn't speak until they got back to the driveway at the physical therapy ward.

"I want to leave here."

"I think that will happen soon."

"Who's gonna take me?"

Sara didn't know how to answer his question. He leaned toward her as if he wanted a hug, then turned toward the truck door, opened it, and slid out. Sara followed him, and they walked in the ward together. When they passed the nurses station, one of the nurses called to Jimmy.

"Jim, you have a letter." Jimmy looked at Sara in surprise and then went to take the letter from the nurse.

"I've never had no letter."

"Well you have one now."

He looked at the letter without opening it and then stuck it in his back pocket. Sara didn't ask who it was from.

She took his hand. "Thanks for going with me today." He dropped her hand and swung his arms around her to give her a big hug. As if embarrassed, he quickly moved two steps away.

"Miss Sara, when can I get out of here for good?"

"I promise I'll talk to the doctor and find out about when, and then we can think about where you are going to be staying."

"Promise?"

"I promise. See you day after tomorrow." She quietly added, "Follow the doctor's orders, Peg-Leg."

She turned and left. The boy was heading down the hall with a nurse, and he had a huge grin on his face.

twenty-six

SPENDING TIME WITH JIMMY HAD taken her attention away from her river guiding. When she checked with the dock office, her next days were full. She was surprised that a lot of the new customers on her booking were customers that had been coming to the dock a long time and had been using other guides.

This might explain why she'd found her lines cut every so often, and her boat untied from its mooring. Some of the guides that used to call her "Heat" were going out of their way to avoid her, too. Except for one friendly young man, Milton, who was a cousin to Red. He had stopped to talk to her a couple times. He wanted to ask what she thought about a girl he wanted to ask to marry him. Sara liked Milton and was glad she had at least one friend out at the dock. She was surprised to see him running to head her off before she got to the dock office.

"Morning, Miss Randolph. I'm glad we had the talk about me wanting to get married. I asked her last night." Milton kept looking at the ground and refused to make eye contact.

"Congratulations, Milton. She's a lucky gal to be getting you."

"Thanks, Heat. There's something I should tell you. Red, well—he ain't my cousin. He's really my pop. He run me off."

"Ran you off? Why in the world would he do that?"

"He was beatin' on mama. I tried to stop him. He took to beatin' on me after that."

"That's horrible. Can I help with anything? Do you still see your mother?"

"I try to see her when he's not around home."

"Good. Don't forget to do that when you can."

"I won't. But there's somethin' else. I'm hearing things. The guides are talkin' about you stealin' their customers away."

"Oh, I've been feeling some of them were upset with me."

"You might want to watch out."

"I'm sure a lot of the customers just want to see if a woman guide can hack it out there on the river."

"I'm hearin' you hack it pretty well, Miss Randolph."

"Thanks, Milton. I'll be careful. If you need anything, you let me know. I've got to get up to the office now."

Sara had been surprised when the dock owner called and said she should come in this morning. She was greeted on the parking lot by the dock owner and a lady carrying a note pad and a camera around her neck.

"Good morning, Sara. I want you to meet Betsy Thompson. She writes for *Fly-Fishing Magazine.*" George Hines, the dock owner, introduced them. "She wanted to meet you, and oh, before I forget, how's the boy you saved from the mountain?"

"He's doing fine, George. I'll tell him you asked about him. Dad's going to take him fishing before too long."

"Bring him by, Sara."

"I will."

"Sara's our hero around here," George said to Betsy Thompson and then added, turning to Sara. "Ralph is taking your morning guide trip so you can meet with this lady."

He turned and walked away.

Sara sighed and gave her attention to the lady with the camera. "Hello, Betsy. Sorry for all the hoopla hero stuff. If you're here to fish for some big trout, I'm your guide."

"I was wondering if maybe you would be available for some pictures and an interview, Sara."

"Why me, ma'am?"

"I learned just yesterday there was a woman guide on the White River that's teaching a lot of folks how to fly fish," Betsy reached for her camera. "And there's a story about a boy, too?"

"Hold on a minute. I'm not sure why you want to write about me." Sara shied away from the intrusion of the camera. "You aren't here to fish?"

"Would you mind guiding me, and I'll just take some notes and snap a few pictures as we go?"

"Well, since they had another guide take my scheduled trip, so well, okay. I'll take you upriver to the headwaters, and we'll cast a few flies."

With the writer seated in the front of the boat, Sara left the dock and steered into the fast current of the river. She opened the throttle of the outboard and hoped the noise would give her time to think about the answers to questions she knew would be coming.

The noise didn't stop the reporter.

Betsy shouted over the engine. "I write for several of the fishing magazines, and I think they are all going to want the story of a woman guiding here on the White River."

Sara nodded and thought, *Oh, hell no to* this *bullshit.*

Betsy took her camera and took a few shots of the fishing boats they were passing before turning and quickly snapping a picture of Sara and the wake behind the boat. Sara realized the picture of her would be plastered all over Betsy's magazines. She shut the outboard down to drift and tried to hand the writer a fishing rod.

"If it's okay, I'll stick with the camera and this note pad."

Shit, she had enough trouble with the other guides without this.

"Sara, you're working in what's always been a man's enterprise. How does that work for you?"

"Most of the men guides are respectful. I'm sure they would help me if I had a boat problem out here." She knew a couple of them would let her fucking drown.

"The dock owner said you're getting as many or more bookings than some of the other guides. Aren't the men upset about that?"

"You can stop there with this subject. Can we be off the record?"

"Of course."

"Yes, they get pissed about it. I don't want to create more problems, so can you move on?"

"I hadn't thought about it like that."

Sara stood with her fly rod and expertly cast a sump bug out into the current.

Betsy snapped the picture. "Great picture. Thanks, Sara. Tell me about what got you started fly fishing."

Sara liked this subject a lot better. She let the boat drift and asked Betsy to sit near her in the boat. She told the writer about her mother's love of tying flies and showed Betsy the small box of her mother's flies she still carried in her creel. She told of the several novice clients that she had begun teaching both fly fishing and fly tying. She could tell Betsy wanted to move on when the questions about fly fishing stopped.

"You're ex-military aren't you? Iraq, right?"

Sara wasn't sure where that came from. "You saw the scar on my face?"

"No. Hell, no. Not that. You called me ma'am when we met. Several of the veterans I've interviewed never got used to calling me by my name."

"I served in Iraq. Two tours there in a Military Police unit."

"Tell me about that. What did your unit do there?"

"We had prison guard duty. But I thought you wanted to write about fly fishing, not just about me."

"I have to say, I think you're the real story out here on the White River."

Their drifting had passed the dock, and now they were near the point where Crooked Creek came into the White River. A strange, flat boat covered from front to back with a tarp came out of the creek. Only the engine and a man with a black hood over his head were visible. The boat came into the middle of the river and then turned directly toward Sara's boat. The guides had had enough. They were out to scare her for taking their bookings.

"Get on the floor back here by me and hold on. This is all about me."

Betsy was on her knees taking pictures of the approaching boat. "Damn. This is crazy!"

"He's picked the wrong person to play chicken with." Sara opened the engine full throttle. With all the weight in the back of the boat, the front of the boat rose more than three feet into the air. "Boy, I'd like to have a hundred extra horsepower on her right now."

The tarp-covered boat came straight on at them. Her motoring downstream with the current gave her a speed advantage over the boat coming up-stream.

Betsy screamed, "He's going to hit us head-on!"

"No, he'll turnoff before that." Sara twisted the throttle harder. "If he doesn't, I'm going to run over the son-of-a-bitch."

With less than fifty feet to go, the man stood. She saw his mouth flapping but didn't hear the cussing he gave her because of the roar of her outboard. The tarp-covered boat turned away hard, giving her a broadside target. With the front of her boat riding high out of the water, she went straight at it. Sara's boat ricocheted over the top of the attacking boat's mid-ship. Safely across the boat and underway, she turned and headed back for the listing boat.

Betsy laughed hysterically. "And I didn't have a GoPro to record that! I don't even know where in the hell to start with this story."

"Looks like he fell out of the boat, and he's having trouble keeping his head out of the water. Maybe we should just go on about our business."

"I can only guess, but I'm really damn sure you're going to pick your son-of-a-bitch up. Aren't you?"

"Pick him up? Hell, I think I'll run over him again." The man had his hood off. "Well, hey, there, Bill. Looks like you're up the river without a boat. Betsy, this guy is one of the guides that's been talking crap about me for weeks." She stopped alongside the floundering man, grabbed him by the collar and pulled him out of the water. "Your boat's over there, headed into the bank. Don't think those rocks are going to do the prop any good, are they?"

"Just get me over there, and I won't tell anybody what happened."

"That's fine. I won't say a word, either. By the way, have you met Betsy? She's writing an article for three national fishing magazines about fishing with me on the White River. I'm not sure I can spell your last name. It's *JONES,* correct? And hold still while she gets another picture or two of you for the magazine."

Bill was no longer in Sara's boat, he had jumped overboard.

Sara pulled alongside the grounded boat and jumped in. After she killed the surging engine, she took out her sheath knife and cut the rubber fuel line running to the engine. "There, that should keep him out of trouble for a while."

BACK AT THE TROUT DOCK, Sara and Betsy sat behind the building. Sara had come up with two beers.

Betsy chuckled. "You know, I'm going to have something a little stronger when I get to my motel. I need it after the action earlier."

"I'm heading for a bottle hid behind the breadbox when I get home."

"I have only a few more questions for you. No more boat rides, please."

"My last for the day. Trust me."

"Sara, you know fly fishing is a whole different ballgame from the trout bait fishing you've been guiding for."

"I know. Fly fishing is an obsession to some men and women that love it. It's not about filling a cooler with fish."

"There are a whole bunch of real serious folks whipping fly rods around. I think you would like the way they study the art of fly tying and fishing," Betsy said. "The men and women that like to fly fish are always looking for guides that specialize in their type of fishing. I'd like to write about you as a specialist in fly fishing guiding."

"I promise to look at the other side of the fishing scene. I'm not sure it would pay all the bills right now."

"I think you would be surprised. Thanks, Sara. I think I have way more than enough for several stories."

"You aren't going to print the story about the other guides, are you?"

"You know I was laughing about it at the time, but it scared the piss out of me."

"Me, too. I think Bill is going to be out of a job when word gets around."

"Wouldn't be surprised. Think we're finished. Let me run out to the car,

I have some back issues of *Fly Fishing Magazine* I want to leave with you."

"Thanks. Glad I got you back here safely."

"Me, too, honey. Me, too. Watch for your story. I'll send you extra copies and the pictures of Bill. You can use the pictures to blackmail him into being nice to you."

"That'll work."

"Can you take a little more time and tell me about the boy you saved from the mountain?"

"Let's sit on the dock porch. That story will take more than a little time."

twenty-seven

FINALLY, WITH A CHANCE TO get back to the cabin at Calico Rock, Sara and Luke walked arm in arm past the tall pine tree. They paused when they heard the whisper of an owl's wings, the bird taking flight from the pine tree. The predator's flight path glided just above the scrub brush along the edges of the rocky cliffs and then with what looked like no effort, the owl rose more than fifty feet to reach a nest high in an oak tree.

She pointed. "Look at all the dark brown patterns on top of its body and wings. What a beauty."

"All the beauty of a great horned owl. It's strange we get to see a great, but I think it likes to have company up here on the bluff. I've watched it drop and glide over the bluff's edge and down into the wheat fields in the bottoms at dusk to hunt mice and snakes. I've been watching her for quite a few years. She's raised several broods up in that old oak tree."

"So much of your work is learning and teaching about wildlife, no wonder you love it so much."

"Oh, trust me. There are some bad parts to my job, but you're right. Being out here makes it all worthwhile to me." Sara pulled his arm tight to her side in a hug.

"Are we near a place where we can get down the bluff to the bottoms?"

"There's a trail about a hundred yards to the east. It's steep, but we can climb down."

Sara liked the challenge of climbing down the bluff. Luke had told her of the caves hidden in the Calico Rock bluffs they could explore. Luke led the way along the bluffs to a break in the edge that opened to a narrow crevice large enough to slide down and through.

"Let me slip through there first," Luke slid into the rock slit and offered his hand to Sara. Halfway down the rock crevice, Luke paused for Sara to wedge in beside him. Together they hung pressed against each other, filling the rock opening. Hidden from all the world. She liked the feel of the tight squeeze of Luke's body pressed against hers and locked her hands behind his neck. The tip of one his fingers caressed her mouth, and she gently nipped it. Luke moved his hand to the side of her face, and their mouths met. Open, inviting, she bit his lip and then slid along its edges with her lips, pressing them with her tongue and probing for the response she sought. Luke slid out of her arms and dropped to her waist, lifting her blouse to kiss her on both sides of her hips before opening her belt and buttons. He slid her pants past her knees and pulled her black thong to the side. She pressed both her hands hard against the wall. Her head tilted up, staring at the narrow slit they had come through but not seeing anything but the pleasure he gave her. She pounded the rock crevice wall with her open hand. The sound of her gasping and pleading for more echoed in the narrow passage until the short breaths slowly trailed off into a gentle whisper. Luke pressed the side of his head against her bare belly, his hands gripping her buttocks in a gentle squeeze. They remained silent for a few minutes.

"Luke, I'm stuck here."

"Really?" Luke pulled up her pants and fastened her belt. He kissed her again in the middle of her belly.

"Too weak to move."

They both slid down the remaining fifteen feet of the crevice and paused at the bottom, wrapped in a tight hug and then a kiss.

"You know we are going back that way, right?" Sara said.

"You think so?"

They leaned against each other for support and walked slowly along the wide passage at the bottom of the bluff. When the trail narrowed, Luke had to lead the way through places where rock falls had blocked all but a few inches to squeeze through. He climbed over the rocks first and then gave a hand to Sara while she climbed over. Just past the rock fall, Luke moved a fallen tree limb to expose the entrance to a small cave. It was tall enough for them to stand and enter the cave.

"Break up some of those limbs, and let's start a small fire," Sara said as she kicked around some old ashes in a rock circle.

Sara gathered small branches and leaves to sustain the fire until the larger limbs would start burning. As the small branches began burning, Luke added the larger pieces. The brightness of the dancing flames lit the ceiling in a mosaic of orange and scarlet flashes reflecting off the walls and onto the couple resting tight in each other's arms on the cave's floor.

"I love this place to escape to, Luke." She pressed against his side and pulled his arms even tighter around her. "Would it be all right if we talk about Jimmy? I'm worried."

"You hadn't mentioned him, Sara. I wondered what's going to happen when he gets out of the hospital."

"I don't know. If his grandmother isn't going to take him, I wish I could just grab him up and take him home for Dad and I to raise."

"You would really consider doing that?"

"Only if my dad was on board. It would make a family for Jimmy. His grandmother isn't going to be able to take care of him."

"But she might be able to help if you really want to be a foster home for him."

"Maybe more than a foster home."

"I wish we would have come prepared to stay here all night. I love the quiet of the cliffs and this cave."

It surprised her he changed the subject so quickly. It stung. Maybe she felt more comfortable with him than she should.

"You know, there's a legend about bootleggers having covered the mouth of the cave with all those rocks we crossed. The bounty hunters came over the edge of the cliff with rope ladders and climbed down right into the line of fire from inside the cave. It was a slaughter. The bootleggers shot four of the 'em dead, and the fifth was wounded and fled down the bluff to the town."

"Okay, this is getting spooky."

"They say if you go far enough back in the cave, you can still see the skulls and bones of the men the bootleggers hid and never buried."

"Darn you, Luke. Now I can never believe a word you tell me."

"I'll tell you something you can believe. Your caring so much for a boy that was lost tells me so much about you. I want to make our relationship something more," Luke said, taking her hand.

She reached and pulled him around to face her. "That's about the sweetest thing anyone has ever said to me, Luke. You've played a large part in my keeping my sanity these last months. I really love being with you, but I want to make sure you really know me better before we make this something more. I'm still working on myself. You know I lost my crew. More than that, I've done things in war that I'm ashamed of. It's all always there, in the center of my mind." Sara offered him a weak smile. "It's hard to open up, but it's also hard to commit to someone without taking that step. I'll get there. Just give me time."

She was afraid to tell him or anyone how the CIA had used her as a weapon to torture other humans. Her talk with him had brought on a familiar sadness she often had and never had been able to overcome. She hated the inhuman ways the CIA had force her to act. It made her so ashamed to think about it. She had to be sure Luke understood the way she thought now.

twenty-eight

AFTER SEVERAL MORE SUCCESSFUL GUIDING trips, Sara was looking foward to a break. When a client canceled a guide trip, Sara called the hospital and asked for them to get Jimmy ready for her to take him for a morning outing. She drove to the ward and went in to sign the boy out. The nurse greeted her and asked her to step into a side office. Sara followed not sure of what was coming.

The nurse spoke first, "I thought you should know. We are going to have to discharge the boy pretty soon."

"Where are they taking him?" Sara asked, putting her hand to her lips when she realized the time had come for some action. Action she had been slow to take in the last couple weeks.

"He's going to be a ward of the court. Anyway, that's what we heard. I don't know any more about it. We have kept him here way longer than our board wanted."

"Thank you for telling me. I'll have to do some checking on what might happen to him."

Jimmy was waiting when she came out of the office.

"Ready for a trip on the river?" Sara asked, motioning him to follow. He was close behind walking with very little limp. Loaded in the truck, she drove through town and down the hill to the trout dock to where she had left her boat. At the dock she led the way to her boat and pointed out the middle seat for him to take.

"Can I help you get in?" she asked, reaching to take his arm.

The boy was way ahead of her. He stepped off the dock into the middle of the boat and settled into the seat. She had made a bet with herself that Jimmy would be a rock skipper. "Where are we going?"

"We're going rock skipping. I think you'll like the spot I've found."

About two miles from the dock she steered the boat into the mouth of a small creek. After a hundred yards she beached the boat on a sandy spot and had Jimmy get out and follow her. Just ahead was an all rock and gravel bank. Jimmy ran ahead to the rock bank and started picking up flat stones. He tossed back a lot more of the stones than he kept. When he had a dozen chosen, he carried them to Sara and gave her half of them.

"Them ones are for you to throw."

"Thanks, Jimmy. Now let's see if I remember how."

She sailed a stone out flat side down and watched as it bounced once, twice, and on the third hit sunk into the water. The glass-like surface of the water let them watch the stone settle a few inches then drop into the darkness. Then after one throw she thought was her best, she said, "I bet you can't beat that throw, Jimmy."

"Better not bet me, Miss Sara."

Jimmy studied several of the flat stones he had lying in front of him before he settled on his choice. He tested the stone in his hand turning it with each edge in front before spreading his feet for balance and hauling back his arm to skillfully send the stone on its path to glory. His throw landed more than halfway across the stream and then ricocheted like it had been shot into a world without gravity—the flat rock came alive and danced a dozen ballet steps. Each tap on the water carried the dance further away—each tap touching softer than the one before—then the last tap carried the dance to its finale. The stone seemed to pause, and then it dropped to the bottom without an encore.

"That was beautiful, Jimmy. Man, I really lost that bet."

He turned to her and smiled. "You just need some practice, Miss Sara."

"Come on, give me another chance."

They continued challenging each other skipping rocks, and then some mussel shells Jimmy found, until she felt the time was right.

"Jimmy, after that first day we talked at the hospital, I went back to the mountaintop where you were trying to build a signal fire."

Jimmy looked puzzled. "Did you find the knife my dad made?"

"Yes, Jimmy, I did."

She handed Jimmy the surprise she had been keeping for him. The knife sat safely encased in a new tooled leather sheath.

"My dad made the leather sheath for you, Jimmy."

The boy sat quietly, taking the knife out of the sheath and testing the blade's sharpness against the edge of his thumb and then sliding it back and forth into the new sheath. She watched the boy's tears drop and darken the leather. He quickly wiped them off and turned with his arms outstretched to hug Sara.

"I don't have nothin' else to my name, Miss Sara. Thank you."

"I've had it a while for you. Just wanted you to get better and to let my dad make the sheath before I gave it to you."

"Will you thank him for me? It sure means a lot to me."

"Would you like to thank him yourself? He's aching to take you fishin'."

"Fishin'! When can he take me?" He did a little turn around and almost fell on his weak leg.

"Soon."

"He's gotta come get me."

"He will. Jimmy, let's talk some serious stuff for a couple of minutes." Sara led the way to a long dead tree trunk for them to sit on.

"Is it okay if I wear my knife for a while?" Reaching for his belt buckle.

"Sure, till we get back." Jimmy unbuckled his belt and ran it through the sheath's loop. He pulled his belt tight and looked up and smiled at her.

"I know the sheriff has talked to you. Has he said where you might go?"

"He said to be with my grandma, but she might be too sick to keep me." He kicked away a big rock lying near his feet.

"Maybe I can talk to her and see what she thinks."

She picked up a rock lying nearby and put her thumb into a polished crevice just the shape of her thumb. She rubbed the crevice and remembered her mom telling her about finding worry stones in the creeks along the river.

"She never came around much, before I went to live with her all the time. She could really cook, and she hummed all the time. It was okay living with her—she made me take baths and stay clean."

"But you were at your mom and dad's place?"

"I got to go there on weekends."

"Do you want to talk about your mom and dad?"

"It scares me when I think how I last seen 'um. I hear him scream sometimes when I'm asleep." He wrapped his arms around his middle. She could tell by his hand how tight he was squeezing. She tightened up the grip of her thumb on the worry stone.

Knowing she needed to get the boy into a different mindset she said, "Tell me about other times. Some good days, Jimmy."

"I try to remember some. Then all of it gets dark like a storm, and I see him burnin' again."

"Jimmy, here's something I found for you. Just take this rock and press your thumb in the groove."

"Like this?" he asked, pushing his thumb back and forth on the slick spot.

"Yes, like that. Just think about how good that feels to rub the rock when you feel bad."

"Can I keep it?"

"It's yours."

"I may need it a lot sometimes."

"So, Jimmy, what did your dad do when you were younger?"

"He had a log truck. I seen him haul loads ten feet high, all cut down pine trees."

"Did he let you ride with him in the truck?"

"When it was empty, he would. He even let me steer it a couple times." Jimmy sat up and turned the imaginary steering wheel in his hands.

"Wow! Was he teaching you to drive it?" She offered him a high five, and their hands met in a loud clap. "Way to go!"

"He was. Then one day he was hauling, and a wreck happened."

"Was he hurt?"

"He couldn't work anymore cause his back was bad."

"Did your mother work?"

"She did until my dad started getting into shit." She could tell his thumb was buried hard in the worry stone.

"What do you mean, Jimmy?"

"Some fellows would come over, and I heard them talking about how he could make money."

"Did your mother know?"

"He didn't tell her. Just one day he told her to get out of the kitchen he had to work."

"You didn't know what he was doing?"

"I found out from kids at school. They said my dad was a fucking meth cooker, and they didn't want nothin' to do with me." Jimmy's thumb was again pressing into the grove of his worry stone.

"That must have been hard for you."

"No. I hit the big pisshead in the mouth. He went crying to the teacher. That got me in trouble." Sara started to chuckle but held back. What he said was so much like what she would have done.

"I'd say he deserved that but—"

"I know, Miss Sara. I was wrong hitting him."

"Do you remember how you got to the mountain, where I found you?"

He stepped away from her a few steps. "Can we go back now?"

"We can. I didn't mean to pry."

"No. That's okay. I've been wanting to tell you, but I'm tired now."

Sara walked by the boy's side back along the creekbank to the place where she had beached her boat. His limp was nearly gone. He would be leaving the physical therapy ward soon.

"The sheriff's deputy came to see me. He said I had to go stay in the court."

"He did?"

"I don't know. Are they going to put me in the court jail?"

"No, Jimmy, that's not what they meant. They just have to make sure you have a safe place to live."

"I don't know, I kind of liked my cave. Don't you feel bad if I run away, Miss Sara."

"I would feel really bad, Jimmy. You would miss the fishing trip with Dad, and what would I do without you?" She hugged him hoping that something she had said would keep him from running away.

"I'll try and stay, but I ain't going to let them put me somewhere I don't wanna be."

"Look, I promise I'll talk to the sheriff tomorrow and see if you can stay with your grandma or if there is a nice place here in our town you can stay."

"Okay, but don't forget you promised me. Here, keep this for me." He handed her the worry stone he had been carrying. "This is the best rock we found. Would you keep it for me?"

"Okay. I'll keep it for next time." With a sigh of relief, she put it deep into her jean pocket.

Back at the boat, she had Jimmy sit at the back by the motor with her. When she turned out of the creek into the main channel of the river, she had him take the motor handle and steer. She loved seeing the big grin on his face when he turned in circles several times before heading back toward the dock. She took the controls before they got to the dock and steered into her slip. With the boat tied up, she promised an ice cream if he would hurry with her to the truck. Their last stop for the day was at the drug store where they both got chocolate cones. When they finished, Sara drove back to the clinic.

"Remember, Miss Sara, I ain't going to no court jail."

"You won't, Jimmy." She smiled but also bit her lip really thinking what would become of Jimmy.

Jimmy hugged her and left her at the desk watching him walk down the hallway. She had forgotten to ask Jimmy about the letter he had received after their last trip. She headed outside, and before she got in the truck, she called Luke.

"Luke, can you get away for a day trip?"

"I'll ask. Where're we going?"

"Over to see Jimmy's grandmother and maybe the place where he lived."

"That's near Ponca, I think. I'll check with the sheriff to be sure."

"Tomorrow, Luke. We need to go tomorrow."

"That urgent?"

"Yes."

"Dinner tonight, then? You can explain what's going on. Okay?"

"See you at seven. Love you." She hung up quickly, the words had just slipped out. For all her insistence that they take things slow, apparently her heart knew what it wanted, even if she wasn't quite ready yet.

twenty-nine

THEY DROVE INTO THE BOXLEY Valley in Sara's truck before midday. The blacktop roadway wound through the green pastures of the valley. It was scarred with long dirt lanes that paused at branches to cross narrow wooden bridges before leading again to faded red barns and hundred-year-old, two-story houses. The lush pastures ended sharply behind the houses at the tree line's solid wall that signaled *no further, because the mountain starts here.* Only the grazing cattle provided proof that anyone still lived in the houses.

"It's beautiful, Luke. It must be peaceful to live here."

"It was a lot more peaceful before the Commission introduced elk back into the area."

"Really?"

"Traffic picks up along this road come late afternoon. It all starts when the bull elk show up and call down the herd of cows from the mountain. It's really quite a sight."

"I'd love to see them."

"The locals are tired of lookers blocking this narrow road. It fills with tourists coming to see them."

"So, it's not quite so peaceful then."

"Just too many people for a few hours."

Luke pointed to the narrow lane that crossed a field before disappearing in the trees on the steep mountain side. "Turn here."

Sara turned off the blacktop and stopped at the dense treeline before starting up the gravel road.

"Want me to drive?" Luke asked, with his hand on the door to get out and change sides.

"No. Hang on, going four wheelin'." She turned the shift switch to four-wheel drive, stepped on the accelerator, and started up the steep inclined road that looked more like a rock-climbing trail. The scrub trees lining the road blocked out the sun and leaned toward them, brushing the truck's cab. Sara was certain the trees would claim the road and hill someday.

The truck gained one tire hold and then would lean hard before the other tires grabbed the next rock ledge. Shaking from side to side in the cab, Sara quipped, "Is there an end to this climb? Damn, hope we don't meet somebody coming the other way."

"Somebody would be backing up for a long way."

"How can anybody even live up here?" she asked, slowing to let the truck climb over another six-inch-tall rock ledge in the bed of the road.

"You'll be surprised at how the ground levels out at the top of this. The map shows the road running along the ridge top for a couple miles before it drops down into a creek bottom. Somewhere along there the sheriff said we would find Jimmy's burnt-out home. He said they lived in a house trailer with a shed built on the side of it."

When the road leveled, Sara eased back on the accelerator and shifted the truck out of four-wheel drive. When they passed the second house and barn, she pointed to the pinto horse grazing in a small, fenced lot.

"Did I tell you our neighbor Marty took me trail riding on her pinto mare?"

"Don't think you did. Do you like to ride?"

"I did. The next morning, not so much."

"I've had that feeling."

"I talked a lot to Marty that day on the ride. She helped me realize how much I needed help."

"After that you went back to the hospital?"

"Yes. Why is it we listen better to someone that doesn't have much invested in us?"

"Invested?"

"You know. Like Dad tried to encourage me to get help. I did my best not to listen to him the first couple weeks I was home. Then things got worse. We would try to talk, but sometimes it's hard to work things out with someone so close to us."

"I want you to know you can always talk to me about anything bothering you. I'm never sure though just how much I can ask."

"You can ask me anything. I want you to know the real me, Luke. I thought I would be normal someday. I told you in my letter I wanted to be normal for you. But I'm not sure whatever the hell normal means, because I'm clearly never going to be it."

"From what I've seen carrying a badge, I'm not sure there are normal people anymore. Only a lot of people trying to be their own version of normal."

"I guess you will have to make a decision, Luke. Am I normal enough for you? Let me explain. The terrible nightmares I was having are gone now, but I still have trigger thoughts that pop into my head during the day. I can mostly control them and not totally lose it now." She had slowed down the truck and pulled into a turnoff.

"That happened at the bar on the night we met. Didn't it?"

"Yes. It was just my female warrior side that cut loose on Ruiz at first. Then something clicked, and I was getting shot at in Iraq. I beat him up so much I must have wanted to kill the people shooting at me."

"I didn't know about that part of the fight you had. Did other things like that happen?" He reached and took her hand into his.

"Yes. They happened way too often. I got desperate to end it all. If Dad's old .38 revolver had worked, I wouldn't be sitting here now."

"What are you saying?"

She reached for him and pulled him toward her. "Don't say anything more, just hold me for a minute." She felt for a moment she was sliding back into a flashback to Iraq. The feel of his body against hers and his grip around her shoulders strengthened her focus on the present. Her mind was clear of the past for now. More than a minute passed before either of them spoke. She wanted to hear from Luke first.

"That's frightening—I'm sorry to have to ask, but have you tried again?"

"Only the one time. I had a talk with Dad a few days later, and I think it did more to ground me than all the talk with the docs at the V.A." She paused for a few seconds and looked down at her wrist.

"This minnow tattoo on my wrist is like a guardian angel for me. I put it there to stare me in the face each time I hold a weapon. It speaks to me in my mother's voice. 'I'll protect you, Little Minnow.'"

Luke took her arm and ran his finger over the tattoo and then pulled it to him and gave the minnow a long kiss.

"Keep her safe, minnow. I love this woman."

"I love you, too, Luke."

She pulled back on the road. Two quiet miles passed before Luke pointed to a driveway. "Pull in here."

Crows sounded the alarm and flew from brush growing up around the burned-out trailer shell. One landed in a tall tree not far away watching like a sentry guarding a death scene. With the truck parked, they got out and crossed the road and stood looking at the trailer floor sitting on black melted tires and wheels. The shell of a shed lay flopped over on top of the floor.

"Why doesn't somebody clean this up?"

"The county will get around to it someday."

"His bicycle." She pointed to what was left of a bicycle sitting against a tree covered with rust. "How did Jimmy ever survive this?" She walked closer to the trailer trying to peer into the blackness.

"Don't go that close, Sara. The whole place is toxic from the meth explosion."

"Why isn't it all blocked off with yellow tape? Won't they bury all of this?"

"This is about as backwoods as you can get. Most of the meth explosions fires here just sit. Rains wash the poison into the gullies and streams."

"How far is the river?"

"It's a half-mile down the ridge." He pointed to the west and down a cleared slope toward the valley.

"He went that far with his hands burned?" She took a picture of the slope and the woods on each side.

"Must be a tough little guy with all he's been through."

"I've got to help get him a place where he won't go into foster care. I forgot to tell you dad is taking him out on the river today."

"The sheriff and his wife are foster parents now for one child. Could that be an option?"

"I've talked to Dad about another idea."

"There's a vehicle coming from the south." He took Sara's hand, encouraging her to follow him back across the road. "Let's get by the side of your truck."

"What's wrong?"

"Just stay close. They'll probably just go by."

The rusted-out truck with a load of brush hanging over the side slowed. One rear tire locked up and slid as the driver braked to a stop.

The driver pointed at the burned-out trailer and yelled, "If you're lookin' for them, they're dead. Both of 'um died right here." His shaggy beard hung over the arm hanging out the truck's window. The gaping opening of the back of a dirt-colored cap topped off his image.

"That's what we heard," Luke said and whispered to Sara. "Stay here." He stepped around the back of the truck.

"What happened here?" Luke pointed toward the burned-out trailer.

"Why you out here asking questions? Folks in these here parts don't take well to strangers asking questions."

Luke stood his ground. "Why? Is that a problem for you?"

"It will be if you don't turn that truck around and get on the hell down the ridgeback."

"We'll do that after we get some pictures of what's left here."

"Luke, let's go." She felt danger was coming and had quietly opened the truck door to get her Beretta. She let the thought linger just enough to wonder why her reliable sixth sense hadn't kicked in that fateful day. Maybe she wouldn't have lost her crew.

The two men got out of their truck and walked to the front of it. The shorter of the two carried a lever action rifle horizontal across the back of his neck. He turned his body and the rifle in half circles with his arms. Sara knew they were being taunted. She worked the breach on her pistol to load a cartridge. The two men walked past the front of their truck and into the middle of the road.

Luke had had enough, he pulled the edge of his jacket open, the gold of his badge and his sidearm now in full view. Easing his hand down, he slipped the safety strap off his pistol. "Crossing the road and threatening a law officer while carrying a weapon is a bad fucking idea, guys. Why don't you back up, get back in that truck, and get on down the ridgeback yourselves?"

The fellow twisting the rifle lowered it to his side, turned, and walked back around to the other side of the truck.

"That fucking badge don't mean shit 'round these parts, mister. Just saying." The other man slowly backed around the truck and climbed in. Sara watched as he slapped his partner with his cap and drove off, cussing and shouting.

Luke turned to Sara. "Must not have liked being left in the road to face us alone."

"Us? You knew I had the Beretta cocked and ready?"

"I wouldn't have expected anything less."

She lowered the hammer on her pistol and holstered it before sliding it under the seat.

"Not to worry. I could have handled this alone." He pulled the safety strap over his pistol and straightened his jacket.

She slapped him on the shoulder and said, "Sure, Big Boy."

"Now, let's go get some pictures of the trailer. Then we'll head down to the river. I want to see what Jimmy had to swim in to go so many miles downstream."

With pictures of the trailer and the burned bicycle on her cell phone, she climbed in the passenger seat of the truck. "You drive, Mister Lawman. We need to go find Jimmy's grandmother now. She lives somewhere north of Ponca."

With Luke at the wheel, they turned and backtracked down the steep road to the highway. At the river bridge crossing he slowed and turned down the road marked "river access." He drove to the edge of the gravel bank and both got out.

"I checked records on river levels back around the time the explosion happened. The river was high at that time."

"Think he might have stolen a boat?"

"Sheriff didn't have any records of that."

Sara reached for her ringing phone. "It's Dad. Well hi. How's the fishing?" Luke turned and walked a few steps away.

"Luke, wait. You need to hear this. Hang on, Dad, I'll put you on speaker."

"Hello, Luke. I just told Sara Jimmy is gone. He left the hospital sometime last night."

"Did someone pick him up? Maybe the sheriff?" Luke moved closer to Sara to listen.

"Not the sheriff. He was here at the hospital when I came."

"Dad, he wasn't happy staying there any longer. He promised me when I took him back the other day he would stay."

"I think he overheard the sheriff talking to the staff about moving him. I'll let you know if they find him, Minnow."

"All right. Call me." Puzzled, Sara looked at her phone as the call ended. "Any ideas where he could run to?"

"I don't know, but we need to finish this trip and talk to his grandmother. You drive," Sara said, already halfway back to the truck. Luke followed and slid into the driver's seat. Thirty miles north he turned at a mailbox marked with the address the sheriff had given him. Two-foot-tall grass and scrub trees filled the acre of yard in front of three brick buildings each with its own share of green moss gracing the front. A faded sign looking like it had been bumped by a car leaned to the right but still declared this place was *"The Manor."*

They looked at each other. Sara was the first to say it, "What the hell?"

They got out and went toward what she thought might be called an office. Luke opened the screen door after purposely sticking his hand through the empty door frame that was short of any fly protection. A counter covered with magazines and dirty water glasses was the only greeting they received. Both walked past the counter and then into a hallway. Sara covered her nose to block the strong bleach smell out. A man in a wheelchair sat at the end of the hall with his head down.

Luke stopped alongside the wheelchair. "Hello, sir. Is there someone in charge here?"

The man looked up and smiled. "Would you want to be in charge of this?"

"No, sir. I wouldn't. My name is Luke. This is Sara. We're looking for Sally Wilmore. Could you tell me where we could find her?"

"All the women that are still here are in the east building. State's been trying for years to close this place down."

"Before we go, is there anything we can get for you?" Sara asked.

"No. They come back and fix us two meals a day if they ain't drugged up or drunk."

Sara led the way back out. She couldn't wait to get out of the pee-smelling pigsty of a building.

"Damn it to hell, how does anyone get away with this?"

"The hair on my neck stood up when I saw the inside of this place. I wanted to choke the owners. Call the local sheriff, Luke."

"I'm going to do more than call the sheriff. This mess is going to be on my list to help get fixed when I get back to the office."

At the east building they were greeted at the door by a frail lady who smiled at them.

"Won't you come in?"

"Thank you. We would like to," Sara stepped inside and held the door for Luke to follow. She was quick to size up the place and know the well-kept lady's building was probably being cleaned by the women residents.

"We don't have many visitors here. Most of our friends are all gone to be with God."

"Could you tell us where we might find Missus Wilmore?"

"Yes, Sally is down this hall in the second room. She doesn't get out since she broke her hip and they operated on her." The lady led the way down the hall and stopped with her hand on the door sill. "Sally, sweetie, you have some visitors."

"Can they wait? My hair up and all."

Sara stuck her head in the room, "It's all right, Missus Wilmore. I've seen a lot of curlers in my time. We won't stay long."

She went in the room to the bedside while Luke stood in the doorway. The lady in bed looked younger than Sara expected for a grandmother. Her chalk white face was surrounded by dirty blonde hair wrapped up tight in large brown curlers. Sara could tell the bed sheet covered a large body cast.

Mrs. Wilmore reached for her glasses. "Sorry I look this way right now. The girls put my hair up to fancy me up a bit!"

"That's all right. We just stopped to tell you your grandson is fine."

"Oh, my. I heard a rattlesnake bit him, and he was bad off." She held a washcloth to her eyes and sobbed.

"He's much better now."

"They said he run off after the fire and all. They wouldn't tell me what happened to my girl. Do you know?"

"I know there was a fire."

"Did Kip burn her up with his cookin'? He was a poor excuse of a man. My daughter should have left him long 'fore it happened. Jimmy would at least have his mother to take care of him."

"I'm so sorry. We just know about Jimmy. I found him snake bit in a cave and took him to the hospital."

"Where'd he get to?"

"Clear over near the White River."

"How'd he get so far?"

"He must have found a boat, I think."

"He ain't no thief. Is he in trouble with the law? It's always been hard for that boy to go back and forth and staying with me most of the time."

"No trouble with the law. He's almost well now."

"They told me he was in the hospital. I wrote him a week ago."

"I think he might have gotten it." Sara took a seat near the bedside.

"Who is that good-looking man standing at my door? Tell him not to look at me. I look so bad."

"This is Luke Matthews. He's a policeman and has been helping me with Jimmy and all."

Luke stayed in the doorway. "Hello, Missus Wilmore, I wish we would have come sooner to tell you about your grandson."

Wanting to get on with why they came, Sara took the lead. "Would you mind if we ask some questions about your grandson?"

"Anything you want to ask is fine, but please call me Sally." She reached for a long dowel rod lying by the bed. "This thing is gonna drive me crazy." She slipped it under the covers, and Sara could tell she was scratching an itch inside her cast. "You'll will have to excuse me."

"Does Jimmy have any other family?" Sara asked, feeling she was being nosy but still wanting the information.

"I only had the one daughter, his mother. Jimmy was an only child."

"What about his dad? Is his family from around here?"

"His dad's mother and father died years back, and he never mentioned having brothers or sisters."

"Have you been taking care of Jimmy?"

"I did till I fell. Then he went back to stay with his mother."

"Jimmy's going to want to see you, Missus Wilmore. We'll bring him if it's all right with the county judge."

"It better be all right. That boy belongs to me. They signed him over more than a year ago. I'm his legal guardian."

"His guardian?"

"Yes, he's my boy. When my daughter's husband started making drugs, she got him to let her give me guardianship of Jimmy. He came to live with me. He was only on a visit when they were both killed. Somebody gonna have to take him. He's such a good boy."

"You're his legal guardian?" Sara rebounded from what the woman had just told them and leaned in toward the bedside. "I'd hoped there would be a way Jimmy could stay in Cotter with a family there."

Her head was spinning. She couldn't stand the thought of Jimmy getting put in the foster system. She knew he might never get the help he would need with the kind of PTSD he was dealing with. She would have to draw her own line in the dirt of Arkansas—whatever she could do to prevent the foster system from getting him she had to do.

"Bring him back to see me when things are ready. If I'm still alive, I'll sign papers if he has a good home to go to."

"We'll do our best to find a good home for him." She leaned over the bed and kissed the old woman on the forehead. "Thank you, Sally."

Sara had trouble holding back the happy tears. They thanked Sally for her time and headed for the truck and the long drive home. She let Luke drive the trip back to Cotter.

"What his grandmother told us should keep the Department of Family Services from getting involved and putting him in some foster home. I think I see a lot of what I went through in Jimmy's thinking. He needs professional help with it. Seeing his father and mother die like they did is going to work on him and keep coming back in nightmares. It won't be a surprise if he starts acting out in school."

"Did the doctors at the hospital say anything about how he was adapting?"

"From what they said I'm guessing he's a little bit like I was—I would adapt for a while then something would set me off. It can still happen with me but not so often anymore. They think he's at the point of getting better."

"Have you been talking with him trying to help?"

"Yes, but I may do more harm than good. It scares me to play psychologist with him."

"How's he doing?"

"I have to pull information out of him. He says his health is good and he feels fine. I just need to go with him to his doctor if he'll let me...."

"Will he stand for that?"

"I can ask him. He'd probably let me if nothing serious is wrong."

"My dad's the same way about talking about his health. Just keep asking him."

"I will, but first we have to find Jimmy. Where could he have gone?"

"Not far with that sore leg."

"He's tough as nails, Luke. He wasn't raised like kids around here."

"Different?"

"Yes. I think he had to really make his own way."

"When I get to a radio, I'll alert the state's Conservation Police to watch for him."

Sara yawned and took her jacket off to roll it into a pillow. When she rested her head against the coat on Luke's leg, she fell asleep. The miles rolled by, and no restless dreams came. It was midnight when they pulled into Cotter, and Luke drove straight to the sheriff's office. The lights were on, and two of the deputy's cars sat outside. Sara got out of the truck and was through the station door first.

She walked past the counter and through the swinging gate to where the deputies were talking. "Have you found the boy?"

"We're working several leads that have come in."

"Can Luke and I help?" She had both of her hands on the counter, leaning forward.

"We just got a call from someone who saw a boy walking on the road east of here. He was a couple miles from the horse ranch out there. We're going to search the barns there when it gets light out."

She grabbed Luke by the hand, "Come on."

"Thanks, guys. I have a feeling we are going to be in the barns tonight,"

Luke missed the handshake of the deputy as Sara pulled him to catch up.

thirty

THE MORNING FOG ROLLING OFF the waters of the river had drifted up the bank and now floated like a white carpet in the lights of Sara's truck. She was wide awake and ready for the hunt.

"Sorry I'm driving so slow." She leaned forward and used her hand to wipe the windshield.

"I'm glad you're driving. I can't tell where the road is half the time."

"I've got a bad feeling we're not going to find him sleeping in a horse barn."

"Where else could he go? Would he try to go back to where he lived with his grandmother?"

"Her letter may have told him she had to go in a nursing home," she said, reaching and touching his hand. "We'll probably find him before the sheriff's deputies get out here. He's had enough trauma to last a while."

Sara knew the horse farm of her friend Marty Johnson was just ahead. She had tried Marty's phone but got no answer. Pulling into the barn lot, Sara gave a short honk and then turned off the truck. After getting two flashlights from the backseat, Sara left the truck lights on. They got out and went to the side entrance leading to the Johnson's living quarters in the barn. She saw the hall lights come on before they got to the door. Sara didn't have a chance to knock. Marty had the door open.

"Marty, I'm sorry if we scared you, but Jimmy has gone missing. We think he might be around here."

"Hell, give me a minute to slip on some jeans. Did somebody see him around here?"

"Maybe on the road back toward town, the sheriff's deputy said."

"I'll be right back."

Sara leaned back pressing against Luke's chest. "I used to like nights. Walking guard duty with Tank when most of the unit's men were asleep sure beat the hell out of days. I always felt there were dozens of eyes watching us in the daytime."

"You don't like nights now?"

"Only when I can be with you," she said, turning her head for a kiss. The door opened as the kiss ended.

"Need a room?"

Both of them laughed at Marty's quick wit.

"Hang on a minute I'll light up the place like a football stadium."

"She's not kidding," Sara said. "She rides in the arena a lot at night. Come on we can start looking in the horse stall area." Sara led the way to the big sliding doors and went in when the lights come on. "Jimmy are you in here?" she yelled.

A muffled voice came from somewhere down the line of horse stalls.

"He's in here, Luke." Sara ran ahead. "Jimmy, where are you?"

Sara heard the voice again and went to the last of the stalls. The horse in the stall was standing with its head down looking at the curled-up pile of hay in the corner.

"I'm sorry, Miss Sara. I couldn't take it there any longer."

"Come on out, Jimmy."

The pile of hay shuffled, and the boy stood up. He reached and petted the curious horse's head. Luke opened the stall door enough for Sara to get through. She ran her hand along the horse's withers as she walked past it. Jimmy was covered with hay, dirt, and some of what the horse had eaten the day before. Marty arrived as Sara and the boy came out of the stall.

"So, this is the boy from the mountain. Son, you look like you have been cleaning stalls for a month."

"He was hiding back in the corner stall," Luke said.

"Am I in trouble for running away?"

"No, son, but you caused a lot of folks to worry," Luke said.

"Come on all of you. Let's get this kid cleaned up. I've got a full horse tank just outside."

Jimmy lagged behind the others. "What's she mean about a horse tank?"

Marty gave a big wave of her hand for them to follow, "Just come on, boy. I'll show you." She led the way out of the barn.

Jimmy followed. Sara noticed that his limp was barely noticeable. At the tank, Marty turned on the hose and helped Jimmy get his shirt off.

"These folks are going to wait for you over a ways."

Sara and Luke moved to where they were still in earshot of the boy and Marty.

"I need to wash my pants, too. Can't I keep them on?"

"Turn around let me hose you and your pants. Just keep them on."

Marty didn't spare the boy when she hosed him down. She got most of the dark spots off his pants before she stopped.

"Now climb in that horse tank, son."

Jimmy slipped his leg over the edge and stopped, "Ma'am the... water is cold."

Marty gave him a little shove, and Jimmy slid on into the tank. He sat up on his knees with his arms wrapped around his chest shivering.

"Move around. You'll warm right up." She turned the hose off and went to stand with Sara and Luke. "What's going to happen to him now?

Sara spoke first. "I don't know. His grandmother is his guardian, but she can't take care of him."

"We would be glad for him to stay here for a while, at least 'til things get settled for him. I've got to get him a towel. I bet he's cold as heck. I've got some sweatpants and a sweater, that will warm him up." She headed into the barn.

"Thanks, Marty." Sara turned to Luke. "I'm not surprised Marty would make that offer. Being here close would let Dad and I see him often."

Marty was back and had the boy out of the tank and wrapped in a large bath towel. She was rubbing the towel on his back to get him warm.

"I'm okay, ma'am. Let me do it."

The drying stopped, and Marty invited all of them to come into her downstairs kitchen. With Jimmy outfitted with Marty's husband's clothes, they all settled in on the couch and chairs to wait for the clothes Marty had put in the dryer to dry.

"Jimmy, we saw your grandmother today. She's really worried about you."

He got up and went to stand beside her. His bathrobe drug the floor and almost tripped him. "Can I go to our home now and be with her?"

"Jimmy, your grandmother is in poor health, and she's in a nursing home."

"When can I go see her?"

"We'll make sure you get to go." Luke sat forward on the couch. "I'll be right back in. I'm going to let the sheriff know we found Jimmy."

Marty yawned. "It's very late, gang, and I don't see any reason this can't all be worked out in the light of day. I'm heading up to bed. Go ahead and spread out on the couch and lounge chairs."

With a promise from Jimmy he wouldn't run away again, Luke turned all the lights off but one and took over one of the lounge chairs for himself. Sara joined the boy on the couch—he wasn't asleep.

He leaned toward Sara. "I get scared at night. Fire comes in my sleep, and it's all around me."

"I'll keep it away tonight, Jimmy. Put your head on my shoulder. I'm so glad we found you."

———————

SARA AWOKE AT DAYBREAK TO the smell of frying bacon in Marty's kitchen. Luke and Jimmy must have gotten up earlier as they were both not in the room. Sara left the couch for the bathroom on the way. "Do I also smell coffee brewing, Marty?"

"Hurry back, it's finishing now."

When Sara got back to the kitchen counter, a steaming cup of coffee was waiting there for her.

"I remembered you take it straight, right?" Marty had the bacon lying out on a foot-long strip of paper towel, and now the huge cast iron skillet was crackling full of eggs. "I hope those boys are hungry. I think I've fixed enough for all of you."

"Marty, you were more than kind to put us up last night. Thank you."

"I enjoyed having you young 'uns under my care. Do you think the boy is going to sit still for another stay at the hospital?"

"He isn't. They want him out of there, and he's ready. Showed us that for sure, didn't he?" Sara picked up a piece of bacon and bit off an inch. "Marty, I can't remember how long it's been since I tasted bacon this good. What the heck?"

"Did you forget the feral pig we shot and butchered? We cured the hams and bacon in a little smoke house we put together."

"Darn, it's good, gal."

"Not to change the subject, but you're not going to let the boy get taken away to foster care, are you?"

"No. Hell no. His grandmother is his guardian, and she's willing to give him up if I can find a place for him."

"She doesn't want him?"

Sara was slow to answer—she had just bit down on the rest of a bacon strip. "She's in a cast now and probably too ill to ever care for him again."

"I see."

"Marty, he saved me up on that mountain from getting snake bit in the face. He's been through some things like I went through. We can get him some professional help." Sara put the last half of the six bacon strips on the counter and leaned with both her hands in front of her on the counter. "We'll adopt him if we can."

"Are you and your dad ready for the responsibility?"

"I just need a little more time to work it out. To make sure what's best for the boy, not just Dad and me."

"Why not leave the boy here for now, Sara? We can get him enrolled in school and on the bus every morning. He seems to like the place, and your dad can come over to see him as often as he wants. Jimmy's out there cleaning out stalls right now, in fact. He wanted to earn his keep for last night. I like that in a kid."

"You would do that for him?"

"Already talked to your Dad about it. Right?"

"Not yet. I'll ask Luke to talk to the sheriff to be sure it would all be legal. I think they're coming in." Jimmy led the way to the table.

"Boy, oh, boy, Miss Marty. Somethin' smells really good."

"Well, do a quick wash up and then pull up a chair, boy. You are about to have a real cowboy breakfast," Marty set a plate of bacon, eggs, and some fried potatoes she pulled from the stove.

"Oh, my. Look at that boy's eyes," Sara pulled up a chair across from Jimmy. "Luke come sit down. There's a country breakfast awaiting you."

Luke scooted the chair back and then sat down beside her. He put a slice of the bacon on his plate and whistled. "Marty, this looks mighty fine."

Marty bit the end of a piece of the bacon. "Enjoy, folks."

"My mom used to fix us a breakfast like this, 'fore things got all bad at home." Jimmy reached for the plate of eggs.

"Help yourself, young man," Marty pushed the plate closer to him.

"How about you, Luke? Did you help with the cooking when you lived at home?"

Luke choked on the bite of toast he had just bit off before he could answer.

"I'm sorry," Sara said. "Both these boys are hungry, I think."

Luke finally recovered. "When Mom and Dad found out I could eat them out of house and home, they started letting me fix my own breakfast. They knew I was lazy and would probably settle for a bowl of corn flakes."

Sara chuckled. "My mom would have to set her foot down since Dad always kept the fridge full of trout and say, 'No more damn trout, John.'"

Marty and Luke both laughed. Jimmy was too busy with his fourth piece of bacon to even notice.

Luke finished first and pushed his chair back.

"Luke, hang on a minute," Sara finished the last potato on her plate and took a big wipe across her mouth with her napkin. "Come with me. I want to show you the horse Marty had me ride." They both left the table and went through the kitchen door into the horse barn area.

"I just needed to talk to you for a minute before we tell Jimmy something that might not happen."

"Sure, go ahead."

"Marty said she's willing to keep the boy here until other arrangements can be made for him. She'll get him in school and all."

"Well, his grandmother let on she would be willing to go along with whatever could be arranged for him."

"Can we be sure it's okay with the sheriff's office? We need to run it by his grandmother also."

"I'll do that with a phone call to the sheriff now. If you're sure Marty and her husband are okay with it."

"She says she rules the roost here. I'm fine with it. It would keep Jimmy out of trouble. And keep him from running off." Before he could say more, she headed back to the kitchen feeling happier than she'd felt for some time.

thirty-one

AFTER MEETING WITH THE SHERIFF, Sara arranged for Jimmy to stay with Marty and her husband until other arrangements could be made for a permanent home. She also had a long conversation with her father and, with his blessing, called for an appointment with a lawyer.

She headed for the trout dock to see if they had booked any trips for her. The only place left to tie up her boat was on the river side of the dock. She eased the boat up, patted the Mercury on the top, and jumped to the dock. The dock manager, Sam, popped his head out of the office when he saw her pull in.

"Morning, Sara. We've called the guides up to have a quick meeting."

"I'll be right up. Gotta get this old jon corralled up tight." She pulled the front rope up and wrapped it to a cleat to secure the boat against the current.

She found the eight other guides in the dock's office filling up the four log benches. She found an open space to stand and leaned against the frame of the door. The man on the seat next to her had on his dirty coal-covered railroad cap topping off four-inch tuffs of rust colored hair all blending with his beard.

It surprised Sara when Red stood and brushed against her while going to the door. He turned and growled. "Sit there, bitch."

"Oh, that's all right, Red. I'll stand. I don't want to take your place like last time." She heard snickers from the other three men sitting on his bench. Red pushed the screen door open and left, slamming it behind him.

Sara kept her place against the door frame.

The dock manager stood behind the counter holding a calendar and the schedule book for the guide trips. "Okay, if we can get started. We've been asked to host a weekend float for a large group from Little Rock. We'll set up our campsite on the sandbar below Buffalo River."

"How many boats you needin'?"

"We'll need at least four more guides, plus men to drive the trucks carrying the tents and cooking pots and pans down to the camp area. Signup sheet is up here on the counter—first comes gets the jobs."

"What group will we be guiding?" Sara asked.

"The Arkansas Game and Fish Commission is having its annual outing here this year with us guiding them, so make sure you have all your licenses up to date. It will also be important to have your safety equipment in good shape. Treat them like our regular customers. I'll let you know when we have the trip set in stone. Joe, I see you have some customers waiting on the porch, so that's all for now. Thanks for coming in."

Two of the guides followed Sara out the door and stopped to talk with her.

"We both know Bill tried to scare you. Wasn't right. Still, you're getting a lot of the best tippers we used to fish with," one of the guides told her.

"They'll come back, guys. I'm starting to take folks who want to fly fish, So I won't be having as many bait fishing trips." What they didn't know couldn't hurt them, right?

"We know you wouldn't steal our clients. But still... we wanted to tell you how we feel."

"Thanks for telling me, guys. I really don't advertise to get them." She remembered the magazine story she'd interviewed for and realized it would cause her even more trouble with these guys. She sighed and led the way down the steps to the dock.

"Son of a bitch!" She ran to edge of the dock. "My boat's gone!"

"Did you have it tied in front and back?" one of the guides asked.

"Front only. Look here. My rope's cut. That bastard!"

"Come on, Heat. Jump in my boat. It hasn't had time to get very far down stream. We'll catch it."

Two more guides joined in the boat to help. She saw the boat when they rounded the second turn from the trout dock.

"Thar she blows, gents. At least he didn't drag it off and sink it."

"I wouldn't put nothin' past that man."

"If you don't mind sticking around and letting me make sure he didn't screw with the engine," Sara said, climbing in the boat and yanking the starter rope. The engine started and sounded fine. "Thanks, guys, I owe you. I'll buy you a beer up at Bear's." She was pleased to have learned that at least two of the guides didn't hate her.

WHEN SHE GOT BACK TO the dock, she found Luke and her dad in the parking lot waiting for her.

"I had to run down my boat. Someone cut the tie ropes while we were in a meeting. Red was the only one that left before the meeting was over, so I'm sure it was him."

John took off his cap and scratched his head in frustration. "I'm going to have a big-ass talk with him."

"No! I don't think talking to him is going to help. He hasn't gotten over a put-down I gave him."

"Good for you. I told you not to let them get a foot up on you."

Luke shook his head. "All that said, Red could really cause some shit for you. Be careful and put me on speed dial. If we're on the river, I'll come as fast as the boat will travel."

"Thank you, babe. I just came from one war. I sure don't want to get into another right now."

"I'm heading up to the cabin this Thursday after work. I'd love for you to join me."

"I'll let you know. I promised Jimmy a fishing trip. I'll see if I can arrange it to do both."

"Want me to go along?"

"Thanks, anyway. I'll take this trip with just the two of us. I'm hoping I can get him to open up and talk more. I want to know how bad he might be feeling about not going back to live with his grandmother."

"You guys count me in on a day's fishing with both of you later."

Her mind chased some wild ideas about what she might do and say the next time she got near Red. None of the ideas fit under the definition of a legal operation.

thirty-two

SARA WAS ON THE RIVER in the jon boat a mile from their cabin when the first bullet hit. The motor's control arm ripped from her hand and off the motor. The Mercury engine went full throttle without the blown off control arm. She didn't hesitate a second—her war training had taught her this was real. Sara threw the fishing rod she was holding in the air and dove over the edge of the boat. She heard the thud from the next shot when it hit her engine. Her adrenaline rush fueled her war memories. She pushed them away this time. Panic came next. She started to gasp and realized she was four feet under water. Now it became all about staying alive. The outboard shuttered and stopped. Sara came up on the far side of the boat away from the shooter and then dove to get back underneath the boat. Sara felt bullets shred the wood sides of the boat. The two shots echoed across the river. She came up alongside the boat and heard the hiss of another bullet pass above her. She had her pistol in her hand but knew it was smarter to stay down. Badly shaken and mad, she held onto the side of the boat just behind the engine.

The boat had drifted more than two miles, and Sara's legs were starting to cramp from the cold water before she felt safe in climbing back in the boat. Still not sure the danger had passed, she rolled over the edge of the boat and laid shivering on the bottom. Being back in a shooting war didn't ring well with her plans to continue guiding on the White River. She stood and tried to squeeze as much of the cold water out of her clothes as possible. Still shaken by being shot at and the cold, she picked up the boat's paddle and dug in to hurry. The Buffalo River Resort was just around the bend.

Sara saw the resort owner walking up the hill toward his log house built high on the riverbank above the flood stages. When she yelled, he turned and hurried back down to meet her.

"What happened out there, Sara?"

"I got my engine and boat shot up. That's what happened."

"What?"

"Don't ask. I don't know who shot at me."

"Did you call the sheriff's office?"

"My phone is ruined. It was in my pocket when I dove in the water."

"I'll call."

"No. Let me handle this." She stepped out of the boat and tied it to the dock.

"All right. If you're certain."

"I am."

"You're shaking from being in the water. Come on up to the house. Let's get you in some dry clothes and that camo outfit in the dryer." he said. "Then I'll take you home."

They walked up the hill together. He opened the door for her, and they went into the house's living room. Sara was embarrassed because she had forgotten the man's first name. Well, might as well get this over with. "I'm sorry, with all that just went on this afternoon, I totally forgot your first name, Mister Johnson."

"That's all right. Ron is not a very memorable name, now is it?"

"Thank you for the offer, Ron. I do need to make a call. Could I use your phone?"

She took the cell phone and stepped out on the porch to call. She entered her dad's number but then stopped, erased it, and entered Luke's number instead. He answered quickly.

"Luke, I had some bad trouble down near Buffalo River—"

"What—"

"Hold on. This is *not* for my dad, understand?"

"Go on. What trouble?"

"Some son-of-a-bitch either tried to kill me or scare the hell out of me. He darn near did both."

"Kill you?"

"I've got a shot-up engine and two bullet holes in the boat. I'm okay, I just need one hell of a big hug. Can you come get me? I'm at the Buffalo River Resort." She was trembling and about to cry.

"I'm leaving now."

"Luke, listen... Telling Dad about this right now is going to send him off in a rampage."

"Sorry. He's standing next to me in your kitchen."

"Shit. Bring me something warm to put on. I'm cold and wet."

She stepped back into the house and handed the phone to Ron.

"Thank you." She looked around for a bathroom.

"I have a robe for you. I hung it in the bathroom just down the hall. It belonged to Rose, my wife. You can change, just down there." He pointed down a long corridor.

"Thanks. I've got help coming, but I'm shaking from the cold."

She headed down the hallway and undressed, throwing her wet clothes in a heap. She took a towel he had laid out for her and rubbed it across her shoulders and back. The feel of it against her cold skin made her shake. The pink robe just made it past her knees. She remembered it was his wife's. Must have been a short lady. What he had told her about how she died caused her to think of her dad and all the times he was on the river when storms came up. She often worried about him when she walked guard duty at night at Bucca Prison, knowing he would be on the river. She pulled the edge of the robe to her mouth and kissed it, sending a message to Rose, his wife. She knew Ron had kept the robe because he missed his wife. She picked up her wet clothes and shoved them into her shirt. She tied the arms around them and then went back to join Ron.

"This feels a lot better. Thanks so much."

"I made hot chocolate. I can slip a little bourbon in if it's your pleasure."

"Oh, God, yes." She needed the bourbon.

Sara followed him out the front door with the cup in her hand and took a seat in the sun on a wooden bench. She heard a fast-moving vehicle coming toward the resort while it was still a half mile away. The Jeep pulled down to the dock and slid to a stop alongside the ramp.

"Sara, are you on the dock?" Luke yelled.

"Luke, hang on, I'm coming." Sara emptied the cup and sat it down, then ran down the hill to meet him hurrying up the hill.

"I was at the house when you called. Your dad knew from your voice that something was wrong. He's standing by the Jeep."

Sara threw both her arms around him and pressed her head against the side of his face. "I was afraid to tell him what happened out there today."

"What?"

"Just hug me until I stop shaking."

Luke wrapped the jacket he had brought around her back and then hugged her.

"She's okay, John," he yelled.

"Wait till you see the holes in the boat and motor. Dad's going to want to kill somebody."

"Is everything okay, Sara?" Ron asked.

"Good, Ron. I think you know my friend, Luke."

"Hello, Luke. Glad you came to pick her up. I'll leave you two to talk. Take the robe. It's time for it to go."

"I'll get it back to you. Thank you. Luke, get your flashlight and Dad, I need to show you both the boat," Sara said, leaving his arms and heading straight for the boat dock and the shot-up boat.

John walked out to the slip where the jon boat was tied. "What's going on, Sara?"

"Shine the light on the engine."

"What the hell? The tiller is gone. Looks like it broke off."

"Broke off, hell. It was shot off. Right out of my hand. The next round went right into the crankcase of the Merc. Two more rounds went through the side of the boat after I bailed out." She pointed to the pair of holes in the boat's side.

"Who the hell did this? You could have been killed." John pulled her into a tight hug. "I'm sorry, Minnow. You're okay? Didn't get hurt?"

"I'm fine. Felt like I was right back in the middle of another war. I couldn't call—my phone is at the bottom of the river about two miles that way." She pointed upriver in the direction of their cabin. "I'll be right back. I've got to thank Ron for his help and get my wet clothes. He kept me from freezing to death."

thirty-three

WITH THE OLD JON BOAT on sawhorses in his garage shop, John and Sara repaired the bullet holes in the boat's sides. John thought a piece of tin nailed down over the holes would be fine. Sara argued the boat meant too much to her. Her search of the garage turned up a fiberglass repair kit. With the wood filler paste from the kit, she filed the bullet holes level. A touch of gray paint would come later to finish her repair. Done for the day, they both headed into town. Sara had spent more than an hour the night before telling the sheriff about what had happened on the river. She was to meet the sheriff and Luke at noon to go out where the shooting had occurred. John dropped her off at the trout dock on time and told her he was headed out to look for a used thirty-five horse outboard.

She joined the sheriff, Luke, and Gwen for a trip down the river on the Commission's airboat.

"Let us know when you think we're getting close to the spot," Gwen said, easing back a little on the boat's throttle.

"The shots scared me. I went overboard so fast. I'm not sure exactly."

"Just get us in the general area, and we can check the bank for signs of the shooter," the Sheriff said.

Sara watched the several miles of bank and bluff pass the boat.

"Sara, we're almost to the Buffalo River Resort. Did we miss the location?" Luke asked.

"We'll be right on the spot if you set your GPS for two miles and head back," Sara said. "It's easier having the resort as the point of reference."

The GPS system on the Commission's boat sounded at the two-mile waypoint. Sara pointed to the large gravel fill on a road washout. "This is it. I remember the washout. Pull in here."

"Could he have been up on the top of the bluff?" Gwen asked.

"You didn't get to see the holes in the boat, Gwen. The shots came in at a low angle," the Sheriff said. Gwen eased the airboat close enough for the sheriff, Luke, and Sara to jump to the bank.

"Don't touch anything you see up there along the dirt road. Show me first," the Sheriff said. "We'll do a grid search and see if we can find the shooter's stand."

Sara walked the grassy edge of the road. Her enemy sniper training had taught her where to expect them to lay in wait. She stopped and called the others to see the imprint in the dirt of the shooter's elbow.

"Luke, get a picture of this. We need to check the ejection side of this shooter's position for spent cartridges," the Sheriff said.

Sara knew she had probably policed more brass than either of the two men, so she kept looking when the others quit. Both of the men had gone on to look for signs of a parked car when she saw the cartridge lying halfway down the bank toward the river. "Hey, here's the one he missed picking up," Sara yelled.

The sheriff lifted the shell with his pen and dropped it in an evidence bag. "Let's hope this guy wasn't wearing gloves when he loaded this one," the Sheriff said. "I checked the loose dirt along the road and don't see any car tracks. So, did he get here by boat?"

"If he was up here waiting for me, where did he sit or stand to wait?" She started walking into the trees on the north side of the firing site.

"If he was careless, we might find a cigarette butt or a water bottle along here," the Sheriff said, taking the lead into the trees.

"He didn't just catch me here by accident. He knew I'd be coming back this way, so he spent some time waiting. I was gone a couple hours at least."

"She's right," the Sheriff said, pointing to a stump with footprints alongside it. "Stay back while Luke gets this picture. Luke, there's a rifle stock impression on the other side."

Sara pointed. "There's a cigarette butt lying over here. He must have flicked it when he saw me approach."

"Your dad's report about the slashed tires said Ruiz threatened to kill you, and we've been wanting to get something on him for a long time. I believe you did make a report about the car following you and scaring you. The Feds keep pushing and knocking on our door to help them take him down." The Sheriff put his hands on his hips. "Is there anyone else you can think of?"

"He's had chances to kill me and hasn't, so I don't know. Other than him, there's maybe a dozen guides are mad at me for taking their clients away from them."

"Anything serious there?"

"Nothing I can't handle with the guides. I think this shooting was a warning. He could have just as easily hit me instead of the outboard. This guy is mean, but I don't think he's a killer. I don't think it's Ruiz."

"We had word from some our field agents Ruiz has been running drugs again up through Arkansas from Texas. He's built up his operations a lot," Luke looked up at the older man. "I think you should still be worried about him."

The Sheriff shook his head. "We've had word the DEA has people assigned in Texas trying to stop his operation."

"I just want him to stay away from here," Sara said.

"If we're ready, I'll have Gwen pull the boat back in to pick us up." Luke lifted the mic on his shoulder.

"All done on my part." The sheriff gave a short wave for Luke to go ahead.

IT WAS A WEEK LATER when the sheriff called her to a meeting at the trout dock to discuss what evidence they'd found at the shooter's position. Sara pulled into the dock in her jon boat, tied it up, and then walked up the steps from the dock to meet the sheriff and Luke. The sheriff took out a small notebook and opened it and said, "I wanted to give you an update on what we found on the shooting scene. First, we had a good print on the spent cartridge, only it wasn't from anyone in the federal fingerprint registry. We didn't get the final DNA result, however, the first test showed the DNA didn't come from a Hispanic person, so it wasn't Ruiz."

"I think if Ruiz had shot at me, I'd be dead."

"I think you're right about that, miss. He may not be beyond harassing you, however. We could put the word out to pick him up if he's connected to the black car that's been following you. Get a plate number if you can. I'll run it. Problem is, he and most of his family have left this area. They cleaned out the house and left no sign of ever being here." The sheriff closed his notebook and put it in his backpack.

"I'll keep you informed if we learn any more. I've asked for anyone seeing anything up on the river road the other day to let us know."

"That's good news about Ruiz being gone, but who shot at me, sir?"

The sheriff sighed in frustration. "I don't know yet, but you can be sure I'll do everything I can to find out. This makes me mad as hell when things like this happen in my county."

WHEN SHE SAW THE NEW cardboard box sitting tall in the back of John's truck, she knew he had just spent big bucks for a new engine. "You couldn't find a used engine?"

"Had to go on over to Baxter. The shops here didn't have anything I would want to put on the boat. What did the sheriff have to say about the shooting?" John set the outboard's manuals on the trout dock's wooden bench.

"Sorry I've cost you a new engine, Dad."

"It was about time, anyway. Sorry I missed the meeting with the sheriff."

"He came up with some interesting data. They got a fingerprint off the shell. It didn't match anyone they have on record."

"What caliber was it?"

"I didn't see it up close. The sheriff picked it up and bagged it right away. I've been trying to remember the first two shots. They didn't come from an automatic weapon, too long between shots. I even think I heard a lever action loading between the shots, like your Marlin 30-30."

"The 30-30 is more of a game rifle. Not one a sharpshooter would use to shoot at you." John walked back to the truck with the manuals.

After Sara told him the information about Ruiz's family leaving town, she remembered she needed to get back to the cabin. "Do you mind taking me out there? Luke asked me out tonight."

"Let's go. You know I think Luke is a great guy."

"So do I."

With John driving the truck to the cabin, she sat running the guides' names through her mind. Two kept coming up at the top—Bill Jones and Red Ferrell. She felt certain Jones had enough of her after he tried to ram her on the river. She would need proof Red had it in for her.

She promised herself to go back to the river crime scene.

thirty-four

THE SUN HAD JUST CLEARED the hill to the east when Sara pulled up to the front of Marty's barn. She had promised to take Jimmy fishing, and she found Jimmy and his dog waiting for her in the doorway of the barn. Somehow the boy had come up with an old Zebco rod and reel. He carried it and a tin can to the truck to meet her. He stood on his tiptoes and dropped the rod and reel into the truck bed. Sara smiled when she saw Jimmy walked with only a slight limp.

"Got me something to fish with, Miss Sara." Jimmy jumped up into the truck seat without using the step bars. Blue followed right behind him and shared the passenger seat.

"I see. Do you have anything to use as bait?"

Jimmy lifted a five-inch-long worm out of the tin can he was carrying and set the can on the truck's console. He shook it straight for her to see. "Do you think they bite on this?"

"Oh, I think the trout will love that beauty. My boat's waiting for us at the cabin dock, so let's go." Sara started the truck and headed home.

"I gotta tell you a secret, Miss Sara." Jimmy dropped the worm back in the black dirt of the can and shook it to cover the worm.

Sara had hoped Jimmy would open up and start to talk more about his life. It surprised her when it was this early in the morning.

"Jimmy, you can just call me Sara." She waited, not sure what might come out of the boy's mouth.

"Miss Sara... Sara, don't tell nobody. All that horseshit around that barn is full of these here big worms. We don't want everybody digging them up before we get 'um."

Sara choked trying to hide her laughing. "Jimmy, we're going to catch some mighty big 'uns with those horseshit worms you dug." What he said surprised her. His serious tone had led her to believe he was going to say something about home and a new family. She realized maybe she didn't know children as well as she had thought.

The drive to the cabin was a short one. Jimmy sat looking over the dog's ears and head.

"He's got a bunch of them damn ticks on his head. Don't like me pulling on them. Just gets him growling." Jimmy tried clamping down on one with his fingers. "My fingers just slip off the things."

"It would be better if you didn't pull them off in the truck, Jimmy. I'll help you with them later. I'll get you some stuff you can put on Blue to keep ticks and fleas off."

"We'll both like that. I let him sleep with me, and I get to scratching sometimes."

"You'd better check yourself for ticks, and it'll be best to not let Marty know the dog sleeps on the bed."

"Promise you won't tell her, Miss... ma'am."

"It'll be our secret." She turned into the cabin driveway and parked.

"Is this your place?"

"Yes, my dad and I live here. He used to work as a fishing guide down on the river."

"I bet he knows all the good holes where the bass hide."

"We don't have a lot of bass in this river. We have scads of trout that we can catch, though."

"I bet I can catch 'um!"

"I bet so, too." Sara led the way around the cabin and down the steps to her boat. She had set out four of her best fishing rods and reels for them to use. "Take a seat up front, Jimmy, and we'll get started pulling in the big ones. Slip on that lifejacket that's draped over the seat."

"I never had to wear one of them before."

"We always have to wear them when I'm captain of the ship."

"Yes, sir, Captain."

Blue followed them into the boat and went to lie down by the boy. "That dog likes you a lot."

Jimmy was busy pushing and wrapping one of the big worms from the can around a huge hook.

"Hold on, Jimmy. Take a look at the hook on my fishing rods." Jimmy stopped threading the worm on his hook and reached to pick up one of Sara's rods.

"But, Miss Sara, them little hooks won't hold hardly nothin' at all."

"The fish here don't have big mouths like the bass where you lived."

"I'll change my hook then." He stripped the worm off his hook and bit the line in to just above the hook. Sara shuttered and never said anything when Jimmy didn't wash his fingers in the river.

"Untie the front rope, and let's head out."

"We gonna get to go swimming?"

"The water is really cold here because it comes from under a big dam upstream from here."

"Oh, well I love to swim."

She slipped the outboard into reverse and backed out of the slip into the current and headed upstream. She wanted Jimmy to experience a favorite spot loaded with trout. She stopped the motor about a hundred yards past the spot and checked Jimmy's hook and pole.

"Looks good. We're going to drift kind of fast so cast out to the side and let the bait follow along. I'm going to try a salmon egg on mine."

"I ain't never fished like this, Sara." He worked his pole in short yanks.

"Just let the worm drag along the bottom. The trout will find it themselves."

Jimmy gave a hard yank on the pole and came up empty when he reeled in the hook.

"It done got away." Jimmy tossed the rod down on the floor beside the dog.

"You're giving up so easy?"

"Not givin' up. I just don't remember how to fish anymore."

"Sure, you do. It's just a different kind of fish. Look at your hook. See how it's bent. Just give a little tap when you feel a bite, and you'll catch 'um. Here, take this pole. It's all ready to fish." She handed him a rod and reel like the one he had stolen from her boat.

"Go ahead. It's all baited and ready. Throw it out toward the bank." Jimmy's cast landed halfway to the bank. Before the bait hit bottom, his rod was bent and surging against the pull of a hooked trout. Right then, the boy bought into the fun of trout fishing. He stood in the boat reeling the line and working the fish up from the bottom.

"Get it up to the side, and I'll get the net on it." Sara reached out with a six-foot-long handled net, ready to snag the fish.

"Let me get him. I ain't stupid 'bout fishin'." Jimmy played the fish until it slowed its fighting and came up alongside the boat. He reached with his hand to grab the fish around its body. The trout would have no part of that. It jerked the rod from Jimmy's hand and swam off dragging the rod.

"No! Jimmy. Let it go!"

It was too late. Jimmy jumped in the water and grabbed the rod in his hand. Blue jumped over the bow of the boat and belly flopped right alongside the boy. Sara reached to help him, but the boat was drifting too fast. She rushed and started the motor. Jimmy was bobbing along in the swift current getting drug downstream toward her. She steered the boat alongside him.

"Grab the boat, Jimmy. Grab the boat!" Jimmy reached and got ahold of the boat's side with one hand. He was holding the fishing rod over his head with the other. Blue was dog paddling downstream right behind the boy.

"I still got him, Miss Sara. I got him."

Sara killed the motor. She reached, got him by the lifejacket, and rolled him into the boat. Blue came up alongside and looked like he was more than ready to end his swim also. Sara grabbed his collar, and the dog got its front legs over the edge of the boat. Another jump and it was in the boat. The shaking dog gave Jimmy another bath. He was reeling again and reaching to grab the fish again. It was too late for that. Sara's net went under the tired fish and swept it up in the air and into the boat.

"There. That was one hard fish to catch, Jimmy."

"But we got the son-of-a-bitch, Miss Sara!" Jimmy took the hook out of the fish's mouth. Sara showed him where to drop it into the boat's live well.

"Maybe let's call it something else okay?"

"Oops, I'm sorry. It was just something my dad taught me to say."

Sara saw a break, a chance to talk to the boy about his mom and dad and what she had in mind for him. She started the motor again and this time beached the boat on a gravel bar island. Blue hit the gravel first.

"Let's get you dried off, and we can have some treats I brought for us. Gather up some dead limbs, and I'll get a fire started."

Jimmy was quick to collect enough dry limbs and branches to make a small fire. Sara got the charcoal lighter fluid out of the boat her dad always carried to quickly get a fire started. She poured it on the wood.

"Back up, way back, Jimmy," she said and tossed a match into the wood pile. The whoosh and flash of the explosion scared Sara. Jimmy screamed and fell on his back. He turned and huddled up with his legs pulled tight against his chest.

"Make the screaming stop, make it stop." He was beating on his ears with both his hands.

The screams and the fire from the rocket hitting the Humvee grabbed her mind. Then she willed it away. "Jimmy! It's Sara. Look at me. I shouldn't have done that to start the fire. We should have lit it with your knife and flint like you did on the mountain. Jimmy. I'm so sorry."

She knelt beside the boy and pulled him to her, giving him the shelter she wished she'd had when her terrors returned. She stayed right next to him. He didn't relax until Blue returned. Blue huddled in close to the boy and licked his arm. Sara understood all too well the dog's intervention. Jimmy looked up, unsure of what had just happened.

"I heard my mother scream."

"I'm sorry, Jimmy. That had to be terrible to hear your mother."

"I seen her in my dreams. She's burning up in the trailer." He reached for Sara and put both his arms around her waist. She was surprised he wasn't crying by now.

"Do you wake up when you have the dreams?"

"Sometimes I do. Miss Marty comes and shakes me awake, I think. She gives me a hug, and sometimes I don't have to cry then."

What he just told her rattled her. She tried to remember what the V.A. doctors had told her to do. Nothing they said helped with her own nightmare until the V.A. put her on meds. She reached deep trying to think of what to say to help Jimmy. She came up with nothing. All she could do was hug the boy and tell him he was safe now. She was certain that Jimmy needed a lot more help then she could offer. She got a spare coat out of the boat and slipped it over Jimmy's shoulders. They sat not talking with Sara rubbing his shoulders to warm him up. After a few minutes she could tell Jimmy was getting restless.

"Come on, boy, let's catch some more trout." She led the way to the boat, got Jimmy seated with Blue beside him, and then shoved off the gravel bar. "Jimmy, promise me you'll stay in this boat."

"That water's a whole lot colder than I've ever been in before."

"Current's faster too. Makes it easy to drown."

They stayed on the river until Jimmy caught three more trout. She could tell he was getting tired and still cold from being in the water. With their dock close by, she steered the boat into its slip. With the four trout cleaned and the lifejackets hung over the back of the boat's seats, she took Jimmy and Blue to her cabin.

Her dad had the door open for them. "Come in. Somebody looks like they've been for a swim."

"Jimmy was determined not to lose a fish."

"I got 'um all right."

"There's a little fire going in the woodstove. Sit over here, Jimmy," John said, pulling a chair over next to the stove. Jimmy took a place next to the stove. Blue came over and laid next to the boy.

Jimmy was quick to say, "This warm feels really good."

After a few minutes at the sink, Sara had Jimmy's catch on ice in a small cooler and ready for him to take them to Marty's.

With a hearty lunch over, Sara loaded the boy and his dog into the truck, and took them back to the horse ranch.

They pulled up in front of the barn. "Miss Sara, how much longer am I going to stay here with the horses?"

"Aren't you happy here, Jimmy?"

"Ya, it's fine, and Marty can really cook, but it's just I like being with you."

Sara choked up for a moment before she could speak. "I want us to be able to do more together, Jimmy."

"I'd like that!"

"We need to go and see your grandmother and see what she has to say about us spending more time together. Would you go with me to see her?"

"She wrote me another letter saying for me to come see her."

"Okay. I'll plan for us to go on a Saturday when you don't have school."

"I like school here, Miss Sara. The kids don't know about my dad cookin' and all."

"That's good. You study real hard, okay? I'll come over if you need any help with homework."

Jimmy gave Sara a hug. Blue leaned over and got a really good lick in on her forehead for good measure.

"Bye, Miss Sara."

The boy and dog both jumped out of the truck. Sara watched Jimmy waving as she drove off. She felt elated Jimmy had told her he wanted to spend more time with her, and she was working to keep the promise she made to herself to keep him out of the foster care system. Being around the boy made her feel her life as a soldier had slipped away for a while, and she could feel human with her new purpose in life to help Jimmy.

thirty-five

WITH A WEEKDAY WITHOUT A guide trip, Sara loaded the jon boat to go fish the catch-and-release area just south of the trout dock. She loved to preplan where she might take her clients. She remembered seeing a long slab of rock on the bed of the river where she felt certain the large trout might hide.

When she passed the first of the big new houses along the river, she saw the black Dodge sitting along the bluff. The sheriff's information that Hector Ruiz had left the area didn't jibe with the black car still being around and watching her. Now she felt sure Ruiz was having someone watch and torment her. She didn't like the odds of facing Ruiz on his turf along the road.

A mile down the river, there the Dodge was again. It sat pulled down into a boat ramp. The telltale exhaust smoke told her the engine was idling. Now this was *her* turf.

Sara passed the car and went into a narrow channel cut off from view by an island covered with willow trees. She quickly beached the boat and grabbed the old baseball bat her dad had tethered under the front seat. She reached in her boot and felt the assurance of the pistol holstered there. Running through the brush, she came out just behind the black Dodge. The tinted windows offered no hint of what awaited her. With little regard for the danger, she squat-walked to the driver's side of the car, stood, and smashed the window. The scream she heard came from the woman in the driver's seat.

"What the hell are you doing following me?" Sara pointed the bat at the woman's face.

A flurry of what Sara felt sure were Spanish cuss words were spit in her face, then in English she said, "Why you do that?"

"Get out of the car."

The woman got out and went to stand at the rear bumper carrying a tire iron in one hand and an open cell phone in the other.

"Stay there," Sara commanded. She slipped into the driver seat and set the car into neutral, rolling down the ramp, and stopped half-covered with water.

The woman stopped waving the tire iron. It hung limp in her hand. "Ruiz is going to kill us both."

"Why've you been following me? What does Ruiz want with me?" She held the bat across her waist with the end resting on her left hand. She patted her hand with a slow rhythm.

The woman let the tire iron slide out of her hand onto the ground. She smiled at Sara.

"Are you laughing at me? This isn't funny, woman." She took a step toward.

"You calm down. Ruiz isn't going to hurt you."

She got even closer. "Not after I take you to the sheriff and they find him."

"No sheriff. They come for me."

"Who's coming?" Sara stepped to the side and looked at the bluff road coming from town.

"Ruiz said you one crazy ass bitch, and he wants you in his crew. I've been watching you for him. I'm his, how you say, recruiter."

"Recruiter? For what *crew?* Tell him I said to go to hell." Sara pulled her Black Widow pistol out of her boot. "If this happens again, I'm going shoot somebody."

"You'll find out when he's ready. You really are one crazy bitch." Another black Dodge skidded to a stop at the top of the ramp. The woman ran to the car and disappeared into an open back door. She lowered her pistol when she saw the AR-15 pointed at her out of the passenger side of the car.

Neither of the men in the front seat was Ruiz. They were both laughing at her. The blacked-out license plates on the car offered no clue to who owned them. She opened her phone to call the sheriff, then closed it. She didn't want it known she had run the car into the river.

She ran for the willow trees and the narrow channel where she had left her boat. She needed to find Luke and tell him she had done something really stupid.

She was a half-mile from the trout dock when she cut the boats engine and hit Luke's speed dial number. She waited through four rings and started to close the top of her phone. She heard him answer.

In a panic, she said, "Where are you?"

"Gwen and I are down river about three miles. Somebody drove a Dodge into the river down here. The window's been broken out. We're checking if the driver went into the river and drowned."

Shit.

"The driver left in another car. I saw it. I'll be waiting at the Cotter Dock when you finish. We need to talk. Privately."

"Privately?"

"Yes, hurry."

SHE PACED AROUND A WOODEN bench in the city park waiting for him. She had the feeling another war had started in her world, and it could surround her. The word from the woman's mouth, "recruiter," spun in her brain as she tried to tie it down with Ruiz, the cartel, and her being followed for weeks. She found no connection that jibed with him thinking she was a "crazy bitch."

What crew? It didn't make sense that his recruiter had followed her.

She heard the Commission's airboat pull into the dock and then leave. She needed Luke. He came rushing across the gravel driveway to her.

"Gwen had to go on another call."

She stood and wrapped her arms around him, kissed him, and then her words blurted out. "Damn, I really don't know what just happened down there on the river."

"Slow down and tell me." He gave her a hug back and then eased her to his arm's length. "You look pale. Are you okay?"

"Can we sit down first?" She pulled away and went for the board seat on the picnic table. "This has to stay between us."

She reached for his hand and gave it a tug for him to sit beside her. He continued to stand with his hand on her shoulder. She started by telling him how the driver of the black car had acted differently than when she had seen it before, that it had come down the boat ramp, closer to her than ever before. She felt certain they wanted to confront her.

"I was tired of the car following me. I broke the fucking window out on a woman. Then I drove the car in the river. The woman stood looking at me holding a tire iron and a cell phone."

"*You* put the car in the river? I wondered why you didn't call the sheriff."

"She works for Ruiz and told me he wanted to recruit me because I'm one crazy-ass bitch."

Luke took a seat alongside at the table. "There's some commission actions going on that I'm not allowed to talk about. Here's what I can tell you. Ruiz is recruiting non-Hispanic women."

"What the hell?"

"He pays them big money and puts them in nice cars so they can run drugs for him up through Texas and Arkansas. No one notices them."

"And he wants me for that?" She gave him a hard stare.

"He may have wanted you to head up his women drivers."

"Who knows about this?"

"I can't tell you any more except the DEA has been called in and is working with some undercover commission agents to stop him."

"What do I do now? I told the woman if anything happened again, I was going to shoot somebody."

"That won't make any difference to that bunch. From what you told me, he may give up on you."

"Are you going to call the sheriff about me and the car?"

"Hell, no. The car is leaking oil into the river, and you don't want to be on the hook for that."

"I'm sorry for that."

With a strong assurance from Luke that he wasn't going to share her story with anyone, they walked together to her jon boat. She kissed him, pushed the boat off from the dock, and headed down river to the cabin. When she passed the ramp where she had the run in, the car was gone. The ramp was wet where a wrecker must have towed it out of the water. She promised herself John would never know about what happened.

thirty-six

LUKE HADN'T TOLD HER WHERE they were going, only to dress for hiking. He picked her up in a green official Arkansas Commission truck with an ATV loaded in the back. He said they were headed north toward the Missouri border on Commission business. Luke said he had been filling in for other agents and working calls all across northern Arkansas.

"Damn, it's great having a tall brunette riding along with me. I'm sorry you can't sit over here right next to me like all the country boys and girls do in these parts." Luke put his hand on her leg.

"Do that some more and you might have me on your lap," Sara put her hand on his and gave it a squeeze. "Only thing we're missing is a really old pickup truck with a gun rack in the back window, and—oh, yes, a Confederate Battle flag flying just behind the cab."

"Sounds like you've got the country boys around here figured out." He rolled down the truck window and stuck his elbow out.

"Not all of them. I've never heard you mention sides with either the north or south."

"My parents moved to Arkansas from Iowa a long time ago. They never tolerated racism in our house."

"I thought my dad was a racist for a long time. I would hear him talking to mom about seeing an out of place black person in town, only he didn't call them black. But when he came home from 'Nam, I never heard him use the 'N' word again. I think he fought with a lot of black marines and learned to respect them. Are you ever going to tell me where we're headed?"

"We do a lot of public relations calls these days. It helps to tamp down little problems before they get too big. We're going to meet a farmer who has a lot of his garden and crops rooted up by feral pigs. He's asking us to bring traps up and kill off the big herd he says he keeps seeing."

"I saw some of the damage they cause. Our neighbor has been shooting them. Hope it's legal. We had some really great pork chops a while back from one he butchered."

"It's legal, but setting traps and catching the whole sounder does a lot better."

"Sounder is a pig?"

"Whole herd of them. Shooting one just makes them scatter, and it's harder to get them in a trap later on."

TWO BLACK LABS GREETED LUKE'S truck when he pulled in the farm driveway. Both of the dogs walked slowly to stand in front of the truck.

Sara grabbed Luke's arm. "I need to pet those boys really bad."

"I think those boys are girls. They look really friendly. Go ahead."

Sara jumped out of the truck and dropped to her knees with one dog on each side of her. Trying to hug one was nearly impossible, the other would keep pushing to get in on the action with her. The two excited animals quickly pushed Sara off her knees and started licking her face. When Luke walked up, she was trying her best to shield her face and laugh without opening her mouth.

"I didn't know you loved dogs so much." He knelt on one knee and quickly had one of the labs halfway in his lap. Sara sat up, and the other lab leaned against her side. She had her arm wrapped tightly around the animal and her head on its shoulder. She started to cry.

"Are you hurt?" He reached for the other dog's collar.

"No, it's just memories of Tank, my K-9 partner in Iraq. We lived together all my second tour. He was killed the day we got shot to hell. I loved that dog."

"I'm sorry, Sara."

"He protected me when I walked guard duty. I knew he would give his life for me. He did." She gave the dog a last hug and stood up turning away from Luke to wipe her eyes.

"Hey, you girls! Leave those folks alone," the farmer called out, walking over to greet them.

"Mister Murphy, hello. I'm Agent Matthews. We talked about coming up and seeing what could be done with your feral pig problem."

"I'm glad you could finally make it. You folks come along. We'll head over back of the barn to our garden."

Luke stopped at the edge of the garden and took out his cell phone to take several pictures of the rooted-up ground and plants.

"Looks like you have a big sounder of swine tearing up things."

The farmer pointed to a field of prairie grass. "They come out of the grass most anytime they like now. One of the hogs chased my dogs nearly back to the barn Saturday. Go on girls, get back to the house!" Both of the dogs turned and went only a few feet before deciding to sit and watch.

"If you don't mind, I think Sara and I will walk through the prairie grass and see where we might set a trap for them."

"Nope, fine by me. By the way, just across the grass is the Missouri border. My place sits right on the damn line. Make me pay taxes in both damn places."

"How far out in the field is the state line?"

"Survey showed it right on the other side of the grass field."

"We'll see if there's a place we can set a trap without getting into Missouri's territory," Luke headed toward the six-foot-tall prairie grass field.

"That grass is taller than I am, babe." Sara followed behind Luke as he parted the grass with his hands and pushed into it. After five minutes of pushing grass aside, they were still faced with more grass.

"Stand still. I've been hearing some grunts. I think the pigs are coming into the grass. I'm going to yell and scare them out."

"Too late. I've got a little pig right by my foot."

"Shit. Don't touch it. I think they're all in front of us," Luke pulled out his service pistol. "Move up tight behind me. No matter what I do, when the pigs realize we're here, it's going to get crazy. Start walking back real slow."

Taking two steps, they both realized the grunts and squeals were louder.

"They know we're here."

"Is this like walking into a nest of copperheads?" Sara whispered.

"Never been in that, either. I'm going to fire up in the air. Be ready to run. Here goes."

The shot touched off a wild storm of hogs racing away from them. Except for one sow looking for the little pig now squealing and trying to find its mother. The running sow bumped into Luke's legs and knocked him off his feet on top of the screaming piglet.

"Damn it!" Sara saw the sow turn and come back for Luke. She jammed her foot into it's side. It wasn't enough to stop the runaway freight train, but it was enough to deflect the direction of it's charge just a bit. "Shoot it!"

Luke rotated on his knees, sprang to his feet, and pulled the trigger. The single slug hit the sow between the eyes, and she dropped at his feet.

"Come on. I've got to see where the hogs are going back in the woods."

He grabbed Sara's hand and pulled her, and they headed for the Missouri side of the field. When they busted out on the other side, they saw the pigs coming out of a shallow draw, headed for the Missouri timber.

Luke stood with his hands on his hips, trying to catch his breath. "This'll be where we set the trap for them."

"You aren't going to say a word about what happened back there, are you? That scared the shit out of me."

"You saved me from getting bit by that sow. Do you always move so fast?"

"I do when it happens so fast you don't have time to think about it." She smiled and took his arm.

"You're smiling."

"Let's just say the memory of my own battles have started to fade and not haunt me at every crazy crisis."

"I'm glad." He turned her, and their lips meet in a promise for more soon. "Welcome to the everyday life of a Wildlife Agent, Miss Randolph."

"I like it, Officer Matthews. I like it."

Mr. Murphy stood waiting for them at the edge of his garden when they pushed their way out of the prairie grass. When the farmer said he would like to take the pig to get butchered, Luke unloaded the ATV from the back of the pickup. With Sara's help, they loaded the two-hundred-pound sow on the back of the ATV and then back to farmer's pickup.

After a thank you from the farmer, Luke promised he would be back with a half-dozen agents and a hog pen trap. They loaded the ATV back in the truck and left.

"I'm proud of you, Sara. The sow would have made a mess of my leg. She was out for blood."

"What about the baby? Will it starve?"

"It's probably sucking teat on another sow right now. The pigs share duties raising young."

"Oh. I didn't know that." She slid in next to him and laid her head against his shoulder. "Is this okay?"

"Can you get closer?"

"Before I do, there's something I've got to tell you." She had been holding off telling him until just the right time. She knew her recent decision could be life changing for both of them.

"Yeah?"

"I really like the life you have as a Conservation Agent."

"You mean chasing pigs and all?" He laughed and tried to pull her a little closer.

"Well that, too. Anyway, I need to tell you this." She leaned away.

"Go on, please." He gave up on getting her closer. She had pulled away and sat with her back to the passenger door of the truck. "That serious?"

"Yes. I applied to the Arkansas Commission to take their tests to become a Wildlife Officer."

A short pause. "That's great. I've thought for a while you might just want to do that."

"Whew! I'm glad to hear you say that."

"You thought I wouldn't like the idea?"

"This position is so life-changing. It's not like an everyday job. I see it's such a large part of anyone's life that signs on to it. I didn't want you to feel like I'm butting into a career you love."

"I'm excited for you. I wanted to ask you a while back if you might consider doing exactly this. Your Military Police background and love of nature makes you a natural for the commission."

She scooted across the truck seat to his side and gave him a hug and a kiss on the cheek.

"Have you heard when you go for the interview and testing?"

She pulled back a little from his side again. "Not yet. Luke, don't do anything to help with this. Don't talk to anybody you know there. If I can't get in on my own, then forget it."

"I won't. I promise. I can help you get ready for the test."

"No thank you, sir. This is mine to do."

"I knew you would say that."

She squeezed his arm, feeling a little bit apprehensive her application may not make muster. She had heard how tough the commission was on sorting through the hundreds of men and women applying for the position. However, it would turn out she had set the goal, and reaching it had to be totally in her court. She had remembered the easy promotions that came in Iraq when she slept with her superior officer. It made her sad. It would never happen again.

thirty-seven

WITH THE MORNING TO SPARE, Sara headed down the river to the shooting scene. She cruised along the bank and behind a small island where the stream split into two parts. Halfway through the split waterway she found a small creek branch entering the river and hidden by trees. The branch was so hidden no one had found it on the sheriff's trip there. She slowly guided the jon boat into the branch and stopped before stepping over the bow to wade and tie the boat to a tree. A few yards up the branch, she found what she had been looking for. The clear imprint of the front of a jon boat. Footprints in the bank showed where someone had struggled to climb the steep bank. She took pictures of the tracks and then scrambled up the bank. The tracks and the type of rifle used had given her good clues to believe a local person had shot at her.

The muddy tracks at the top led right to the spot the shooter stood in the trees waiting for her. She spotted the dent in the mud where the shooter had placed his elbow to steady the rifle and laid down with her elbow in the same location. She imagined the rifle and looked through the scope. She pulled the trigger. Bang. She pledged to find the shooter. Sara had seen enough. She went back to the hill leading into the creek branch and started down the slope. Holding on to a willow branch, her hand slipped, and she slid the rest of the way down the mud bank on her butt. Her foot caught in one of the deep footprints she had found and tore the mud away. A piece of cloth stuck out of the mud. She had found a worn dirty glove. The reeking smell of pig-shit coming off the glove gave her the last clue she needed as to who had shot at her.

AN HOUR AFTER DARK, SHE drove up the backroad the folks at the dock said led to Red's place. She pulled up with the truck lights shining on the front of the cabin. The smell of the place blowing through the truck window made her almost sick to her stomach. A dirt path led to the steps to the porch. Only the top and bottom boards remained with an open space between them to step over. A single light bulb hung from a chord in the middle of a cracked window and did little to light the inside of the room behind it. Glimmers from the light came through two places in the log cabin's chinking. The front side of the cabin sat tilted, the foundation of large rocks supporting the cabin floor leaned dangerously. The live moss on the wood thatched roof glowed green in the truck lights.

A woman looking more weathered than the cabin itself stood on the porch with her hand shading her eyes from the truck's headlights. The woman came down the two steps, lunging forward at the bottom and catching herself against the railroad tie gate post. One side of the gate still hung from the post—the split pieces of the other side lay scattered across the dirt path.

Sara patted her pistol in the leg holster before getting out. She felt good about it being there. The old woman's gray hair hung around her emaciated face and over her stooping shoulders. Her faded pink dress hung straight across a flat chest and gaunt stomach to the tops of her feet. She hadn't seen someone look this hungry since Iraq.

"Hello, I'm looking for Red, the guide over at the trout dock. Is he here?"

"Good Lord, what's he gone and done now?"

"I just need to talk to him about something."

"Are you that guide woman he's been talking to himself about?"

"I'm afraid I am. I'm Sara." Now she began to feel certain she had stepped into something too deep for her to handle. "Are you his wife?"

"If you even want to call it that, I'm his wife. He paid my daddy for me. Took me to a preacher before he brung me out here. I was fifteen. Been here forty years. Don't know why I stayed, 'cept things were worse at home with Daddy coming in to tell me goodnight."

"Oh, my. That's terrible."

"I'm sorry I sprung all that talk on you, Miss Sara."

"It's all right I can be a good listener. I didn't see his truck when I drove up. Is he home?"

"Ain't home. He takes off to a whorehouse over in the next county when he's had a bad day on the river and spends his earnins. He calls it vistin'. My name's Annie."

"Annie, he had me in his rifle sights. He shot out my engine and then kept shooting at my boat and me. I jumped in the water to get away. I thought he was trying to kill me."

"I heard him mumbling about scarin' somebody."

"Well, he sure as hell did that."

"He took his old deer rifle and had them put one of them scope things on it about a month ago. I'm sorry if he shot at you."

"He's had it out for me for some time now. Since I let him know he couldn't push me around."

"I've tried doing that, but it don't never work," Annie said, kicking at the squealing pigs nosing at her ankles. "A damn feral sow came in here lame leading a bunch of them little pigs. She was looking for something to eat after the herd must have ran her off. She died last week, and now he has to bring home slop from the restaurants in town to feed 'um."

"Is his deer rifle in the house?"

"Is he gonna have to go to jail?"

"I don't know yet. Could you help me by bringing the rifle here, please?"

Sara watched as Annie reached to hold a porch support as she climbed over the open space in the steps. She turned the cabin doorknob and leaned with her shoulder against the sticking door to get it open. Sara knew she only had seconds to think about what to do with the rifle. Taking it to the Sheriff would get a dangerous idiot off the river. She didn't know what the man would do next. She had to think quickly. Annie returned to the top of the steps and held out the rifle to Sara before coming down the steps.

"He's gonna go to jail, ain't he?"

"When he gets home, tell him I found his glove out at the shooting site and got pictures of his boot prints. I knew the glove was his—it smelled just like he does all the time."

"His pig-shit smell, ain't that right?"

"Well, I wasn't going to say, but yes, pig-shit. The Sheriff got his DNA and a fingerprint on the cartridge. The sheriff doesn't know it's Red's print."

Hanging her head, "That ain't Red's fingerprint. It's mine. I was gonna shoot the old son of a bitch last week and loaded the gun to get ready."

"I guess he just got lucky you didn't shoot him."

"I'll be lucky if he don't go to jail. At least 'til he gets these pigs ready to butcher."

Sara knelt on the ground holding the rife while she loosened the screws holding the new scope. When the last screw came loose, she took the scope and threw it on the rock driveway and then stomped it until it bent and cracked. It made her feel good that Red would not be using it to shoot at her again. She handed the rifle back to Annie.

"I know you probably need this rifle to hunt for food. Let Red know I busted his scope into little pieces, so he doesn't blame you."

"I'll put the pieces on his dinner plate when I tell him you was here."

"Is there anything I can bring you? Anything you need?"

"Nope. Unless you got a good man tied up somewhere that would like a wore out hag like me."

Sara touched the old woman's shoulder. "I'll keep watch for one, Annie. Send word if you need help. Either me or my dad will come."

The truck lights lit the portrait of the woman's face. It captured the rounded and sunken lips no longer supported by teeth. But when the woman lifted her hand over her brow, Sara saw her eyes. Beautiful eyes with brilliant green around the iris. Eyes that were almost lost in a forest of wrinkles and frowns. Sara saw the pain and misery buried there deep behind those eyes. Then Sara remembered seeing the same green eyes before.

"Annie, does your son ever come to see you?"

"How did you know 'bout my son?"

"Milton told me Red was his father. I had been talking with him about getting married, and he just let it out."

"My old son-of-a-bitch man don't claim our boy no more. Milton beat the crap out of him over something he done to me. Red ran him off for good that night. I've only seen him a couple times since. He sneaks out here when Red's on a visitin' trip."

"He's a good boy. I'm sorry his dad treated him that way. When Red gets home, hold off on shooting him, Annie."

"I 'spect if he shoots at you again, you'll do that for me?" Annie said.

"No. I don't think he'll be doing any shooting when he finds out I know who it was."

"Good. He goes to jail, I'm hopin' my boy can come home."

Sara left the woman leaning against the broken gate with her hand still shading those beautiful eyes. She waved once and then turned and went slowly up the steps. Sara watched as the frail woman leaned and pushed hard again against the cabin door. And then Annie was gone into the place she thought of as home.

thirty-eight

THE OLD STAINED OAK SLATS of the fish cleaning table were often left baptized with slime and fish entrails. A galvanized slide turned brackish and green graced the back of the table and provided a scoop to push the fish leavings out to nature and the bottom feeders of the river. Sara remembered telling her father if anything happened to her in Iraq to spread her ashes out to the balance of nature. She chuckled as she thought of the gross site in front of her and where her own balance of nature would be.

Sara set the bucket of trout on the floor of the dock and reached for the handle of the cracked red cistern pump. She seldom used the pump, so she didn't have to prime it. Two strokes on the pump handle today brought the clear river water splashing across the dirty cleaning table. She swept the slime other guides left into the scoop with the back of her fileting knife before reaching for the first of ten trout she needed to clean for her customers.

The stripped string of guts and a small bundle of roe slid through the scoop and into the river where the chase began for first dibs on the leavings—the bottom feeders were at work. Sara finished cleaning the last fish, brushing the slime across the table and into the scoop. Reaching below the table, she picked up the Billy club she had borrowed from her dad's truck. Knowing a showdown with Red would happen soon, she had been carrying it for protection. With the club in one hand and the fish bucket in the other, she started up the steps to the trout dock.

The hunk of red beard and pig-stinking boots stood blocking the top rung of the steps. Sara stopped halfway up and set the bucket of trout on the steps before she reached into her boot for the security she always carried hidden there. She touched the minnow tattoo with her left index finger for good luck and slipped the pistol in her pocket. She stepped off the boards to the dirt hill side, ready. No way did she intend to ever have another adversary to fight that was above her like the Iraq ambush she couldn't forget and came on her last day in theater. She climbed the hill and walked around Red to face him. She hoped she could stare past the beard and find the bird-shot eyes hiding, sunken in the whisky burnt face. This needed to be eye-to-eye if it were to end.

Tall enough to look down on the man, Sara took a deep breath and wedged forward into his space. "You stink like pig shit, man," she said, about to retch at his smell.

He pointed at the club in her hand. "That there ain't going to stop me."

"Well!" Sara jammed the end of the club with all of her strength into Red's belly.

He fell on his knees, holding his belly and gasping to get a breath.

"I'm gonna... beat the hell out of you, woman."

"No, you're not. I've got the pictures of your footprints and glove I found hid away ready to go to the sheriff. What you did out there on the river shooting at me is going to land you in jail for a hell of a long time."

"I was just trying to scare you."

"Let's see if this scares you, pig shit." Sara had her Black Widow pistol twelve inches away from Red's head and pointed between his eyes. "Let me hear you say you're sorry."

"Ain't gonna say it. You done got me run out of my own house. She took two shots at me with my rifle as I was running."

"She must not be a very good shot. You're still standing. Been me, you wouldn't have a dick left for all that visitin' you've been doing on her."

"Put that nasty lookin' pistol away, and maybe I can say something."

Sara lowered the pistol a bit. "Go ahead. I'm waiting."

"I'm sor—"

With the pistol back between his eyes, she said, "Damn it. Say it loud, and you better ass mean it."

"I'm sorry! There. You be one mean woman."

thirty-nine

SARA WAS WORN OUT FROM HER run-in with Red. She took the late afternoon time to relax on the cabin's back deck and wait for Luke. A pair of young eagles on a cottonwood just across the river from the cabin caught her attention. Only half of the sun remained above the horizon, and she thought the eagles were roosted for the night, but then a flash of a white head and a *whoosh* of six-foot wings just above the water grabbed her attention. The eagle's day wasn't over yet. Talons crashing into the water's surface, it hooked the unlucky trout trying for a late day meal of its own. The eagle rose with the captured fish, then turned away from the young eagle's tree. It flew to a separate tree, landed, and began feeding itself.

Sara couldn't wait to tell Luke about the lesson the young eagles had been taught. She was sure the parent was saying, *it's time, children. Time to fend for yourselves.* The eagles reminded her of Jimmy's running away. Where would he go if he did it again? It may have been time for the young eagles to fledge and leave their nest, but it wasn't for the young boy she worried about.

"Are you sitting out here waiting for Luke?" Her dad came out of the cabin with two frosty bottles of beer and passed one to her. He sat down in the old white chair beside her.

"I just watched an eagle teach her juvenile offspring a lesson. Two are in a tree across the river."

"I think the young eagles have been roosting there for about a week. Their nest is upstream from here."

"Dad, you know it's strange what I thought about while walking guard duty in Iraq. Thinking of the eagle, our symbol of freedom, was sometimes the only thing that kept me sane. I would try to remember all the times we watched them here along the river. My memory of them flying low above the water for a strike always made me feel better."

"They sure are good parents." He pointed to the eagle flying a few feet above the water. "The female's making a last pass and heading for her roost."

"It still makes me shiver when I see them fly. I missed this so much while I was gone."

"When I went out on the river alone, I felt the darn river missed you too."

She leaned over and gave her dad a little hug. "That's so sweet, coming from an old ex-marine."

"The marine thing never wears off. Getting old just sweetens it up a bit."

"Love you, Pops." She turned her chair toward him and gave him a peck on the cheek. "You sound happy. Is that the truth?"

"Yes. I'm happy you're home, Minnow. Happy we're sitting here like your mother and I used to do. You're a lot like her. She always wanted me to tell the truth about things. Sometimes I hid things like what happened in 'Nam."

"I guess I am like her in the ways that keep bothering you. You need to tell me what your doctor is saying."

"I talked myself right into this trap, didn't I."

"Tell me."

"I came out fine from all his tests. He said my stopping smoking and drinking years back did a lot to help my health. Only thing he wants me to be careful of infections and let him know if I get one."

"Did he say why?"

"He thinks it's leftover problems from the damn jungle rot and crap I went through."

"I'm sorry, Dad."

"Don't be. I've got buddies a whole lot worse."

"That reminds me, I've got to write my old sarge, O'Dell. He pulled me out of the Humvee when we got hit."

"I haven't heard you mention Iraq for weeks now. Are you able to stay away from the flashbacks like you were having?"

"They haven't stopped—it's only that I can control how intense they get."

"I know you're getting around to talking to me about the boy."

"Pretty savvy for an old fellow, aren't you? Well, would you want a new face in our family?"

"He needs a family. I think it would be good for me to have him around to hang out with. From what you say, he's a heck of a good outdoorsman."

"Before we go on about this, I have to tell you a little secret I've been keeping. I've applied to the Arkansas Wildlife Commission to become a Wildlife Agent."

"Well, now. That's stepping up some, Minnow." John sat up in his seat and offered her a high five. Their hands clapped together.

"I know. Applying doesn't mean I'll be accepted. Luke has said only a few out of a hundred applications get in."

"They need agents like you, Minnow. Look at your background."

"I know. We'll just have to see how the testing goes."

"Did you tell me this because of Jimmy?"

"Yes, if I'm accepted, I'd likely be away for days. Leaving you to take care of him."

"I'll not only take care of him, but if we can adopt him, it's going to have to be me, especially with you gone. I think I can be a father he could look up to."

"Is that why you have been spending so much time with him?"

"We both like to talk to each other. Darn boy knows as much as I do about hunting and fishin'."

"You can teach him some life lessons he might never have gotten at home."

"Yes. We both know what PTSD is. We may not know how to treat it, but I'll know the times he's hurting most. I want to do this, Sara." John got up and picked up the two empty bottles.

"Wait." She stood and went to her Dad to give him a hug. "He may be a handful, you know."

"Oh, and you think you weren't?"

"Maybe a little?" Sara didn't hold back the tears that were getting her dad's shoulder wet.

"Easy, girl. Want another beer?"

"Nope, I'm okay just sitting here, Mister Randolph, sir."

"I'm going to take that boy fishing. We're going to go up the Buffalo and catch some smallmouth."

"Jimmy will be really happy."

"I'll go over tomorrow. Tell Luke howdy when he shows up." John patted her on the arm and went inside.

Sara touched the hot button on her phone for Luke and waited four rings before he answered.

"Hi! I just wanted to know if you're on the way."

"Hang on a second. I'm loading our boat back on the trailer. We just finished on a call for a sunk boat. I ended up in the water to save this guy and his buddy."

"You're okay?"

"I'm fine. Both the guys got stupid with their drag line and got their boat swamped and sunk."

"Whew! Dad and I noticed the river was up and flowing fast."

"It was a crazy day out there, lady."

"Why don't I meet you in town and save you a tired drive?"

"Are you sure? That would be great and give me a chance get some dry clothes on."

"I'm sure."

"Back to where we first met, okay?"

"Save a place for me if you get there first. I'll be on the way." She slipped her phone in her back pocket and opened the cabin door.

Sara started the truck and drove onto the gravel road. She slowed at the water crossing and, looking up, noticed Marty's husband had repaired the fence she had knocked down. Driving in the evening along a country road with very little traffic gave her a place to let loose with her truck. On the blacktop now, she held back waiting for the two-mile-long section that was ahead to come up. Clear of traffic, she floored the gas pedal. The truck's engine took the shock of getting a rare full throttle command with a loud cough and grunt and then accelerated toward six thousand rpm. Sara yelled with her hand out the window.

"Come on, damn it. I need the feel of the wind in my face." The speedometer swept past eighty-five headed for a hundred for sure. Out of the corner of her eye she caught the glint of the black cruiser sitting in a half-hidden driveway. The cloud of dust the cruiser's tires stirred up was almost as heavy as the black smoke from Sara's tires as she braked to slow down.

"Shit. Shit. *Shit.* I'm stupid as hell."

The cruiser's flashing red lights lit the inside of the truck's cab like a moment from a psychedelic dream. She wished it was. It surprised her the deputy was at her window so fast.

"I didn't have to run your plates, ma'am. I knew the truck when you passed by like a damn fool kid."

"I just blew it, didn't I?"

"You've been helping that kid you brought off the mountain, right?"

"Yes, but—"

"You can shut up now, Miss Randolph. I haven't radioed anything, and I don't plan to."

Sara got perfectly quiet.

"Do you plan another space launch like this again?"

Sara shook her head no.

"Now I want to hear you say it."

"Never again!"

As he walked away he said, "Tell Luke he owes me one."

"What's your name, Deputy?"

She got no answer and came to the realization there really isn't anything like small town life. She barely touched on five miles an hour over the speed limit the rest of the way to town. In spite of being stopped, she got to Bear's Bar and Grill before Luke. She parked and sat back in her seat to take a deep breath. All her thoughts about a relationship with Luke began spinning in her head. She wasn't sure how he would take to the idea of her dad and her taking in the boy to raise. She felt almost afraid to ask him the question directly. She felt certain she wanted much more of Luke in her life and didn't want to blow her chance. Just then, Luke's green conservation pickup pulled in beside her. They both left their trucks and met in front.

Luke gave her a hug.

"Sorry I stood you up at the cabin." He took her hand, leading toward the bar's door.

"Wait. There something that happened on the way here. I need to tell you about."

"Come on, Sara. Let's get a beer. That cat's already out of the bag, girl. I got a phone call a few minutes ago about talking to you about slowing down."

"Shit. I'm going to need more than a beer. Come on, you damn lawman."

Luke reached to open the door for her but retreated when the door swung wide open in front of him. Four men came out, and the last of the four stopped to hold the door for both Luke and Sara.

Sara went in first, then turned to thank the man. The man had stopped Luke, and they were talking softly, she thought in Spanish.

"Just a second, Sara." Again, he exchanged a few words with the man and then turned to follow her in the bar.

"Sorry. He's been helping me."

"I didn't know you spoke Spanish."

"My department has some interface with Hispanics. So, I had to learn to speak a little Spanish."

"*Compredo, señor!*"

"*Si.*" He led the way to a table in the middle of the bar.

"Can we get a booth? It'll be a little quieter for us to talk." She turned from the table and led Luke to the same booth where they had met.

"This must be serious. We're back to the same place we started." He slid into the booth beside her and leaned to get a kiss. The kiss came, but she held back on it a bit.

"What's wrong? Are you mad at me? Want me to sit over there?"

"No. Sit by me, but I'm starving, and I want to talk about Jimmy, too. I don't know which to do first."

"Can you hold onto your thoughts about the boy?"

"Barely," she said, reaching to replace the tap of a kiss with a meaningful one. "Go ahead, get the waitress. Let's order."

"Are you thinking pulled pork sandwich or ribs?" Luke asked, standing to go place the order.

"You choose and lots of steak fries. Get a tap for me. Please!"

"Done." He headed for the bar.

Sara wasn't sure where to start the conversation about John and her making a home for the boy. After all, her idea might not become a reality. Luke returned carrying two tall taps of what she was sure would be her favorite, Dos Equis. After setting the beers down, he took a seat across from her. His sitting across from her made Sara feel he was ready for a serious conversation about the boy. Suddenly the feeling of not having Luke in her life hit her.

She started the talk, "I want you to know what Dad and I are considering."

"You mean about the boy?"

"Yes, that and more. I don't want to complicate it for us. But—"

"I know you want to help Jimmy." He moved around the booth to her side.

"More than help him. Dad and I want to provide a home for him. Dad has applied to adopt Jimmy."

"Taking on a child with PTSD and bad memories might be more than your dad can handle."

"Memories and PTSD like I have."

"But you've told me you learned to control the bad memories."

"Oh, hell, I have to fight to keep the memories from coming back and swamping me. They don't ever completely go away."

"You don't let on. You're so much better now."

"I am. But I have to work at it to keep my head clear."

"Won't having someone around with those same problems make it even harder for you?"

"It won't. When I talk to Jimmy it helps me. I don't know yet if it helps him. I do know we'll need to get him professional help and not fall into the trap I fell into when I first came home without the help I needed."

"Just tell me how I can help. I want to get to know Jimmy, so I can help you and John raise him. Let's plan some things we can do together with him."

"Thank you for that. How about Silver Dollar City soon?"

"Amen to that!"

forty

SARA HAD PROMISED JIMMY AN early morning start for the trip to see his grandmother. She and John arrived at Marty's before the sun came up.

Sara saw him first coming out of the barn carrying a box. "He's coming out of the barn, Dad. Pull up anywhere."

"Okay."

She opened the door and slid out. "Good morning, Jimmy."

John touched the brim of his cap. "Hello, Jimmy."

"You going with us, too?" Jimmy leaned into the truck cab.

"I wanted to meet your grandmother. What's in the box?"

"It's a cake for her. Miss Marty baked it and let me put the frosting on. It sure was good."

Jimmy's grin had already told Sara that. "Well that was very nice of her." She took the cakebox and set it in the backseat of the truck. "Let's all sit up front, Jimmy. You sit in the middle."

Jimmy climbed in. "I told Miss Marty I wanted something to take."

"That cake will make your grandmother happy," Sara said.

Jimmy was dressed in a stiff pair of never washed blue jeans and a western shirt with snaps.

"You look like a cowboy in that shirt."

"It's my favorite shirt ever. She said I could wear it when I ride the paint horse again."

"We'll have to come see you ride that paint, son." With everyone buckled in, John turned out of the barn lot and headed for the curvy roads leading to

Western Arkansas. Sara waited until she felt the small talk was over before she was ready to tell Jimmy what she and her dad were planning.

"Jimmy, Dad's going with us so he and I can have a talk with your grandmother."

Jimmy turned to look at Sara. "'Bout me?"

"Yes, it's about you. We want to ask your grandmother's permission if you can come live with us."

"When can I come?"

"Soon we hope. We want to be sure you understand what we're doing."

Jimmy looked down before he spoke. "Would you... be like my mother and dad?"

Sara was stumped for a moment. "Sort of. Do you know what adoption means, Jimmy?"

"Would it be like when I adopted Blue?"

"Adopted Blue?"

"I adopted him from a man that was beating him."

John patted the boy on the arm. "Good for you."

"I stole him, and he never got to go back there."

Sara bit her lip and held back a smile. "I guess it's sort of like that. Only when you adopt someone it has to be done legal through a lawyer."

"So, my grandmother has to say it's okay?"

"It has to be okay with you *and* your grandmother, and she has to sign some papers."

"What if she could keep me like before?"

"I think she's too sick. I'm afraid she'll have to stay in the nursing home from now on."

"Then you get to steal me legal and all?"

Grinning, Sara said, "Only if you want that, Jimmy."

"I hope she signs them papers. I want to come live with both of you. Will I still get to go to the same school?"

"Yes, and it will give us a chance to talk about your friends and teachers at the end of the day, and we'll help you with your homework."

"My grandmother never used to talk to me much about school. She always wanted me to tell her what my dad was up to. She wanted to know stuff. Everything he did."

"Did you tell her, Jimmy?"

"I was afraid to tell. My dad would whip me if he found out."

Sara's follow-up question was cut off by their approaching turn. At the last second, she pointed. "There's the turn, Dad."

She gave Jimmy a reassuring smile, a silent promise they'd talk about this later. She would like to know more about Jimmy's father. She knew it would have to come with time.

Not much had changed since she had been there. At least the sign had been fixed and the weeds were cut along the driveway.

"People live in there?" John asked. "Damn, Sara. I would bring a mower if we were closer."

"I could help," Jimmy said.

"The women's ward isn't too bad, at least. They keep it up themselves."

"Somebody needs to speak up about this mess." John stopped the truck and got out. He started walking toward the men's ward.

Sara stood on the driveway with Jimmy at her side. "Over here, Dad. You really don't want to go in the men's ward. We can do that on another day. It'll just make you madder."

She led the way along the concrete walkway to the women's ward. Jimmy followed carrying the cakebox. John followed, still muttering about the poor upkeep of the nursing home.

No one met them at the front, so Sara headed down the hallway to Jimmy's grandmother's room.

John ran his hand along the hallway banister, and it got covered with the weeks of dust still on it. He paused for a moment in front of two framed pictures. The glass had been broken on both of them, and the photos of the man's and woman's faces had been covered with black marker ink. "Don't think the ladies like them very much."

Sara knocked on the open doorway and leaned in the room. "Hello, Missus Wilmore. Can we come in?"

"Yes, dear. Is my grandson with you?"

Jimmy slipped around her and was the first one in the room, proudly carrying the cakebox and laying it on his grandmother's lap. He stood waiting with obvious excitement.

"Well now. What's in this box?"

Jimmy grinned. "It's a cake. I even helped make it for you, Grandma."

"A cake for me? Open it up, Jimmy."

Jimmy took off the cakebox cover and proudly stood back a little from the bed. "See what I wrote on top? Miss Marty mixed up the red stuff for me. I got most of it on my fingers. It sure tastes good."

"It's beautiful, and you spelled my name almost right, 'Gradmother.' Thank you so much."

"It's cook-a-nut cake—I was sure you liked that best."

"I kind of remember coconut cake was your favorite, too, Jimmy."

"Yep!"

"Give me a hug, boy." Sally had both arms out to the boy. Jimmy made sure the hug was as short as possible. "Boy's always been bashful with his hugs."

"Sally, he's been wanting to see you."

"Boy, I fell and broke this here hip. Doctor, he doesn't know if it is ever gonna be right again."

"Is that why I can't be home with you?" Jimmy stood close by her bedside.

"Jimmy, I can't be at home to take care of you myself, boy."

"Are you sure, Grandma?"

"I'm afraid I won't be walkin' no more, son."

Jimmy sobbed and laid his head on her shoulder.

"Don't cry, son. I want you to spend some time with these folks. They'll take you hunting, and I bet fishin' all the time, won't you? This fine lady is going to bring you over to visit me often. Ain't you, Miss Sara?" Sally held her hand out for Sara to hold. Sally squeezed it hard and then let it go.

"Yes, I will for sure, Sally."

Sally's attention went back to the boy. She was holding him and whispering something in his ear.

Sara quietly spoke to her dad. "Let's give them some time alone."

John led the way down the hall until she caught up to him and took his arm. "It's gotta be sad for her I know. She got Jimmy away from his dad and now she won't be able to take care of him."

"I think she's doing her best to hold back. Breakin' down and all."

"I do, too. She's being strong for Jimmy."

"Times like this, I sure as hell need a smoke."

"Me, too, Dad."

He wiped off a wooden bench and offered her a seat. She sat close by him with her hand on his arm. "I'm proud of you for this. I only wish Mom could be here. I think she always wanted a son. She would have raised a boy with a fishing pole in one hand and a .22 rifle in the other to hunt squirrels."

"She almost raised you that way, Minnow."

"We'll make a good family for him."

"Hell, who knows what would happen to that boy if he got tossed out into some foster family."

"We can do better for him. I think as he gets a little older it will be important that he's had some professional help with how he lost his mother and father. We've got to do that for him."

"Girl, I know this adoption means me stepping up here. I'll be calling to get him the counseling he needs."

Jimmy came running from the ward. "Hey! Grandma said for you to come back in. She wants to cut the cake I brought."

"That mean me, too?" John asked.

Jimmy ran to him and pulled him up off the bench. "Come on. I say you, too."

They followed the boy down the hall. He paused in the doorway. Sara followed and stopped at the door to listen.

"Come in, John. Boy's been talking about you."

"Hello, ma'am. You've got a fine grandson here. I've gotten to know him when we were out on the river fishing."

"He ain't had nobody pay that much attention to him in long time."

"I've been planning some squirrel hunting for us when it's time."

"It's gonna surprise you, my boy here can shoot their eye out when he hunts squirrels. He said he was proud to be with a Marine soldier."

"Sara and I are proud... you would want us to be his folks."

"You all bring him back to see me. Hear?" Sally held her hand out to John. She took it and pulled him closer, then gave his hand a kiss. She rubbed his hand in the tears running down her cheek. "Them's real, mister. I love this boy. You know that, don't you?"

John reached and took her hand. "We'll love him, too."

"Miss Sara, come in. Bring Jimmy here." Both Sara and Jimmy went to her bedside. "If you can work it out to adopt this boy, all I have left to say is God bless you all for doin' this for Jimmy and me."

Sara leaned over and kissed Sally on the cheek. When she straightened up, her tears had blended on the bedsheet with the Sally's—a bond of her family to Jimmy's grandmother.

"Ain't somebody going to get some forks and plates? I want to share this cake my grandson brung. Holler down the hall for my friends to come."

It didn't take long for the entire cake to disappear when several other residents of the home showed up to join the celebration. With the cake gone and the paper plates cleaned up, Sara and John left Jimmy to say a private goodbye.

forty-one

THE LONG-PLANNED GUIDE TRIP for the Arkansas Game Commission came almost before the guides and the dock crews were ready for it. Rushing, they got the camp set up and ready downriver on the sandbar. After a great first day of fishing, eight jon boats with fishing rods sticking up along their gunwales like tree limbs rested on the sandbar, docked for the night. The guides would be hard at work at daybreak getting the rods ready for the new day on the river. New fishing line would have to be wound on many of the rods and reels, and others held the strong smell of all the fish caught that day. Lifejackets that had just come off the backs of the twenty men, women, and children along for the ride hung everywhere to dry, as though they were trying to protect every chair, branch, and boat from the fall breeze blowing off the fifty-degree river water.

The damp oak logs snapped and popped, fighting against the efforts being made to get a campfire going. Two fishing guides fanned the small kindling strips they had lit under the logs. More than a little tired, half of the trip's clients were already collapsed in the waiting tents. The other half were standing around the rock fire circle, rubbing their hands and hoping the fire would get started soon. Sara secured her jon boat and selected an empty tent to stay in. Without helping the guides get the fire started, she made a mental note to tell the dock owner next time to have the cooking fires started an hour before the day's float ended. Dinner would now have to be served in the dark. Except for the late dinner, the first day of the weekend fishing camp had gone well.

The next morning, after a quiet night sleeping in the tents and breakfast cooked by the guides over open fires, the eight boats motored several miles down the river to float and fish for the day. While her clients were eating lunch in the boat, Sara had pulled to the bank after noticing some threatening clouds. She climbed up the steep bank to the top trying to get a weather app on her cell phone to work. With no indication of a cell service, she slid back down the bank to her boat.

"Nothing doing, guys. The towers must be down."

The black ledge of clouds had grown higher by the minute. She knew the strong gusts of the incoming front would catch the boats before they got to the island camp. She wasn't alone in realizing what might be coming. Both her weather-wise clients from the Arkansas Game Commission stowed their rods before she asked, and both were pushing buttons on their cell phones.

"Keep trying. We need to warn the other boats. We're still five miles from the camp. We may need more than a tent to be in anyway with what might be coming. I'm going to head back upriver and dock so we can get to higher ground. With luck, we can make the Buffalo River Resort before this thing hits."

"It's all in your hands, lady. Let's get the hell off this river." The older of the men shivered. "I'm still trying to get my wife on the phone. She's in the boat that left before us."

Sara opened the throttle on the Mercury, afraid they might be in the path of a tornado. The treetops gave way to the cold blast of air being pushed by the hands of thunder god, Thor. It raked across the water, trying to scuttle them as they approached the resort.

A red cooler tumbled across the dock. It rose in a high dive and landed in the river. A plastic lawn chair belly-flopped right in front of the boat. Sara ran over it and steered into a dock slip.

"Go ahead, run for the lodge. I'll tie things up here." She held the boat steady for the two men to leave.

"Go ahead, Jim. I'll help Sara," the older man said.

"I need to get back out there and help, mister. Some of our boats aren't going to be this lucky." She pointed for the older man to head for the lodge.

"I'm going with you. I spent twenty years in the field before getting stuck in an office. I'm responsible for these folks."

"Set the full coolers on the dock. I know who you are, Brad Johnson. Get the hell off my boat."

"Look, my wife and daughter are out there in the middle of this. I'm not getting the hell off anything, understand?"

"If you get tossed in the water, don't blame me. Tighten up that life jacket. We're heading downriver. Sit flat down in the bottom of the boat."

The old comparison of a cow pissing on a tin roof didn't come close. Wash tubs of water and wind gusts pounded them from the west. Sara pushed the tiller of the motor hard to keep the boat headed down stream, but it wasn't enough. The boat still needed to be tacked into the currents.

"I'm going to be surprised if there isn't a funnel in this mess," Brad shouted, holding on with a hand on each side of the boat.

"Grab the bucket tied under the seat. You need to bail water, or we're going to sink."

A lighting strike boiled the white bark off a sycamore.

"Damn, that was close," he shouted.

The wind gusts gave her no time to adjust, no time to scream. No time to rub her good luck tattoo. She saw the trails of rockets fired from the roof tops of buildings on each side of her Humvee. She went where her therapy had trained her. A deep breath, then to realize the now of what was happening. She tried to catch her cap as it blew off. She was back on the river and needed to act now.

"Keep bailing. There's one of the boats up on the bank." Sara pointed and waved at the guide and his passengers.

"Looks like they're okay. My wife and daughter were fishing in the boat just ahead of them. Maybe they made it to the camp."

Sara knew his wife and daughter were in a boat with the newest guide on staff. She hoped he had been able to beach the boat before the worst of the storm reached them. She saw the open width on the bank where tree trunks stood like stripped remains of a battle with a tornado that had been lost. Fifty yards past, Sara pointed to the red cooler caught against a broken treetop still hanging on to its trunk. An empty life jacket stretched out in the current, snagged on the longest limb of the treetop.

Sara started to steer away from a mountain of tree limbs, but then she saw it. "There's a jon boat jammed in those tree limbs. It's up on its side."

"I see it!"

She steered the boat into the bank. "Get out, Brad. I'm going in there."

"Not without me you're not. *Go!*"

Damn him!

Sara backed off the bank. She set the boat into a side drift toward the floating log jam. They smashed into it broadside.

"Grab a limb, and try and keep us upright."

They both heard the cries for help coming from the other side of the lodged boat.

"It's my wife. God, we have to get them out of there."

"Tie the front to anything you can reach." She took off the bulky life vest and jumped into the tree limbs. She climbed to the top of the tipped boat and saw his wife and child with the tips of their fingers barely gripping the edge of the boat. The boat shuttered from the rushing water. She knew from the squeal and cracking of the boat's bottom boards it would break apart any second. She dropped to the inside edge of the tipped boat and grabbed the back of the young girl's life jacket. The mother started to reach and help.

"No, don't. The current will suck you under. Just hold onto the boat. I've got her. I'll be right back for you." Sara dragged the little girl across the limbs and lowered her into Brad's arms.

His arms tight ened around his daughter. "Is my wife in there, too? For God sake, save her."

She didn't answer. She had climbed back into the nightmare. With a hold on the mother's life jacket, Sara pulled her up out of the water.

"Climb out there. Brad is waiting. Where's your guide?"

"He was trying to help us get out. The water just sucked him deeper into the tree branches."

Sara held the woman's arm until her husband grabbed it and helped her into the boat.

"Brad, the guide is still somewhere in this mess. Get the boat out and around to the other side of the limbs. Just beach it there and wait for me. I'm going through to find him."

Sara pushed back into the limbs. Only the gunnels of the boat remained. She climbed over the boat's frame and into the broken branches. She heard the weak cry for help coming from under the tree limbs. Pushing the limbs aside she saw the guide turn his head and look up at her.

"Hang on, Randy. I'm coming." She dropped lower in the limbs and locked her legs under a branch. "Give me your hand."

Randy reached for her. "I'm caught. My foot's caught."

Sara pulled on his arm.

"I ain't got no more pullin' left in that arm, ma'am. Ain't none left in the rest of me, either."

"Shut up, Randy! You're going to have to go under and loosen your boot. Do it now!" The man ducked under and came up coughing, spitting out water.

"Is it off? Get down there again. Untie the laces."

He came up again. "It's loose."

"Push it off, now. This whole mess is going to break apart along with a jon boat that's going to take your head off at the shoulders. *Move!*"

"It's off. God, it's off."

"Climb. Crawl on the limbs, and I'll grab you and push you through the rest of this." Sara didn't wait for the man to be clear. She shoved his back hard through the last of the branches and into the open stream. Randy went under and out of sight. Sara dove into the currents after him. When she came up without him, Brad waved her further downstream. She dove again. This time her hands touched his back. She wrapped an arm around his waist and with a stroke of her free arm, she reached the surface. She turned him on his back and locked an arm under his throat before backstroking toward the bank. Brad grabbed the guide before they got there and dragged him up on the bank. Sara turned the coughing guide on his side to help him get his breath.

"Get the boat, Brad. Your family?"

"They're cold, but they're safe."

Sara helped Randy onto the floor of the boat and then climbed aboard. She dug out an old coat from the boat locker for Brad's daughter. With all four people on board, she headed back up the river to the resort. What was left of the wind carried the pungent reminder of the close lighting strikes. Her dad had warned her if the lighting was so close that you could smell the stink of the ozone, you might be dead or dying. His reminder to get the hell off the water before a storm was so close that you didn't have time to count between the lighting strikes and the thunder played through her mind. Distant rumbles rolled across the east bluff signaling the end of today's immediate danger. Brad draped his jacket around his wife's shoulders and pulled his daughter close in his arms. Sara had changed the way they had been seated so the husband's back faced into the wind from the moving boat. She was worried about how hard the child was shivering and afraid she might go into shock.

Steering into the first slip of the dock, she saw Ron, the resort owner, stoop to steady the boat as it bumped the back of the dock.

"Ron, the little girl is close to going into shock. Get her to some place warm. Her dad will carry her." After she helped her passengers from the boat, she jumped back into the boat and slipped the engine into reverse.

Randy stepped back into the boat. "I'm going with you. I can help."

"Stay here, Randy. Go help Brad and his family get up to the house." With the guide out of the boat, Sara backed out of the slip.

Ron shouted, "Sara, your clothes are soaked. Better get on up here."

"No. I'm okay." Opening the throttle on the boat's engine, she headed back downstream.

WITH THE SWIFT RIVER CURRENTS helping, she quickly reached the downed trees that held the other jon boat captive. The boat had flipped completely over and was now upside down. She took a deep breath and continued on.

Another mile of broken treetops and rockslides on the east side of the river brought her to the first of the guide boats coming upstream headed for the trout dock. The two boats were overloaded with six people in each. Sara slowed to see if she could help, but the boats didn't stop. One of the guides gave her a thumbs down as they passed.

There were three boats ahead. Two were hugging the side of the river with two of the guides in each boat scouring the water looking for something. The third boat was in the middle of the river. Sara knew they were searching for someone. She pulled alongside the boat in the middle. Red sat at the tiller of the boat.

"Red, I came to help. I can run ahead and look for places with hang-ups."

"Woman, you look more beat up than I ever saw. We lost my cousin, Milton, out here. Big gust blew them over back up there some ways. Both his people had on vests, and we picked them up when they came dog paddling past camp. They said the boat may have hit him in the head when it went over."

"Asshole, quit lying about the cousin crap. Everybody knows he beat the hell out of you before you ran him off. He's your son. He may have found a place to crawl up on the bank. I'll run on yonder." She cracked the throttle wide.

"He's gonna be way past dead by now, woman."

Sara shook her head in disbelief. What was *wrong* with this man? "Son of a bitch doesn't give a damn about his own boy."

The bottom of the river bore traps unlike any man ever dreamed up. Tree trunks long ago having lost their will to float sank in place or moved along with the bottom currents of the river feeling and bumping for a place to lodge, if only until the next flood. She scoured the clear water, looking for rock ledges and drop-offs where the currents of the river turned and churned, trapping chunks of loose moss against the bottom.

She saw the blue denim of his overhauls rolling against a rock ledge first and then the pale skin on Milton's water-soaked hands and face turned toward her and then away, time after time as his body rolled. She took the deep breath she needed to push back the memories of body bags of prisoners she had seen.

She reached for the Glock under the seat of the boat and chambered a round. She fired three shots in the air to signal she'd found the spot where Red would find the son he had run off. Sara slowed the Mercury and hovered the boat in place against the current, sadly waiting for the hard-ass father to arrive. To see death wasn't new to Sara. Still, it shook her to see it so close and wrapped in the pale body of someone she knew and liked. She tried to imagine Red's reaction when he found his son's body. She gave up quickly, though. She'd wait and see for herself.

BACK AT THE CAMP, CANVAS tents didn't have good odds against a freak downpour armed with tornadic forces stripping and tearing at the thick seams along the edges of the tents, chewing them apart and then ripping them like a delighted dog tearing paper to shreds.

She needed a break from this tragedy on her river. Sara lifted the torn canvas of her tent and grabbed the strap on her bag. She brushed the water droplets and then the sand off her name painted in black letters on her army duffle bag. Her pulse and breathing raced when she remembered the sands in Iraq, how it got into everything. Even the rations on patrol had the gritty feel and taste of Iraq earth. Sara opened the snap at the top of the bag and found everything inside wet. With her cap having been swept away, she gathered her tangled wet mess of hair and pulled it to one side. Her breathing slowed as she worked methodically to braid her hair and then tie it with the old bandanna she finally found at the bottom of the duffle bag. Shoulders now relaxed, she went outside the tent to throw herself into the work at hand.

Men that the dock owners had hired arrived and were cleaning up what was left of the campsite. Sara went to her jon boat, checked to be sure she had enough gas, and started the engine to back off the sandbar.

She didn't hear the horn but she saw the uniformed officer running toward her. Sara didn't bother to kill the engine. She ran across the jon boat's exposed bottom, jumped to the sand and into the arms of Luke.

"Are you all right?"

"No! Milton drowned out there."

Luke held her until she relaxed her grip on his back. "No one got the word to us. The cell tower got torn up. The resort owner called after you dropped off Brad and his family and told us about the tornado going through. He said you went back out to help."

"It was too late to help him. God, I found his body rolling in deep water against a jetty."

"Gwen is on the way. She was on Norfork Lake when I called her on our satellite link. She's going to bring the boat and trailer to the resort and launch from there. What can we do to help?"

"Red and the guides will be bringing his body here once they get him up. They say all the other boats and people are accounted for."

Luke slipped his regulation jacket off and wrapped it around her. "You really need some place warm, young lady. I'll radio for the coroner."

"We can still help. I think the boats are coming in now."

Sara grabbed the last standing tent and pulled the stakes to make a sling. She went to the boat that was carrying Milton's body and helped carefully center his body on the carry she had made. After they helped carry Milton's body to a waiting area, she and Luke pulled her boat high on the sandbar. She slung her duffle over her shoulder and told him she wanted to just sit in the Jeep. Luke started the Jeep's engine and turned on the heater before going back to the river's edge to wait for the coroner to arrive.

forty-two

THE TATTERED WREATH, WHICH WAS dug out from Christmas storage, graced the bow of the jon boat burdened with a cardboard Garcia reel box. The ashes in the box had a small candle rising from the center of the mound. The guides in the funeral boat procession, who spent their lives on the river fishing and had no black suits to wear, only hastily washed tattered jackets with sides unraveled clear to the underarm and blue jean pants stained from too many days of cleaning fish. Milton's sixteen-year-old bride sat just behind the Garcia reel box. She wore a hand-me-down pink overcoat that did little to hide her third trimester. His father, Red, sat at the boat's tiller and steered the boat ahead of the funeral cortege of eight jon boats. Sara, John, and Jimmy, in their old jon boat, brought up the rear of the cortege. It had surprised her when Red had actually acknowledged Milton as his son and agreed to lead the boats.

Red led the jon boat convoy of mourners to a small inlet just down the cliff from a side street of Cotter. After the boats circled and the engines were quiet, a parson watching from a church's open door on a bluff pulled a rope and rang the church bell once for each year of the man's life. The count stopped at eighteen.

No one in the boats was quick to offer a prayer. Sara remembered standing in front of empty boots and a rifle pointed at the ground and offering a prayer for a lost comrade. Now the eighteen-year-old needed her to pray for his soul. She hoped God would accept her prayer.

Sara gave three pulls with a paddle, guiding her boat to the middle of the circle. Then she stood. "Please bow your heads and join me in saying the Lord's Prayer." Her clear voice reached across the boats and helped those struggling with the words of prayer to somehow keep in step and finally end with a chorus of *amen.*

Before the echo of amen died, the engines on the boats had been started. Red led the way again, stopping at midstream. The young widow picked up the Garcia reel box and handed it to Red. He made quick work of getting the top off with his filet knife. Showing tenderness few had ever seen from Red, he lit the candle in the box and set the box on the water. A Viking funeral with a cardboard burning boat and ashes for the boat to carry. Sara, her dad, and Jimmy hung back as the eight boats started circling the sinking cardboard box, spreading the rest of the boy's ashes on top of the water.

Three rusty shotguns came off the floors of the boats and started blasting into the air, a goodbye to the young guide. Two moonshine jugs were passed from boat to boat, and finally they were tossed back and forth, even though there were only drops left.

With the funeral over, Sara's father took over the tiller and headed their boat downriver to their cabin. It was then she saw the solitary figure standing in the shadows of the Cotter bridge arches.

"Pull over to the bridge, Dad," Sara said. "There's someone I know."

She jumped from the boat before the front beached and hurried to the woman, who stood half hidden behind the bridge column. Her slim, frail figure was clad in a hand-sewn black dress. Her long, grey hair was coiled and pinned behind the back of her head. Sara stopped with her arms outstretched to the boy's mother. The grieving mother stepped into her arms. The beautiful green of her eyes had been replaced with the blood-shot eyes of sorrow and the pain that only a mother would know.

"Annie, I'm so sorry about your son. I would have come and stood with you."

"I ain't never going to get in a boat with that boy's papa. He'd use any excuse to drown me."

"Did Red bring you here?"

"No. He don't want nobody to see me. One of the old guides came and brought me here."

"The parson at the church has been praying for your son. Can I take you to the church so we can join him?"

"I would like that. Thank you, Sara."

With a car borrowed from the dock owners, Sara and Jimmy took Annie to the church on the bluff. John took the boat downriver to the cabin to get their truck. The parson welcomed them at the front of the church and led them to the front pew. After he said a prayer for Milton, he took a seat beside Annie with his arm over the mother's shoulder.

"Milton was a good boy, Miss Ferrell. He came with his wife last week and told me when their baby was born they wanted it to be baptized in this church."

"Annie is there anything I can do for...." Sara's voice failed her. She rose and went to kneel at the altar. She prayed for forgiveness from three other mothers who lost their sons to war in Iraq. Slaughtered because of her weakness. Forgetting what happened for a few hours or even a day had become easier for her. Clemency for herself? She knew would never happen. Sara felt the woman's arm press against her shoulder and then a hand pulled her in against the frail body.

"You're troubled?" Annie whispered.

"I try to imagine what losing a son feels like. I can't."

"I feel empty, Sara. My heart is empty."

"I got overcome being in church. It has been so long."

Annie stood and reached for Sara's arm to help her rise. Together they walked back to a pew and sat down with the preacher and Jimmy. The three of them sat quietly with Annie.

"It's all right. We can go now. I said a prayer for my son."

———————

AFTER DRIVING HER TO HER cabin, Sara and Jimmy returned to the dock. After thanking the dock owners for the loan of their car, she joined Jimmy sitting on the swing on the dock porch. They saw John returning from the cabin with his truck.

"Jimmy, would you please stay here on the swing for a couple minutes? I want to talk to Dad for just a minute." Sara stood outside the driver's window to talk to her dad.

"I've wanted to tell you for a while now who shot at me on the river. I went back out to the riverbank and dug up a stinking glove that led me to her husband."

"Red? I'll kill that old redneck pig."

"Dad, calm down. I went out to his cabin and got his rifle and got Annie riled up enough to want to kill him herself."

"Why didn't you tell me sooner?"

"Maybe because you might have killed him. I did some settling up with him at the dock. He knows I've got enough evidence to send him to jail."

"Well, thinking about it, I am glad it wasn't Ruiz taking shots at you."

"I don't think Ruiz is going to cause me any problems."

"You tell me if you even think he will, hear?"

"I promise I will."

"I forgot to give you the mail that came late yesterday. You had a letter from your Iraq captain, Bartlett. It's lying on the kitchen table."

"That's okay, Dad. I might just tear it up instead of reading it. I had enough of him trying to see me when I went back to the V.A."

She walked around the truck and held the door open as she called Jimmy to join them.

———————

BACK AT THE CABIN WITH Jimmy and her dad fed, she took a moment to think about the letter. She didn't want to acknowledge the envelope lying there in her space at the table. It was evening before she picked the letter up and went to sit in the rusty lawn chair overlooking her river. Without another thought, she ripped the letter in half and threw it on the ground. Her dad came up behind her.

"Are you sure you want to do that, Sara? As much as I don't like him, didn't Bartlett do a lot in getting you into the V.A.'s program?"

"Shit," she said, picking up the letter's two parts and opening them.

Dear Sara,

I hope you found the time at the V.A. hospital helpful. I'm glad I could help in getting you in there. I hope someday you will be able to forgive me for sending you away with the convoy. What happened was terrible. Your letter told me you are blaming yourself for the loss of the three men in your squad. It was war, and I must share the blame with you.

I hope it's not too much of a surprise, but I'm sending Platoon Sergeant O'Dell out your way. He will call you and let you know when the trip plans are complete. You both need to have a talk about what happened the day your convoy was hit. He can tell you why our commander covered up the attack and the prisoner escape. You deserve to know the truth.

Bartlett

forty-three

LUKE'S SLEEPING BREATHS MARKED WITH short, brittle sounds of spluttering graced the back of Sara's neck. She paced his breathing and thought for only a few seconds about the nightmares that still came when she had been under stress during the day before. She knew she didn't need to worry tonight. Sheltered with his arm over her waist, she would spend the night in hard sleep.

They both woke to Luke's day off. With nothing clean to put on, she went to his closet and took down a white shirt to wear. When she passed his mirror, she turned and laughed. She loved the feel of the cotton shirt on her body and the short length that barely hid her backside. It wasn't the first night Sara had spent in his apartment, but she still didn't know all the places a bachelor kept things in the kitchen. After some rummaging around, she found the K-cups for a strong blend and had two cups brewed with his Keurig. Luke came up behind her and gave her a tight morning hug and a kiss on the neck.

They sat across from each other holding their cups in one hand and reached to join hands with the other. The night before, Luke had told Sara how proud of her he was for saving the woman and little girl from drowning during the storm and how frightened he was for her safety when he learned of the tornado hitting the river area. They had spent the night locked in each other's arms.

THE EARLY MORNING KNOCK AT Luke's door surprise them both. Luke answered the door and quickly came back. "Sara, go get my robe from the closet. We have a visitor that wants to see you."

Sara sorted the hangers and pushed them all to one side before she found his white robe. With it on, she pulled her hair out and over the back before joining him in the living room.

"Sara, I think you know Brad."

"Shut up, Luke. Sara, can I give you a hug."

"I need that hug, too," Sara said, hugging him and patting him on the back. "Your wife and daughter, they're okay?"

"Both are resting in the hospital. They were bordering on hyperthermia. Luke, I don't even know how to explain what this woman did out there, saving the lives of my family and going back in there to dig out the guide who was close to drowning. She's the bravest person I've ever met. Sara, you have my enduring thanks. Thank you, thank you. I've got to get back to my family, but I wanted to tell Luke to bring you to Little Rock. I want to give you a tour of the commission. I'd like to talk to you about the possibility of becoming an agent with the Arkansas Conservation Commission."

"Thank you, sir. I'd like to visit the commission." She was about to tell Brad she'd already applied, but thought no, he was high up in the commission chain of command. The acceptance into the program had to be on her own merit.

"Luke, take Sara out with you on some of your trips to the field. I'd like for her to get a feeling for what we do."

"I will, sir."

With Brad gone, Sara and Luke went back to the kitchen and to their cups of cold coffee. She nuked them in the microwave. "What does Brad do at the commission?"

"Do? Sara, he does whatever the heck he wants. He's our number one boss. You've made a good and loyal friend there."

She felt even more glad she had kept quiet about her application.

_____

THE SUN HAD DROPPED BEHIND the mountains surrounding the valley when Luke pulled the commission truck off the road and into a high turnout overlooking the river valley. Both had their eyes trained on the roads crisscrossing the valley floor.

"We want to watch for any sweep of light crossing a pasture." He pointed to a truck driving slowly on a gravel road in the valley. "That's either somebody looking for a place to take his date or a poacher looking to kill a deer."

Sara adjusted the binoculars she was using and focused on the truck Luke was watching.

"I don't think he's using a spotlight." She handed the binoculars to Luke.

"There's a favorite place for parking just ahead. I bet he turns in there."

"His lights just went off."

"Turned off the road. We'll sit tight here for a while and keep watch."

"While we wait, tell me more about what this job is like. Did you start right out of school?"

"I knew it was hard to get on as an agent, and I needed a job right away. I had a bunch of college debt. My law enforcement degree got me my first job as a deputy with a Sheriff's Department in Missouri."

"Does it make a difference I don't have a college degree?"

"Your Military Police service meets their requirements."

Luke took a break from staring through the binoculars and handed them to Sara. "There's a pickup that seems to be not going anywhere in particular. He's just driving around the valley."

"I see the truck. It's headed up a narrow gravel road," Sara trained the field glasses on the truck. "He's stopped just across a creek."

"We're going to head down there. The guy near the creek needs watching."

"Looks like he's driving along a field."

"We'll see if we can catch up to him."

Luke laid back when he saw the taillights of the truck he had been watching. When the truck turned a wooded corner, Luke turned his truck lights off and sped up to get closer.

"Sara, if we have to stop this guy, please stay in the truck. These guys are armed with guns ready. So, I don't know what to expect."

"Ten-four, Sarge."

"There goes the spotlight on the passenger's side of the truck. Listen for a shot."

"They just fired two."

Luke floored the truck's accelerator, racing closer to the poachers before he hit the switch for his topside light bar and flashing red lights.

"Don't run. Let's make this easy, guys."

"They just threw a grocery bag out the window, Luke."

"They just tossed their drugs, you mean."

The truck's back wheels were raising a huge dust cloud. Luke barreled into the dust cloud in pursuit and reached for his mic.

"Baxter County, this is Agent Matthews in pursuit of poachers and possible drug suspects. Headed east on route ten, crossing 2240 North."

"Roger, Matthews, we'll get a car up where ten joins highway five. They'll have a roadblock setup."

"Luke, they just went through a fence. I think they turned over."

"Baxter, better get an ambulance up here on ten. These guys just went off the road and flipped."

"Roger, that. Our car will also be on the way."

Luke slid to a stop on the edge of the road. He lit the upside-down truck with his mounted spotlight.

"Christ, the truck's almost out of sight in that ditch." Jumping out of the vehicle, he rushed down the bank and pulled at the driver's door. It wouldn't budge.

Sara ran up behind him. "Come on, I'll help pull."

"Get back, Sara. It's leaking gas. These guys are all wrapped up around each other." He pulled her back, then raised his voice. "Hey, do you guys hear me? Got to get out of there before the gas goes up."

"Help me out of here. I think my back is busted!"

"Give me your hand. I'm going to have to pull you out," Luke took the man's hand and pulled. "Hurry up, get out of there."

The man came through the window, sliding on his back. Sara dragged him up the bank away from the truck. She was back in a few seconds.

Luke crawled into the truck window and shook the other passenger. "Hey, I'm going to try and get you out of here."

A Deputy Sheriff's car had just slammed to a stop on the edge of the road. The deputy ran to the truck with his small extinguisher. "This extinguisher is too small. It's not going to help. Get out of there, Luke. This whole thing is going to go up."

"He's got a pulse!"

The small explosion in the engine compartment got Sara's attention. Her military training kicked in hard, and she grabbed Luke by the belt. "Come out of there!"

"Stay out of there, Luke," the deputy said. "Get back. The flames are just about to reach the gas tank."

Luke struggled to get back and help the man. The deputy and Sara grabbed Luke's arm and pulled him back.

"Let me go, damn it! That guy's alive."

The stream of gasoline coming out of the gas tank lit in a pop.

"Run. The tank's going now!"

Sara grabbed Luke's arm again and ran with him and the deputy up the bank away from the truck. The tank explosion shot a tower of fire high in the air and a wall of heat too hot for them being so close. The deputy tripped and went down on his knees.

Sara grabbed his arm and yanked him upright. "Come on, Sarge. Get away from the vehicle."

The three of them stopped at the crest of the hill. She stared at the burning truck cab and the sad dark silhouette of the man dying inside. It had been only that one second when her memory took her over. The name Sarge slipped by her defenses.

The pickup truck driver crawled past them and stopped. "He's burnin' up in there, ain't he?"

He backed away from the heat of the burning truck.

"You put him in that fire with the way you were driving," Luke panted.

"If that guy in there wasn't dead, he sure as hell is now." The deputy shook his head. "Damn it!"

"A hell of a way to have to die." Luke turned to Sara. "I was worried this might be too much for you."

"This was horrible."

"You called the deputy 'Sarge.'"

"The name came in a flash. It almost felt we were in a battle."

"We were for a few seconds."

"What just happened would be too much for anyone. It took me back, but I'm good. I'm okay."

They stood together with Sara realizing her V.A. training was working, and it had kept her on point and alert in the moment of danger. She knew being on guard for moments like what just happened would always be needed in her future. She felt grateful for the situational training the military had put her through.

She and Luke walked back to the deputy sheriff and the truck driver. The driver was sitting on the ground with both hands covering his face.

"We've been watching the guy you pulled out for some time. We've been thinking he's been dealing," the deputy said, going to the truck driver and putting cuffs on him and reading him his rights before arresting him.

"There's a trash bag about half a mile back up the road that might put an end to just thinkin' he's dealing. I'm going to have to drag a dead deer out of the field and bust him for that also."

"We both got a slug of charges to file on this guy. I just got the call the ambulance is just about here. I'll need to stay here till the coroner shows up. I'll call the sheriff to drag this guy out of the hospital and take him to face charges when they get through patching him up."

Luke and Sara sat in his idling truck for a few minutes watching the black smoke coming off the four burning tires of the wreck. The flames in the cab silhouetted the trunk of the man's body.

"Are you okay? I know how badly you wanted to save that man."

"He was unconscious—still a horrible way to die. It was a really bad streak of luck for both of those fellows. They'll charge the driver with reckless endangerment. If we find drugs back where this started, he goes up for a long time."

Luke and Sara backtracked to where his chase had started. He pulled off the road and lit the roadside with his flood light bar. After taking pictures, he collected the grocery bag and the several items that he saw fall out. He took a deep breath when he was finished and got his flashlight on the sack's contents.

"These guys aren't cooking meth, they're selling imported stuff, Sara."

"There's more small bags over here," Sara pointed to the evidence for Luke to collect.

"Could it be heroin?"

"I'd bet big it is. That deer they poached is going to have to wait." Luke dropped the drugs in an evidence bag before they headed for the Baxter County's Sheriff's Office.

forty-four

SARA'S FORMER PLATOON SERGEANT'S CALL came the day before he was to arrive flying into Springfield, Missouri. Sara was quick to say she would meet the man she missed and hadn't seen for more than two years at the airport.

She stood at the end of security watching for the man who had dragged her to safety before a sniper's bullet hit him. Mickey O'Dell was a fifty-year-old Army lifer with a crew cut that dated him and a military uniform laced with campaign ribbons and metals. The line of passengers coming from the plane had thinned, and she still hadn't recognized the hero that saved her. She took another look past security and started toward an airline employee. Three light yelps came from the corridor. She turned and saw what could only be a mirage. She started to run past security but was blocked by an agent with his arm out and a loud, "No. Stop." It was no mirage. Coming toward her was Mickey O'Dell with a carry-on in one hand and a dog lead in the other tied to a huge German Shepherd dog. Sara stood speechless. Her hand covering her mouth. She stared at the dog. No one had told her the K9 was still alive.

"Tank!" she shouted, going to her knees with arms outstretched and fingers curling, pleading for a chance to hold him again. The dog stopped in its tracks, looking at the person on the floor, his ears forward, taking loud sniffs of what was happening in front of him. There was no sign of a tail wag. Then a surge forward and Tank jerked the lead from O'Dell's hand.

"Oh, my God. Tank!" She reached for the dog's collar to slow his charge. She fell backward onto her butt. Tank licked her face then crawled to lie close beside her. Sara turned and got an arm over the excited animal. He jumped completely over her and turned to lick her face again.

"Somebody, please tell me this is real."

"It's real, Corporal." O'Dell reached down to help her off the floor.

Sara refused his arm. "O'Dell, I'm so sorry. Give me a minute down here. Tank's alive? God, he's really alive."

Tank whined, high pitch cries of happiness.

"I didn't know, Sara. Bartlett had been secretly trying to get him out of Iraq for some time."

"*Bartlett* got him out?"

"Yes, Corporal."

"Just Sara now, Sarge."

"Some habits are hard to break, ma'am."

She used a hand on Tank's back for getting up and then gave O'Dell a hug. "Why didn't you write me that Tank was alive?"

"Bartlett knew I was coming, and he wanted it to be a surprise."

"Well it sure as hell is. I thought he was killed that last day."

"He crawled out of the Humvee after I got you out. He was hurt bad. One of the medics thought he should be put down. He said the dog shook himself and tried to jump in the ambulance with you. The medic helped him the rest of the way in."

"I didn't know. I thought all this time he died in the attack. How bad was he hurt?"

"The army vet said he lost some of his hearing. Oh, also, you should be careful around strangers—he can be aggressive."

"I think he and I will get along just fine."

"Sara, do you have any idea why I'm here, besides bringing Tank?"

"No. Other than Bartlett wanted to impress me some more. Doesn't matter. You're here, and I'm damn glad to see you." She stood and threw her arms around O'Dell, then held him at arm's length. "I knew you got hit. I thought you had been killed until I heard at the V.A. you were okay."

"That god damn sniper nearly got me. Damn wound still bothers me. Some stuff got hid about that day."

"Let's get out of here and go somewhere we can talk."

Sara leaned over to whisper to Tank before picking up his loose lead. "Come on, Sarge. I'm taking you home with us. I've got a lot to ask you about."

WHEN THEY WERE HALFWAY BACK to Cotter, Sara turned off into a rest stop with a large, shaded parking area. She needed a chance to find out what the army had been hiding, and besides, Tank needed a potty break.

"Let's take that picnic table on the hillside after I take this boy for a walk."

After the dog finished, she waited for O'Dell, who was still at the car. When he joined her, he carried a small package he must have taken from his carry-on. They walked together to the picnic table. Tank walked, pressed against Sara's leg. It surprised her. It was something he had never done before. He had always walked to her side and slightly ahead of her. He always showed the pride of his breed.

She stopped and got down on her knee to talk to the animal. "Easy, boy. You can stay close. I'll keep you safe."

O'Dell stopped alongside both of them. "The vet said he might never be normal. He's cautious and tries not to get close around everyone. His walking against you, he never did that to me or Bartlett."

"I think he knows now he's finally home. Home with me." She stood and continued to the table.

He sat alongside her and took out a copy of her letter to Bartlett about the Humvee incident in Iraq.

"Sara, the captain and I read this and only then realized you don't know all the facts about what happened that day. When I got hit, it only stunned me. I turned and saw the most frightening sight I ever saw. The Iraqi girl stood in the middle of the street between what was left of your Humvee and my lead vehicle. She didn't show any sign of fright. She stood there with her coat open and her body covered in C4. She was about to set off the charge with a switch in her hand."

"She stood smiling at us. I really didn't know what to think."

"She might have been smiling. If she was, it was because she was about to go to some paradise they imagine that awaits them. I had to shoot her."

"I feel terrible for you. I don't know if I would have reacted fast enough to do it."

"Corporal, if you hadn't stopped before hitting that girl, we would all be dead. You shouldn't be carrying around the guilt on this. What I'm going to tell you now is classified. Both Bartlett and I would be court martialed if it got out we told you. You already know the prisoner we were transporting was Aziz."

"Aziz had good reason to hate me. I could feel his eyes watching and tearing at my skin those days I helped torture him. I'm still getting that feeling just talking about him." She wrapped one arm and hand tight across her waist. Her other hand was on Tank's head.

"The fact we even had him was classified. They felt certain under torture he would give up his leaders without the word getting out. After he escaped that day, he went on to blow up I don't even know how many of our vehicles and troops. Later a video surfaced of him swearing he would attack us here in the U.S."

"So where is he now?"

"We don't know. It's scary as hell knowing what he's capable of. The Pentagon wanted to question the CIA officer that used you to torture Aziz and find out what went on in that cell. He disappeared off the map. He was in big trouble for what he had done. They also wanted to talk to you. Bartlett somehow squashed their contacting you. He was trying to save his own ass from them finding out about his affairs."

"That's too bad. I would have gladly talked to them. I've wanted to get that picture of Tank attacking a man tied up naked off my mind. Bartlett seems to keep popping up in my life."

"He wanted me to bring the dog and tell you what had happened."

"I have horrible nightmares about the girl. She comes running out of the alley waving at me. Sometimes I don't stop and run right over her. I feel her body thump against the Humvee."

O'Dell moved closer to Sara and put his arm around her. "I didn't see the girl standing there until I had pulled you out of the Humvee. That's when I saw the detonation button in her hand. I think she was shocked by the RPG hits and didn't have time to push the button."

"I don't remember much after you pulled me out." Sara sat and leaned on the table with her head in her hands and eyes closed. "Still, I can't shake the feeling that there must have been something I could have done."

"We were fighting a vicious enemy willing to sacrifice a child to kill us. They would have wiped out the convoy."

"I can't get the few minutes of that attack out of my brain, Sarge. How do you live with it?"

"Sometimes I relive it in the middle of the day, other times in nightmares, Sara. Sometimes I'm standing in the middle of the street alongside the body of the dead girl and shooting at the walls. Other times I see the girl smile at me after I shot her."

"My father knows it wasn't long after I got home I put a pistol to my head and pulled the trigger. The pistol wouldn't fire."

"Then we're lucky you are still here."

"It wasn't luck. It was fate. My mother had modified the pistol so it wouldn't fire after my dad came home from 'Nam. He tried to do the same thing. She saved both our lives."

"I wish things like that could happen to save others that were in our outfit. We've lost five soldiers to suicide."

"Damn war."

O'Dell opened the small box he had been carrying and took out two medals and laid them on the table before Sara.

"Bartlett said you wouldn't take these when you were back at the hospital. If you refuse the one for bravery, take the Purple Heart. Your dad would be proud to have it."

"I showed no bravery, O'Dell. Taking fire and being hit isn't bravery. I almost didn't survive that attack."

"I'm going to keep this Bronze Star for you, Corporal. Some day you might have a child and will want to explain your get-well story to her."

"We have that child now. Dad is applying to adopt a boy that we have been trying to help. Let me tell you about this kid, O'Dell. He went through some bad shit when his folks got burned up in a meth fire. I see some of the problems he's having are so much like mine." Sara leaned over to O'Dell, hugged him and kissed him on the cheek.

"That's going to be a challenge for you both."

"We're ready for it."

"Sounds like it to me."

"Thank you for always being there for us, Sarge. None of us would have made it off the street in Iraq if you hadn't acted." She took the Purple Heart and handed the Bronze Star back to him.

"Keep it then for me some day." She pulled on Tank's lead. The shepherd had been watching her carefully and sitting pressed against her leg. "Come on, men, maybe we all need a fishing trip tomorrow to relax."

With O'Dell tucked away in the Cotter Motel with a promise she would be back in the morning, Sara pulled Tank against her in the front seat of the truck and headed for home. Halfway to the cabin what he had told her hit home, hard. It had taken that long for her to sort out and come to realize no matter what she would have done men would have gotten killed. The truck bounced to a stop. They were in a ditch. Her eyes were cloudy with tears. Tank stood at her side licking her face. She so much wanted to scream for all the pain she had put herself through. She thought of Tank's trauma and knew he didn't need more—it would have to wait for later.

forty-five

SHE PULLED INTO THE CABIN driveway and waved to her dad standing in the doorway of the cabin.

"Easy, Tank. You're home, boy." She hugged the dog and laid the side of her face against his head before kissing it between his tall ears. "Come on, boy. You've got to meet Dad and Jimmy." She opened the door of the truck. Unsure of what the dog might do, she kept a strong grip on its lead and stepped out.

"Okay, then. Come, Tank."

The dog eased down from the truck's seat and stopped. His low growl told her he was warning of the man approaching.

"My dog from Iraq, Dad. O'Dell brought him and surprised me. Just stand still for a minute I'll bring him to you."

"Tank. *Friend.*" She commanded and stroked the dog's head. "I'm going to let him come to you, Dad. Let him smell your hands before you try and touch him." She dropped Tank's lead and gave him an out command. As she expected, the dog went straight to her dad. After one circle around him, he sat in front of John with his tail wagging.

John gingerly gave the dog a rub on the head. "You didn't expect this. Did you, Minnow?"

"I thought he died the day we got ambushed. My commander somehow got him back from Iraq, and O'Dell brought him to me." She called the dog back and took the lead rope off.

"Go pee, Tank." Tank showed he was more than willing. He circled a grassy spot twice and then blessed the cabin's yard. "He's been holding that a long time."

"You'll have to tell me more about how this fellow worked in Iraq."

"I will. He spent the days at my side and the nights alongside my bunk. I'll take him in the cabin. He's needing a drink about now."

"Then maybe you can some sit with me on the deck and tell me how in the hell your K-9 got here."

"There's a lot more to tell than Tank's story. I'll meet you out back. Come on, Tank."

The dog followed her into the cabin, leaving her side to go to each doorway then stop and look into each room. Sara filled a cooking pot with water and set it on the floor.

"Come, Tank." She backed against the sink and took a deep breath. She watched as a part of her life she was sure was gone came to her side and drank the pot dry. When Tank looked up at her, she could see all the gray hairs starting to grace the dog's muzzle. She knelt alongside the dog.

"You're so old for your years, boy. I'm sorry for what I put you through that day." She stood and walked into her bedroom slumping onto the bed, clucking to Tank to follow. Tank was beside her in an instant. She lay with her face in the pillow softly sobbing at the overpowering flood of memories. The dog nestled against her side and pushed again and again against her arm with its muzzle. Sara turned toward her friend, wrapping an arm over Tank's side.

"I've missed you. You're just the therapy I need."

She was about to go asleep when she remembered her dad was waiting for her.

"Come on, Tank. Let's so outside." She left the cabin and went to sit on the deck beside Tank and the rusty white chair her dad sat in. Tank sniffed her dad again before settling on the board deck beside Sara. She hadn't expected Jimmy to come running around the side of the house. Tank jumped up and bolted toward Jimmy.

"No, Tank. No," Sara yelled, standing without a chance to stop the dog.

Jimmy stopped in his tracks and threw the fishing rod he was carrying onto the ground. Tank slid to a stop—the hair on the dog's shoulders stood straight up. He was poised three feet from Jimmy. Maybe Jimmy didn't know about GSD's and their ability to attack. It didn't matter. He knelt down on one knee.

"Come here, fellow," Jimmy said, putting his hand out to the dog.

"Tank. Friend."

Tank stood in place with a low growl coming from his throat. Then Sara saw a slight wag of his tail. Tank stepped ahead sniffing Jimmy's hand before sitting in front of the boy with his tail wagging.

"Damn."

The dog's sudden reaction had frightened her. He had been trained to wait for her command before advancing on someone approaching. She knew he would need careful watching when people approached.

"His name is Tank, Jimmy. He's a friend of mine from my time in Iraq."

"Does he like to play fetch?"

"I bet you can teach him." She returned to sit by her dad. "Take him and find a stick to throw."

"Come on, Tank," Jimmy walked off with the dog at his side.

"O'Dell must have surprised the hell out of you. Bringing the dog and all, I mean"

"You will never know how surprised. I told O'Dell about Jimmy, Dad. Not everything. Just that we are working on adopting him. I'll tell him tomorrow about all that happened to the boy. O'Dell has been through some terrible things in Iraq. Things like we both went through."

"Speaking of Jimmy, are you hearing anything from our lawyer? I gave him your cell number so we don't miss his call."

"Not yet, Dad. It's like hell waiting to hear from the court. I know he has to be here at least six months for the adoption to be final."

"I haven't told you, but I picked him up at school twice, and we went trout fishing. That boy's a natural on the river."

"Dad! There you are now, teaching Jimmy to skip school to go fishing. Is that why you didn't tell me?"

"Well. Someone just pulled in, Minnow. Whew, saved by a lawman."

"We will talk about that later, Dad. It must be Luke."

"Sit still, Sara. I'll tell him you're back here."

"Tell him I have an army dog back here."

John left and walked around the side of the cabin. Sara heard him yell to Luke that she was in back. Sara called Tank and had him sit at her side. She got a grip on his collar waiting for Luke.

He came around the corner of the cabin. "You have a friend, Sara?"

"Easy, Tank. *Friend.* He's unsure of his new home, babe. Just talk to him."

"Hello, Tank. Want a smell of my hand?"

When she saw the dog relax, she let go of his collar. Tank got up and went to sniff Luke's hand and quickly went back to lie beside Sara's chair.

"Sit here beside me, Luke. There are some things I need to tell you."

"Tell me about Tank."

"He's my K-9 partner from Iraq. He was in the back of my Humvee when we got hit."

"You told me he got killed."

"I thought so. He arrived with O'Dell, my first sergeant from Iraq."

"He's here?"

"At the Cotter Motel. I want all of you to meet him. I'm going to take Tank and him fishing tomorrow. Then we'll all meet back here for a barbeque."

"Count me in. Can I call the dog over?"

"He's working off hand signals and voice vibrations. He lost some of his hearing in the explosions when I got hit. Go ahead—just clap your side with your hand—he'll come."

Luke clapped his side, and Tank looked at Sara for a command. She pointed at Luke, and the dog responded by going to Luke's side and looked at him. Luke turned to the side and patted his side in a heel command. Tank went around him to his side and looked up. Luke walked a few steps with the dog at heel.

"I love this dog, Sara!"

"Not as much as I do." Sara commanded the dog back to her side.

"I saw Jimmy and your dad out on the river Thursday."

"Dad's been a bad influence. Jimmy was skipping school. Dad wanted some time to get to know the boy."

"Do you think he would like to ride on the airboat with us sometime?"

"I'm sure we would, but not on a school day. Hear me, mister?" Tank rose at her loud voice and looked at Luke. "Easy boy." She scratched the dog behind the ear.

"You have a real protector there, lady." He sat back down in the white chair next to Sara and the dog. "Tell me about this boy. I bet you have lots of stories."

"Maybe some you might not want to hear. Mostly Tank spent most of the day and sometimes night walking prison fenced in yards. Prisoners would try and taunt him, and he had no patience for that."

"What would he do? Growl at them?"

"If you have never been in front of a mad dog about to tear your throat out, you wouldn't believe how fucking mean this gentle boy can be. Next time we passed, the prisoners would be sitting at the opposite end of their cages trying their best to just ignore Tank and me."

"He seems to be so gentle and mild." Luke reached and rubbed the side of Tank's head.

"The attack we were in aged us both, I think. Maybe the dog more than me." She spun out of her white chair and sat on the ground pulling Tank's head to her side. "I love this old boy."

forty-six

SARA PULLED UP RIGHT OUTSIDE O'Dell's motel room and flashed her truck lights on the room's window. Sara got her morning laugh when she saw O'Dell come out of his room. She had never seen him in civvies. He wore a pair of tan shorts and a white t-shirt. His military boots made up the rest of his outfit.

"If you're laughing at my boots, I forgot my tennis shoes."

"Sarge, I'm sorry, those boots are funny with the outfit."

"I've lost my tan from Iraq. Need to get some back."

"Okay, that outfit's gonna do just perfect then."

With O'Dell loaded in her truck, she headed for the dock and a morning of what she hoped would put to rest much of what had gone on in Iraq. Her boat was ready with fishing gear and hearty morning snacks. She got O'Dell seated in the middle of the boat and cast off the rope ties.

"Is it always this cold on the river?" He sat stooped over with his arms wrapped across his chest.

"We're sitting on fifty-five-degree water coming from the damn. Want a raincoat, Sarge?"

"No. I'll just tough it out like I made you and the guys do back in the Iraq heat."

"You weren't all that bad, Sarge."

Sara headed her boat upstream toward a small sunny island where she could beach the boat and they could talk. The fishing part of this trip would have to come later.

"Sarge, would it be okay if we just sit and talk for a few?"

"I thought that might be what you wanted. Sure."

With the front of the boat beached, Sara took the lead and stepped out on the sandy beach and sat down in the sun. O'Dell followed and sat down beside her. She slipped her tennis shoes off.

"It's still chilly, Sarge. You okay?"

"Relax, the sun's starting to warm me up. I'll be fine."

"Tell me about you. Are you and Quan living in Washington?"

"We've been housed at Fort McNair since I came back from theater."

"How is Quan?"

"I never know if she's glad or sad I'm back. I spent so much time away, she got used to living and raising our girls alone."

"The last pictures I saw your twins were in cap and gowns for college graduation, right?"

"It was high school graduation. They're both in different colleges now— one studying to be a vet and the other an engineer. It's hard for me to realize they're so different."

"They're not so different. They've picked hard studies." She looked back as she scooted down the sand and put her feet in the water.

"Both of them knew what they wanted to go into back in high school."

"You should be proud of them."

"I am. So is their mother. She had started some college classes while I was overseas and is going to graduate soon to be a language teacher."

"Dang, that's great."

"You've got my story. Now tell me why you wanted to bring me out here on the river?"

She stood in the shallow water and faced him. "This river grounds me, Sarge. It's home—it's my territory. I almost live on it."

"Bartlett gave me a fishing magazine a while back with a story about you and the river. We both sat and laughed when we read it. He said it was all so much like the 'Heat' he remembered."

"I'll have to tell you some of the story behind the article someday. The writer held back quite a lot."

"We thought that might be the case."

"You knew Bartlett got me into the V.A. for treatment in June?"

"Yes. He called in his cards from a fellow officer working at the V.A. Captain had gotten him out of a jam when they were in Iraq."

"I thought it would take months to get in the mental health program. It only took two weeks. Tell me about him."

"Bartlett?"

"Yes."

"Might take all day, Corporal." She could hear him shuffle in the sand behind her.

"Darn you, O'Dell. I'm not a corporal out here."

"All right, Sara. Bartlett's wife divorced him after someone wrote her about his affairs. He's living alone in Virginia just outside of Washington."

"Affairs? More than with me?"

"Yes. The other soldier... she never went up the chain of command and got him in trouble for it either."

"I guess I had chances to spear him, but I kept looking at those captain bars on his collars and realizing it would be my word against his. I'd of lost that battle."

"Is there something more about him? I'm curious why you're asking?"

She turned to face him and said, "He had total control over me and my body. I didn't like the feeling."

"You're lookin' at me like there was something I could have done."

"No, no, no. We were both so far down the ladder of command, anything you would have said would have got you busted down with me."

"He and I drank a couple late one night when we were in Iraq. I flat ass asked him at one point how long he thought it would take for the word to get around."

"Man, that really took some."

"Told me didn't matter if his soldiers knew about you. Most of the men would have liked to be doing the same thing."

"I felt so belittled and embarrassed the first time with him. He got me alone in his office and called me over and pulled me onto his lap. He had me on his desk the first time it happened. It went on from there, never stopping until he sent me away that last day."

"You don't need to explain."

"I'm more or less talking to myself about what I let happen," she said, kicking a softball size hunk of sand into the river. "Just getting it out in the open of daylight makes me feel better. It still bothers me."

"I know how that feels, to talk about things bothering you. Having a wife that lets me vent makes going in for another day of hurry up and wait army a little easier. I think Captain Bartlett has softened a lot since Iraq. We were all up tight over there at the prison."

"You coming out here and risking court martial for telling me what really happened means the world to me. I've just about got the things that happened in Iraq all tied up in a bundle I'm gonna put on the shelf."

"I've still got some of that to do myself."

"Anything you want to get off your chest? I'm a good listener, Sarge."

"Really, no. I've got a new doctor that cares for men still in the service and returning from Iraq and Afghanistan. He's also a good listener. But thanks."

"I know you're the sarge that can do it." She left his side and went to the jon boat and returned with a bag of snacks and two cans of Miller Lite. "Let's finish these, and then I want to show you the fishing this river is famous for."

"Can't wait."

With the beer and the snacks finished, they loaded back in the jon boat. She headed downstream. At the beginning of the trophy catch and release area, she shut the engine down to drift. She handed O'Dell a baited rod and reel with the heavier line she knew he would need.

"When we cross the place just ahead with the rock line jutting up, cast into the swirling water at the base of the rocks. He's going to be waiting for you there. When it hits, these are trout, and we're fishing light hooks, so easy on the jerk to set the hook."

O'Dell had a questioning look on his face but went along with her and made a near perfect cast a foot past the rocks. The look on his face went dead serious when the trout hit and his rod went nearly into the water.

"Easy, jerk. He's on." She started the engine as the line coming out of

O'Dell's rod headed downstream. "Just keep tension on it. I'm going to follow. When you feel him let off, take up the slack. If he heads for the boat, reel in fast as you can."

"What in the hell is on here?"

"One heck of a big brown trout." She watched carefully, advising him as he worked to get the trout near the boat. And then, she netted the fish as it came alongside the boat. She carefully lifted it from the net before removing the hook from its mouth.

"Your catch—want to hold it while I get your picture?"

"Darn right I do."

"Wet your hands and hold it through the mouth and just under its tail."

O'Dell gingerly took the big fish from her and reached to get his hand under the fish. The tired fish gave one last effort at escape. It doubled up and went *wham* as it went flying out of O'Dell's hands and back into the river. Sara got a picture of the fish's launch as it was in midair and O'Dell's mouth was wide open.

She laughed. "I forgot to tell you this is the trophy catch and release area of the river. This fish seemed to think it was past time to release it."

For once, O'Dell was speechless, except for telling her to promise she would never send the picture to anyone in his company.

It was evening the same day, and she and Tank stood at the terminal gate waving goodbye to a soldier who had one day saved her from dying in a burning war machine.

She would miss him.

forty-seven

LOOKING UP FROM BELOW, THE five arches of the bridge resembled rainbows. Like so many of the people of Cotter, the arches were rooted deep in the banks and rocks of the Arkansas river way. The city park below the bridge offered a peaceful place for a stroll and a shady place for a walk for the town folks. Peaceful but not a quiet place today. Right now, the spring pool in the park was surrounded by kids and their families. Luke and Sara walked hand in hand by the pool. Sara led Tank pressed close to her side. The dog acted unsure of what to make of all the people and shouting around the pool. She paused and knelt beside the dog to stroke his shoulder and whisper her command for him to relax. Tank eased away from her a bit and sat looking up at both of them.

"Good boy, Tank. Now come."

The kids in the pool recognized Luke. "Hey, Lawman. My daddy says you caught him fishing with too many fish in his boat," the boy said as he treaded water. "He said you let him go, cause you knowed him well."

"Well, Corky, there was more to the story than that."

Sara tightened her grip on Luke's hand. "Really, Lawman? Why don't you tell us about it?"

"Come on, Sara. Just ask your dad about Corky." Luke started to walk away. "Come on."

Passing the swimming kids and the spring pool, Luke guided them to a picnic table nestled in the hill under tall sycamore trees.

"Gonna tell me about the guy you let go?"

"I didn't feel right about arresting a man fishing for the only food his family would have for a while. He had lost his job."

"Good for you. There is another side to you after all, right, Mister Lawman? By the way, it's great you have a Sunday off. It seems so seldom." She sat next to him with their backs to the tabletop. Tank quickly settled in the shade under the table.

"The Commission gave me the weekend off. Told me to just take some time and consider their offer."

"Offer? Tell me, stubborn man."

"They want me to take over an area in Southern Arkansas. It would mean a permanent move with a good raise in pay and rank."

"I don't want you to go," she said, quickly adding, "I'm sorry. That wasn't fair of me." She placed her hand on his arm and gave a tight squeeze.

"I know you'll be starting training soon for the commission, Sara. The thing is, they don't have a good track record of sending new Wildlife Agents right where we would want to go when you graduate. But I want us to be together. Would your dad ever leave and bring Jimmy to come with us?"

"He'd only leave the cabin and the river in a wooden box."

"I kind of knew that."

"Dad will take good care of Jimmy, I'm sure. He's suffered with PTSD just like me. He knows what Jimmy's going through. He's been calling to get Jimmy in for professional help in Springfield."

"That would be so good for both of them."

Sara stood up and took his hand. "Walk with me."

Tank sprang up at what he thought was a command. The three of them left the bench and went to stroll along in the water at the river's edge. The German Shepherd walked alongside her and then started going in and out of the water chasing and biting the bubbles floating downstream in the current. The feel of the rushing water felt good on her bare feet and gave her ease. After her affair with Bartlett, she had felt it would be hard for her to ever fall in love again.

Being with this man made it much easier.

She stopped and pulled him to her with a look that urged him to kiss her.

Their kiss lasted long and only ended when she pushed him back a little and said, "I love you, and I want to marry you."

"Really?" He quickly kissed her again.

"Really! You didn't know what else to say?"

"Oh, my gosh. I've loved you from the first day we met. I would marry you tomorrow if you say so, my Sara." They started walking again. This time arm in arm. Tank brought up the rear.

"I know you would. Can it happen when our life is a little more settled? You want that, too, don't you?"

"I do for both of us. We're both going to be crazy busy for a while. I can vouch your training to be an Arkansas Conservation Agent will be tough. It was for me. You'll have to be on your toes both physically and mentally. When I take the transfer they've offered, I feel sure I'll be working with drug enforcement, so 'Katy Bar The Door' on getting to see you very often."

"Won't I have weekends off while in training?"

"You might. I spent mine with my nose in law books back then."

"Speaking of the law, I haven't heard a whisper of anything happening after I sent Ruiz's car for a swim. His recruiter sounded like they were going to offer me a job."

Luke stopped cold in his tracks and got close to Sara. He spoke in an almost whisper. "Ruiz.... You'll be able to know more when you get your badge. Things went down with Ruiz in the last couple weeks. The DEA has been partnering with the commission on drug smuggling, and he has been a main target. I've known you've been worried about what happened with the car. It was stupid of me not to think about telling you this. There won't be any more job offers to anyone from him."

"Pardon me, but bend over, I'm going to kick your dumb ass. You didn't think, Lawman?" Tank's ears came up at the rumble of her harsh tone of voice. "I hope this man heard it too, Tank."

forty-eight

IT FELT SOMEHOW EVEN MORE relaxed than usual to be on the river. Sara didn't normally take calls when she was guiding. Expecting a call from their lawyer had her on edge, and she had her phone on vibrate. When she got an incoming call and saw it was from the Arkansas Game Commission, she excused herself to her clients and took the call.

The commission officer on the phone explained that Brad Johnson would like her to be at his office at ten o'clock on Wednesday of this week. He explained she would be getting an award from the governor, and her family was invited to come with her. He explained it had been a special request from Mr. Johnson and Governor Hyder for her to be there.

Sara stood holding her phone in one hand against her ear and a baited fishing rod in the other. Something had to go when the rod tip bent nearly to the water. Sara dropped the phone onto the floor of the boat. She handed the rod to the nearest client to land the fish and then picked up the phone. The officer was still saying "Hello... hello, Miss Randolph." She apologized for the loud noise and assured him she would be there on Tuesday morning.

The reply from the officer came quickly, *"No, it's Wednesday morning. Would you like an email confirmation?"*

She apologized again and said she would remember. With Brad Johnson involved, she guessed the award would be for saving his family on the river. It surprised her, and it was coming at a bad time. She wanted to be just another candidate in the Wildlife Officer's Training.

This would not help.

WITH A PROMISE FROM LUKE that he would meet her at Brad's office, Sara, Jimmy, and her dad set off for Little Rock before it got light. Sara traded her khaki fishing outfits for blue slacks, a white blouse, and a matching blue jacket. John had done his best with Jimmy, taking him for a haircut and buying him a new pair of jeans and a shirt. Sara was happy with Jimmy but not so much with her dad. His outfit was still the same except this one was new, tan pants, tan shirt, and always there on his pocket, the name of his guide service. They arrived a half hour early and found Luke waiting in the commission's greeting center. He said hello to John, and after giving Sara a hug, he offered a handshake to Jimmy.

"Well, hello, young man." Jimmy took Luke's hand and returned the handshake with a firm grip.

"Both of them been making me practice handshakes. Told me to do it like a man!" He let go of Luke's hand and smiled at him.

"That was a great handshake, Jimmy. They should be real proud of you."

"We are, sir." She took Luke's arm in a firm grip and pulled him to her to whisper. "Did you have anything to do with me getting an award?"

"I didn't. Brad's office called me and said to be sure and be here. That's all I know." She relaxed her grip on his arm only a little.

"Brad didn't need to do this," Sara said, letting go of Luke's arm.

Luke just smiled at her and said, "I think that's the governor's car that just went in the garage, so he is coming after all."

"Oh, crap!"

With a few minutes to spare, Luke took them for a quick tour of the wildlife museum attached to the greeting center. Jimmy followed close to Luke listening to him describe the different mounted animals and birds. Jimmy would offer tips on where you might find them.

"Jimmy, you know more about some of these animals than I do."

"It's just that I have been chasing and catching them for a long time." He looked at Luke and smiled.

They were only halfway through the exhibits when the call came for them to go to Brad Johnson's office. Luke led the way back through the greeting center to an elevator. When he pressed the button and the elevator door opened, Jimmy backed up alongside Sara.

"Do I have to get in that room?" Sara realized the boy had never been in an elevator.

"It will be okay, Jimmy. It's like a ride in a car, only this ride only goes up and down."

With Luke and John in the elevator, Jimmy still didn't want to follow. With Sara's encouragement, he followed her in. Luke pressed the button for level two, and the door slid closed. It was too much for the boy. He ran forward trying to open the door. Sara ran to him, pulled him back, and put her arms around him.

"It'll be all right, Jimmy. It won't hurt us. See we're just going up."

Jimmy and Sara were the last to exit the elevator. She took a minute to show Jimmy the buttons and told him if she pressed them the elevator would go to the new floor.

"It's not that, Miss Sara. I'm just afraid to be in a box like that." Jimmy was still shaking from the scare.

"Is there a reason why, Jimmy?"

"It was like our trailer house where my mama died. It scared me."

"I'm sorry, Jimmy. You were brave. I'm proud of you for trying it with me. Now we have to go, okay?"

"Okay."

Luke picked up the pace, leading them to a secretary's desk in front of Brad's office.

"Just a minute, I'll tell them you're here." She pushed a button on her phone and turned her head for privacy. When she finished, the door opened, and Brad walked out to greet them.

"Hello, Sara. I'm so glad I could arrange this so the governor could be here. So, all of you come with me, and we'll say hello to him."

Sara felt sure she would darn rather be back on the White River taking out a couple of beer drinking clients for the day. Luke, wearing his Wildlife Agents uniform and badge, walked alongside her with Jimmy behind sticking close to John's side. When they walked into the room, the governor ended a conversation he was having with two men and turned to walk to meet them. Brad greeted the governor and turned to invite Sara forward. She didn't show her reluctance to step forward, but she felt it.

"Governor Hyder, this is Sara Randolph, the lady we have asked to come and be honored today."

The governor shook her hand as he spoke. "Welcome to the capital, and welcome to the commission's headquarters. Is this your family?"

Sara had to clear her throat before she spoke. She indicated with her hand John and Jimmy. "The two fellows are my family, John Randolph, my father, and his soon to be son, Jimmy. This gentleman in uniform is Luke Matthews, a close friend."

"Welcome Luke and Mister Randolph. Jimmy, can I shake your hand?"

Jimmy got a little closer to John's side. "It's all right, Jimmy. Say hello to our governor," John said. Jimmy took only one step forward and met the governor's hand with his.

"They tell me you're a hero we should also honor," the governor said. "I heard you saved Miss Randolph from a really mad rattlesnake."

"Yea, and the sumbitch bit me."

Laughter filled the room. Sara choked on the laugh she was about to blare out, and the governor took a moment before responding. "You're a hero... young man."

The governor asked Sara to follow and then went to the front of the room. He turned and motioned Sara to stand at his side.

"We're here today to present Sara Randolph "The Outstanding Citizen Award" for her bravery in the face of most dangerous conditions. Her courage saved the lives of a mother and two young people in peril. Thank you, and congratulations, Miss Randolph. Would you like to say a few words?"

She looked at the walnut plaque with the ornate engraved brass plate in her hands before speaking. "I lost a young guide friend to the river that day. I'm told he drowned trying to right a boat that had turned over with a family aboard. Would it be all right if we have a moment of silence for Milton Ferrell?"

Governor Hyder said, "Please everyone." He lowered his head, and the room became silent.

"We all thank Milton Ferrell for his bravery, and congratulations to Sara Randolph for hers. Thank you all for coming."

The governor shook hands with Sara, Jimmy, and her dad before speaking to Luke, standing alongside Sara. "Thank you for being a friend to this lady and arranging this event. I think you know Brad would like to talk to both of you for a few minutes."

"All right, sir," Luke said.

"Good, he's waiting for both of you." With that, the governor waved a goodbye to the others in the room and left.

Luke turned to Jimmy and John. "Would it be okay if I borrow this lady for a few minutes?"

John nodded okay. Luke motioned for her to follow and walked a few steps away and stopped to speak to her, "Brad wanted to thank you again, I think."

They found Brad coming across the room to meet them.

"Sara, a week ago I was still planning to encourage you to apply to become an Arkansas Wildlife Agent. I knew you had the Military Police background, and the classes and training you would receive would be right up your alley. Then I opened the list of new recruits coming in for the next training cycle. There you were, right at the top. One of the best in all the testing our training staff put the recruits through. Congratulations, Sara. You got the jump on me, and I'm proud to see you're on that list."

"Thank you, sir. Getting through the testing was tough. I'm proud to have made it."

"You should be." He reached and shook her hand.

forty-nine

SARA SLOWED THE JON BOAT, loaded with her camping gear, to relish the brilliant orange and red colors exploding across the tops of the river bluff trees. When the sun broke through this morning, it had pushed away thoughts of the blistering sand and dust storms of Iraq that haunted her on cloudy days. She relaxed a moment, aiming her camera at the gold and black dog sitting in the bow of the boat, watching and guarding her. She had tried for days to get Tank to just lie on the floor of the boat and enjoy their time out on the river. He never seemed to stop being on guard duty. She knew the dog's history in the war, and like her, completely unwinding may never be possible for either of them. She realized the best chance they would ever get would be in the wilds of the river country. By the time she reached the Buffalo River, she snapped more than a dozen pictures of Tank and the fall colors of the mountain sides.

Having to rethink her life had become commonplace for Sara. For so many days and months, she had tortured herself, and now the revelation that even though she'd lost her crew, many lives had been saved by her actions. O'Dell had told her as he left to fly back to Washington how he had hoped to tell her earlier. He had even threatened Bartlett he would speak to her while she was in the hospital. She questioned if anything she had learned from O'Dell would have stopped her from trying to blow her brains out. Her answer came quickly—it would not have helped. Like today, like yesterday, like last month, the flashing thoughts still came to her. When it happened, thoughts of her surroundings stopped, only a blankness remained and then a darkness and a noise too monstrous to bear. Sara guided the jon boat into the Buffalo River. She wanted to be alone with her K-9 friend in the wilderness of the mountains and river. She needed the quiet to hear the wispy sound of the breeze floating along the top of the stream. She longed for the deep breaths that would fill her very being with the scent of the pine trees that were encasing the river on both sides. Only here in the wilderness could she reflect and take stock of what her future would be.

She saw them circling long before she got to the sandbar where she had fed the hungry bear. They were black-winged carrion eaters, riding the rising and falling air current flowing down the Buffalo River valley. Thoughts of the poachers running the river made her unhappy that the bear might have been shot and killed. When she got closer, she found the vultures on the ground, ripping at a carcass lying on the sandbar at the start of the woods. Tank was standing and barking his warning when she gave a down command and beached the boat. Carrying a paddle, she slapped the ground and got the birds to back off a few feet. Her actions were too much for the war-torn dog. He was at her side and then running toward the vultures.

"Tank! Back, now!" The dog slid to a stop and started backing toward her.

"Atta boy. You haven't forgotten." She touched his head with her hand and lowered the paddle. It was just a deer, not the bear.

Remnants of the dead animal's hide hung from the bare bones. With a relief she hardly understood, she sighed and backed away.

She heeled the dog and left the vultures to gather back on the carcass. She got back in the boat.

"Still protecting me, my Tank."

She pulled Tank to her side and kissed the top of his head.

"The bear is still out here, Tank. I'll get to feed him again."

Sara motored on upriver for half a mile. Beaching the jon boat, she got out her fly rod. She took a good look in both directions along the bank for the bear she wanted to see before leaving the side of the boat. The dog sat on the sandy bank, watching her every move.

Whipping the flyrod three times, she had enough line floating in the air to cast halfway across the stream. Lifting the rod tip just enough, she let the streamer settle on the water. The four foot of clear leader hid the fact the streamer was really a trap.

Her heart skipped a beat when the smallmouth bass rose from the bottom, going into the air with the streamer in its mouth.

She gave a quick hookset jerk with the rod to ensure the streamer's hook would set in the fish's mouth. The fiberglass rod bowed in a tight arch from the strong fight the bass was making to get away. One pull after another to shorten her long line slowed the bass's swim. Sara backed up the bank, working the tiring fish onto the sandy edge. When she picked it up, Tank ran to the bass, smelling the fish, and then, sitting alongside it, looked at her as if to ask, what do I do now? It was time for a selfie with a nice smallmouth bass and a beautiful German Shepard. She loved showing John, Jimmy, and Luke pictures of the fish that didn't get away. After she got the picture, she lowered the fish into the flowing waters of the Buffalo. Tank watched the fish swim free and took two steps into the water after it.

"Easy, boy. That was one hard-fighting fish. He'll be here to catch again next time we come."

The clay sand of the riverbank stretched along the flowing river for yards. Sara could already feel the pleasure of sitting in the wet sand at the edge of the gently flowing stream. She pulled the jon boat up on the sand, undressed to her bikini, and started to unload her gear. When she thought about the good weather of the coming night, she left her tent in the boat. Tonight, the stars would be her ceiling, and she would try to count them all. When Tank brought her a driftwood branch, she scribed the letters of both their names into the sand. The beauty she drew in the calligraphy of her letters gave away the romance in the new Sara—a woman in love with life and who would cherish being in the wild backcountry tonight.

Tank barked at the driftwood in her hand. She knew what he wanted, and she tossed the driftwood out into the flowing river. The dog's running leap took him almost to the driftwood. He grabbed it and swam back to her, dropping it at her feet. Again, she tossed it. When he brought it back this time, she let it lie. Tank's shake covered her with sand and water. She laughed and took a deep breath of the cool air coming off the water before putting her head back to look at the sky. With outstretched arms, she laid back, turned, and dug her feet into the sand.

After a bit, she dropped to the edge of the water and relished the feeling of her fingers scooping up the wet sand. The cup-sized hole she had dug filled quickly with water as she moved her hands away. Tiny floats of deep brown and charcoal colored wood chips lifted from the sand and graced the top of the flooded hole. Sara dug the sand again and again, making the hole larger and larger. Soon, she knew she could fit her whole self into it. She watched water fill the hole and thought it was so much like life. We carve out our place, and suddenly it's filled, and we're surrounded by what comes to fill our life. She scooted into the hole and twisted to enlarge and make her place fit her.

The noise of Tank barking and a passing boat awoke her. She didn't move from the sand, just turned a bit to the side to adjust her bikini top and then waved to the guide and his clients on the way to end their day of fishing. Surprised at how long she had been asleep, she left the comfort of the sand bed, gave the dog a stay command, and dove straight out into the river currents. Her strokes took her down where the smallmouth and trout lay along the bottom of the waters. The fish would notice her approach and leave a small cloud of sand as they cleared her path in a whip of their tails. Each underwater stroke of her arms and kick of feet rushed her forward. Sara had found her joy for being alive. She had never felt stronger. The deep breath she started the dive with was just about finished. She stretched her arms to gain a power stroke against the water, breaking the surface only a few feet from the opposite bank. She heard Tank's bark even before she surfaced.

Sara froze in place. His black fur glistened in the last rays of the day's sun. A huge bear towered above her at the edge of the water, flailing its paws, paws that bristled with shining finger length claws. It was so close she heard the sniffs and grunts the bear was taking to smell the threat that had come up in the water. So close, the musk of the bear's scent slapped her in the face. The bear beat the water just in front of her with a paw and turned its head and roared. Sara froze in place stooping in the water. Tank hadn't stopped barking. She heard him hit the water behind her. She was afraid to yell at the hero dog coming to defend her.

The backstroke she grabbed propelled her more than halfway back across the river. Her heart was pounding at warp speed when she grabbed Tank's collar and turned him in the water. She felt the adrenaline to the tips of her fingers and in the scar of the wound in her side, but there was no slipping away like she had done for so many months before. She knew she had met a bear untouched by the men on the river. It had come from the wilds of the Arkansas mountains, and it had scared the hell out of her.

Her arms touched sand on the bank opposite from the bear. She rose in the water and paused to look back across the currents, back to where the magnificent animal had stood. He was no longer there. It would take minutes for her to get her breath back and for her pulse to slow down.

"I know you're watching us, Old Bear. Go hide so the poachers don't find you."

Still shaken, she stayed in the shallows. Her butt tapped the sandy river bottom as she held Tank and herself in place with one hand gripping into the sand. "Tank, I don't ever want to see that bear again. It scared the hell out me, boy."

Turning in the water, she crawled onto the sand. The sun had been lost behind the tallest mountain. Darkness would come quickly now. She placed a dozen small driftwood sticks into a pyramid and cut another into chips with her knife. Soon, she had the little pyramid burning.

"Tank, get sticks," Sara commanded. "We're going to need one big fire tonight." Tank looked at her not sure what she wanted, then ran to grab the nearest piece of driftwood. He returned dropping it at her feet and then standing near her, ever guarding his master. Hungry, and realizing she had let her wild, smallmouth dinner go, she sat on the damp sand. Her knees were tucked to her chest, and her arms wrapped around her legs. She hoped the crackling fire would hurry and grow. Their dinner of hot dogs would be late. The fire wasn't enough to warm her, so she reached for a jacket she had borrowed from Luke.

The jacket draped around her with its bottom making a circle on the sand, only her bare toes stuck out into the light of the fire. Digging with her big toe, she carved a canyon under her foot. Soon the other foot followed. Sara danced, seated with both feet, smacking the sand to a beat of a song she tried to remember. What was the name of the song Luke sang to her? Soon she had it in her mind, and she pieced together the words of the Airship song from their Mountain View trip. The scent of Luke surrounded her, wafting from the inner lining of his jacket. It brought back the memory of his lovemaking in the wilds of the crevice on the bluff and again on a boulder splashed with the water from the river. She shivered from the new, fresh memories that replaced the memories of a lover who had cast her away while standing in the desert sand.

The fire pyramid tilted and plopped into the glowing embers of its bed. She reached and added more driftwood to the fire.

"Get the hotdogs, Tank. No, wait. Maybe not."

Cutting a limb, she slipped two of the dogs on and sat holding them over the coals of the fire. Tank sat nearby having quickly finished two of the cold hotdogs she had fed him. She watched and listened as the dogs on the fire simmered and popped. She took them off just before they were burnt. The shepherd got even closer, watching as the bites of hotdog disappeared into his master's mouth. Sara knew he waited for the last bite that she would always give him.

Back at the boat, she found a package of trail mix that had slipped under the front seat during a guide trip. She took it back and sat by the fire. Carefully sorting through the mix, she gathered all the hard chips of banana. A hint of an old memory came—a time when she would have given away a mess hall breakfast and dinner for a fresh banana. She sorted out the raisins next, filling her mouth and turning on her back to start the endless task she planned to do.

Sara counted the stars that made up the Big Dipper first. She quickly counted twenty more in the circle she drew around it. Her count stopped at twenty-seven so she could listen to the sounds coming from far away, muted by the miles traveled around the horseshoe bend of the river. Tank heard it, too. He sat with his ears pointed toward the sound, tilting his head to the side and trying to place what he heard. She knew the sound and had followed it years before with her dad. The sharp barks of the running coon hounds told her the dogs were on the trail of a very unlucky raccoon. She listened as the barks became howls and moans. Tank lifted his head and gave a short echo to one of the howls. The raccoon was treed. It was too far to hear the crack of a twenty-two-rifle shot that would kill the raccoon and drop it out of the tree. But she knew it had happened. The dogs were on the dead animal braying hard, and then they were silenced by the hunter.

She felt surrounded by the hiss and pips of tree frogs only a few steps away. She waited for the deep rumph call of bull frog she knew would soon join the chorus. Instead, she heard a weak cheat, cheat, cheat. She turned, trying to hear where it was coming from. She remembered her dad had been fishing with crickets the day before. This little guy must have escaped and was hiding in the jon boat. Sara chuckled and said to Tank, "Bait for tomorrow."

SHE HAD FALLEN ASLEEP AND awoke to the dog's growl and heard them round the bend of the river. Flying low, the geese came, seeming to be clearing their way with their shrill honking. It was too dark for her to see them. She guessed there were four or more by the racket they poured out. Certain they had left a quiet shoal in the river because of danger—she forgave the awakening. Mentally keeping score, she thought of the other night sounds she loved. Where are my owls? They were quiet tonight. So many times, fishing on the Buffalo just at dusk, they would talk to her asking, "Who? Who? Who cooks for you?" Sara would often question back to them. She tried the question to the mountain's trees across the river.

"Who! Who!" She waited and tried again.

The quiet of the long mountain slope chilled her. She stood and stoked the still burning embers, placing more limbs there to burn. The limbs caught, and the flames cast an eerie shadow across the bow of the beached jon boat. The mountain answered her call. The hissing growl came suddenly, lasting long and filling the valley with a fear that raised the hair on the back of her neck and on the dog's shoulders. Sara shivered and tightened her arms around Tank's chest. Again, the growl grew louder and seemed to rattle the mountain trees. John had taught her years ago it spoke of the mating ritual to call in a female mountain lion.

"I've got this. I've heard you before, old boy. You scared the bee gees out of me when I was a kid. Not this time." Sara pulled the jon boat closer to the fire and laying the last of the wood on the flames, she laid down in the boat and pulled an edge of the tent canvas over her body and her pal. Her day and night on the river had reinforced her love of the outdoors and the animals that filled it. Sara knew a career that made the outdoors the focus of her life was there for her now.

No silver spoons but only hard work doing a job that would help to make her life whole again. She breathed in the night air and slept with a satisfied smile on her soul.